Enter the dark and seductive world of

JENNA BLACK

ROGUE
DESCENDANT

JENNA BLACK

Pocket Books

New York   London   Toronto   Sydney   New Delhi

Pocket Books
A Division of Simon & Schuster, Inc.
1230 Avenue of the Americas
New York, NY 10020

This book is a work of fiction. Any references to historical events, real people, or real places are used fictitiously. Other names, characters, places, and events are products of the author's imagination, and any resemblance to actual events or places or persons, living or dead, is entirely coincidental.

First Pocket Books paperback edition May 2013

POCKET and colophon are registered trademarks of Simon & Schuster, Inc.

For information about special discounts for bulk purchases, please contact Simon & Schuster Special Sales at 1-866-506-1949 or business@simonandschuster.com.

The Simon & Schuster Speakers Bureau can bring authors to your live event. For more information or to book an event, contact the Simon & Schuster Speakers Bureau at 1-866-248-3049 or visit our website at www.simonspeakers.com.

Manufactured in the United States of America

10 9 8 7 6 5 4 3 2 1

ISBN 978-1-4767-0008-3
ISBN 978-1-4767-0011-3 (ebook)

ROGUE
DESCENDANT

The Liberi Deorum

A long time ago, when the ancient gods were still around, they sired children with mortals. Before the gods left Earth, they gave each of their children a seed from the Tree of Life. This seed made them immortal, and the Liberi *thought they were gods themselves as a result. The only limitation they had—as far as they knew—was that they couldn't make their own children immortal, because the gods took the Tree of Life with them when they left. What the first* Liberi *didn't know until too late was that anyone with even a drop of divine blood—in other words, all of their children and descendants— could steal their immortality by killing them.*

ONE

"It's time, Nikki," Anderson said.

I made a very undignified squealing sound and almost dropped my towel.

"Goddammit, Anderson!" I snapped, my heart pounding. The sun hadn't risen yet, and I was still bleary-eyed even after my shower. I certainly had *not* been expecting to find anyone waiting for me in my bedroom at this hour, especially when I was pretty certain I'd locked the door to my suite. The adrenaline coursing through my veins did more to wake me up than ten cups of coffee.

"Sorry to startle you," he said with an unrepentant smile.

"Like hell you are," I grumbled, clutching my towel a little more securely around me. I knew Anderson well enough by now to know a deliberate intimidation attempt when I saw one. He was at his rumpled, harmless-looking best, in a wrinkled shirt, wash-faded cords, and tattered sneakers, but he was anything but harmless. He was a real, bona fide *god,* the son of Thanatos, the Greek god of death, and Alecto, one of the Furies.

"If you hadn't been so determined to play hard to get," Anderson said mildly, "we could have done this differently."

I'd have preferred not to do this at all, which was why I'd spent the last two weeks making myself scarce, finding any excuse I could to avoid the confrontation I knew was coming. Gods are notoriously bad at taking no for an answer, but it was the only answer I could give to the request he was going to make.

"This wasn't going to go well no matter *how* we did it," I said. He had to know what my avoidance strategy meant, and I knew he'd come prepared for a fight despite his so-far mild manner.

"I'm sorry to hear that," he replied, a slight edge creeping into his voice. "I would have thought you'd be eager to rid the world of a predator like Konstantin."

Ridding the world of Konstantin, the deposed leader of the Olympians, sounded like a great idea, in theory. He was vulnerable now that he no longer had the might of the Olympians behind him, and with my skills as a descendant of Artemis, the Greek goddess of the hunt, I was the perfect candidate to find him in whatever hole he was hiding in. It was what would happen when I found him that gave me problems.

"This isn't something I want to talk about while wearing a towel," I said.

Anderson's eyes strayed downward as he took a visual tour of my body. I wasn't much to look at with my knobby knees and winter-white skin, but guys don't seem to care about aesthetics much when a woman is wearing nothing but a towel. I gritted my teeth and kept my mouth shut, knowing he was only looking at me like that to unsettle me. I wasn't about to let him do it. At least, that's what I told myself.

"Why don't you go wait in the sitting room while I get some clothes on," I suggested. "Then we can talk."

"All right," he agreed. "You aren't going to try climbing out the window to avoid me, are you?"

I might have been tempted if my rooms weren't on the third floor of the mansion that was home base for all of Anderson's *Liberi*. "I'm not in the mood for a broken leg, so no." Of course, breaking a leg might be more fun than whatever was going to come next.

"Don't take too long," Anderson ordered. He strode out my bedroom door and didn't even bother to close it all the way behind him.

I gave the door the kind of glare I really wanted to give to Anderson himself, then stalked to my closet to get some clothes. I didn't want to do this *ever,* much less at the literal crack of dawn and with no coffee in my system. I usually don't have any qualms about defying authority, but Anderson was a different story. Most of the time he seemed like a pretty nice guy, but I knew what lay under the surface, and I didn't want him angry with me if I could avoid it.

Knowing Anderson's patience had more than reached its limit, I pulled my clothes on hastily and toweled my hair dry. I had to at least run a brush through it a few times to smooth out the tangles before they dried that way, and I swear I could *feel* Anderson's impatience from the other room. I looked at myself in the mirror over the sink and saw a delicate, anxious woman with bedraggled hair and a faded T-shirt.

Don't you dare let him browbeat you, I told myself as I tried to wipe that anxious look off my face. I stood a much better chance of holding my ground if I at least *looked* strong and confident.

"Hurry up, Nikki," Anderson called, and I knew I couldn't afford to stand there and make faces at myself in the mirror any longer.

"Well, here goes nothing," I muttered, and left the relative safety of my bedroom to join Anderson in my sitting room.

I gave him a few mental brownie points for having brewed a pot of coffee while he waited. I'd gotten tired of having to go all the way down to the first floor whenever the craving hit me, so I'd brought my own coffeemaker from my condo, which I hadn't relinquished, despite having taken up residence in the mansion. Anderson was sitting on the armchair beside the couch, and there were two steaming mugs on the coffee table.

"Thanks for making coffee," I said, picking up my mug and inhaling the steam. I didn't look at him as I reluctantly lowered myself onto the couch. I harbored a brief hope that he would let me get some coffee into my system before the fun and games began, but I knew better.

Out of the corner of my eye, I saw him lean forward in his chair. I realized I was holding my breath, and forced myself to let it out and take a sip of coffee. I'd dawdled long enough that it didn't burn my tongue.

"I would have thought you'd be chomping at the bit to hunt down Konstantin the moment he was forced to step down," Anderson said. "I don't understand why you've been avoiding it."

"I'm sure it's hard for someone whose mother was a goddess of vengeance to understand," I said, though I knew there were plenty of others who wouldn't have my moral qualms, either.

"How can you not want his blood after what he did to your sister?"

That made me flinch. Konstantin hadn't hurt Steph himself, but there was no doubt his late second-in-command had acted with his blessing, if not on his direct orders. If you'd asked me when I first found Steph if I wanted Konstantin dead, I'd have answered with a resounding yes. Even now, I would be happy to dance on his grave. But there was a difference between wanting a man dead and taking it upon yourself to make him that way. If I hunted Konstantin and found him, then Anderson, who had even more of a score to settle than I did, would kill him. I'd seen Anderson kill before, and the screams still echoed in my dreams sometimes. Death at Anderson's hand was neither quick nor painless.

I fidgeted with my coffee cup and avoided Anderson's gaze. "I've told you before I'm a bleeding heart. I'm not the kind of person who can cold-bloodedly hunt someone down so you can murder him."

"You had no qualms about hunting Justin Kerner," he retorted.

But he was wrong about that. I'd had plenty of qualms. Kerner was a serial killer, but he was a victim before that. An ordinary man with an ordinary life who'd been captured by the Olympians and used as a lab rat, forced to take on a seed of immortality that the Olympians suspected might be infected with madness. When Kerner had gone mad, they'd buried him, meaning to leave him in the ground, constantly dying and reviving, till the end of time. He'd been killing civilians. But I'd felt sympathy for him the whole time.

"I hunted Kerner because he had to be stopped before he killed more innocent people," I said, then again met Anderson's eyes. "You want me to hunt Konstantin for revenge. That's an altogether different beast."

"For *justice,*" Anderson corrected sharply. "He can't be tried in a court of law. There is no way to make him accountable for his crimes. Unless we do it ourselves. You know that."

"Yeah, I know. But I'm not a freaking hit man!"

Anderson's gaze was hot enough to burn, and the muscles in his jaw and throat stood out in stark relief. "I'm not asking you to kill him. I'm asking you to *find* him."

Usually, Anderson looks mild mannered and relaxed. The kind of man you'd pass in the street without a second glance. Certainly not someone you'd be afraid of. But that's just his human disguise, and sometimes when he's with me, he lets the disguise slip. Like right now, when pinpricks of white light appeared in the center of his pupils.

I won't say I wasn't intimidated. I'd seen what Anderson could do, and though I liked to think of him as something of a friend, I knew he didn't have some of the boundaries human beings do. I was pretty sure he would hurt me if he got mad enough. But I was not a murderer, and I wasn't going to let him turn me into one.

I put my coffee cup down, as if freeing my hands to defend myself would really help. My mouth had gone dry with nerves, and I couldn't bear to meet his eyes and see that glow. It was hard to feel like I was drawing a firm line in the sand while not meeting his eyes, but I hoped he'd hear the conviction in my words.

"You sound just like Konstantin," I told him. "Remember? He asked me to hunt 'fugitives' for the Olympians and basically told me I shouldn't feel bad about doing it because I wouldn't be the one actually killing the people I found." In truth, there'd been no *asking* involved. The Olympians were on a mission to destroy all mortal Descendants—the only people capable of killing *Liberi,* at least as far as they knew—and they thought having a descendant of Artemis on their payroll would make their mission a lot easier. I was pretty sure that under the supposedly kinder, gentler leadership of Cyrus, they still had the same goal in mind, and still would love to recruit me by hook or by crook.

"If I hunt someone down knowing that person is going to be killed, then I'm a murderer, whether I do the deed myself or not," I argued. "I'm not a murderer."

"You were willing to hunt Kerner down, and you were *hoping* I would kill him!"

Since the alternative had been to bury him alive for all eternity, yes, I had indeed hoped Anderson would kill him. But as a mercy, not as a punishment. I was pretty sure he was being willfully obtuse, but I restated my point anyway.

"I hunted Kerner because it was the only way to stop him from killing innocents. Not because I hated his guts and wanted revenge."

"And you think Konstantin won't kill innocents if he's allowed to live?"

I understood why Anderson wanted me to do this. Really I did. I could even acknowledge that he had a point. Konstantin had raped, tortured, and killed countless innocents in the centuries he'd been alive, and there was no reason to believe he would mend his ways now. Anderson would probably want to kill him even if Konstantin *hadn't* kidnapped Emma, Anderson's now-estranged wife, and chained her at the bottom of a pond to drown and revive for almost ten years. But we'd both be doing it as revenge for what Konstantin had done to our loved ones, not for any great and noble cause, and that would make me a murderer in my own eyes.

"Whatever I do, I'm going to have to live with it for the rest of my life," I said, and with an impressive effort of will managed to meet Anderson's gaze once more. The glow in his eyes had widened, the anger on his face inhuman in its intensity, but I didn't let myself look away. "Unless you're planning to kill me for saying no to you, I'm likely to have a very, very long life. And a revenge killing is something I don't want to have on my conscience."

"You don't think Steph deserves vengeance?" There was both contempt and surprise in his voice, along with the anger. Yes, there was a good reason I'd been avoiding this conversation.

"She wouldn't want me to do this," I answered. "She didn't even want me to kill Alexis." Not that I was capable of killing a fellow *Liberi* myself, but I'd been trying to dream up a scheme to *get* him killed when Steph put the kibosh on it. "She wanted him dead," I clarified at Anderson's incredulous look. "But she didn't want *me* to be involved." *I want Alexis to pay for what he did,* she'd said, *but not at the price of putting a black mark on your soul.* She was the best big sister I ever could have hoped for.

Anderson slowly rose from his chair. I rose just as slowly, my heart pounding, my breaths shallow. My lizard brain really wanted me to get the hell out of there, away from the dangerous predator that was Anderson, but I forced myself to stay rooted in place.

"I *need* you to do this for me," he said in a low

growl that resonated strangely in his chest. He slowly raised his hand, threatening me with what I had dubbed his Hand of Doom. It wasn't glowing, which is what it did when he was about to kill someone, but I didn't much want him to touch me, either. I'd seen him use that hand against Jamaal. He'd been able to make the big, tough death-goddess descendant scream in pain with nothing more than a touch. I did *not* want to know how bad it had to hurt to accomplish that.

"If your plan is to torture me until I agree to do what you want, then you really *are* no better than Konstantin," I said. My voice shook a little, and I was sure my eyes were wide and frightened looking. Under ordinary circumstances, I wouldn't expect him to follow through with his threat, because I believed he was one of the good guys. But he'd never been able to see straight about anything involving Emma, and I was standing between him and his longed-for revenge. It took every scrap of courage I could gather not to run screaming from the room.

We stood there like that—Anderson's eyes glowing, his hand halfway extended toward me while I quaked in my boots—for what felt like forever.

Then Anderson let out a whoosh of breath. His hand fell back to his side, and the glow receded from his eyes. There was still a wealth of tension in his body language and a hint of menace in his facial expression, but at least he looked short of murderous. It seemed like I'd won round one of our game of chicken.

"This isn't over," he told me. "But I guess we have to wait until Konstantin kills someone else before you can feel righteous about hunting him. Don't worry. I doubt it will take long."

He was still so angry I didn't dare move, and I didn't think any response was required. So I stood there like a statue as he stalked out of my sitting room and slammed the door behind him.

Two

Having survived my verbal skirmish with Anderson, I supposed I no longer needed to work so hard at avoiding him. However, I'd already made a couple of appointments for the day to keep myself out of the house, and I saw no reason to break them. Funny how being turned into an immortal huntress and moving into a huge mansion owned by a god didn't make the mundane cares of the world go away. I still had to go to the post office, and go grocery shopping, and get my hair cut. Ah, the glamour of it all.

The problem was the *Liberi* had a way of intruding on even the most mundane aspects of my life. After my haircut, I stopped by my favorite little French bistro to have a leisurely lunch while indulging in some people-watching from my seat in front of the generous picture window.

I'd been expecting to watch strangers, but before I'd even had a chance to place my order, I saw someone I knew crossing the street, headed my way.

Cyrus, the current leader of the Olympians, was Konstantin's son, and you could see the resemblance in his olive-hued skin and coarse black curls. Cyrus, however, gave off the vibe of being an approachable human being, unlike his father, who looked exactly like you'd expect someone who calls himself a king to look. I'd met Cyrus a few times now, and he seemed like a friendly, personable kind of guy. If he weren't an Olympian, I might almost say I liked him. But he *was* an Olympian, and he believed in a world order that was anathema to me.

I hoped that Cyrus just happened to be passing by, his presence nothing but a coincidence. Too bad I don't believe in coincidence.

Cyrus finished crossing the street, obviously not caring about the indignant drivers who were honking at him. He smiled and waved at me through the window and made a beeline for the bistro's door. So much for my plans for a quiet, uncomplicated lunch.

Either assuming he was welcome or not caring if he wasn't, Cyrus plunked himself down on the seat across from me.

"Mind if I join you?" he asked with a charming smile.

"If I told you I minded, would you leave?"

Why I bothered to ask the question, I don't know. Cyrus gave me a mock-reproachful look and helped himself to my menu. I considered getting up and walking away, but as I said, Cyrus is likable enough, and I harbored more than my fair share of curiosity about him. For one thing, I knew he and Steph's . . . Well, I didn't quite know what to call Blake. Boyfriend, I guess, although as far as I knew, they weren't sleeping together. Blake, being a descendant of Eros, is apparently such a supernaturally good lover that any woman he sleeps with more than once will never be satisfied with another man. Anyway, it seemed that Blake's unfortunate ability didn't have the same effect on men, so he and Cyrus had hooked up in the past. Having seen the two of them interact before, I wasn't sure how mutual—or how permanent—the breakup had been. Blake had described their former relationship as "friends with benefits," but I suspected there was more to it than that. If there was any chance Cyrus would play a continuing role in Blake's life, Steph had a right to know, and I figured I could try to work in a pointed question or two.

The waitress came over to take our orders. I guessed Cyrus was staying for lunch, since he ordered a *croque monsieur,* which is a fancy name for a grilled ham and cheese sandwich. I'd gone for a light soup-and-salad combo, resisting the temptation of all that butter and cheese. I felt virtuous and deprived at the same time.

"So to what do I owe the dubious pleasure of your company?" I inquired as soon as the waitress had retreated.

"Dubious pleasure?" He put a hand on his chest as if it hurt. "Why, you wound me." He'd have looked a lot more wounded without the glint of humor in his eyes.

If he weren't the leader of a bunch of rapists and murderers, I might have let myself relax and be charmed. I certainly liked his pleasant, easygoing demeanor a lot better than I'd liked that of any other Olympian I'd met. Which made it even more imperative that I keep reminding myself what he was. It would be easy to become unguarded with him, and that would be a very bad mistake.

"Look, I'm not making a big scene here because I refuse to let you chase me out of my favorite restaurant and because I know I can't get you to leave. That doesn't mean we're friends, and that doesn't mean I actually want you here."

Cyrus's grin faded, but there was no hint that my admittedly rude pronouncement had annoyed him.

"Sorry," he said, and he sounded like he actually meant it. "I'm a dyed-in-the-wool wiseass and I couldn't resist teasing you. But that was overly familiar of me."

Yes, it was. But his admission made me like him better.

"I know we're not friends," he continued, "and considering our . . . differences, I don't suppose we ever will be. But that doesn't mean we have to be enemies."

I frowned at that. "I'm not sure what you're getting at. Assuming you're actually getting at something."

"You're ruining my soliloquy," he said in mock

annoyance, then shook his head and made a face. "I told you, dyed-in-the-wool. I'll just issue a blanket apology now and hope it'll cover our entire conversation. Konstantin did his best to beat the wiseassery out of me when I was growing up, but it never took."

It was no surprise to hear that Konstantin physically abused his kid. From what Anderson had told me, Cyrus was Konstantin's only *surviving* child, but there had been others. Others he'd distrusted so much he'd killed them. I'd spent a lot of years in foster homes, and yet I bet I'd had a better, happier childhood than Cyrus had. I found I couldn't help smiling at him, despite my determination to be cautious.

"I'll let you off with a warning," I said. "But if you could get to the point without too much preamble, I'd appreciate it."

He nodded, leaning forward in a way that signaled the fun and games were over and he was being serious. "I'm the first to admit that Konstantin won't win any man-of-the-year contests. He certainly won't win father of the year. But he *is* still my father, and even though he's stepped down and removed himself from the public eye, I still consider him an Olympian. I talked to Anderson last week, and when I got off the phone with him, I had the impression we had both agreed that he would make it clear to his people that my father was not to be harmed."

My years of working as a private investigator had given me both a good poker face and a nice touch of acting skill. I didn't think my expression gave anything away, though Cyrus was watching me with great intensity. Funny how Anderson had failed to mention this "agreement" this morning when he'd tried to bully me into hunting Konstantin.

"I'm sure Anderson is upstanding and honorable at heart," Cyrus continued without a hint of sarcasm, "but I find myself wondering if his hatred for my father might trump his honor. I wonder if he followed through with his promise to warn his people off. You, particularly, descendant of Artemis that you are."

"If you think Anderson lied to you, then I suggest you take it up with him. No way I'm getting in the middle of that, and I'm not going to confirm or deny what he told us." Cyrus looked like he was about to protest, but I cut him off. "I *will* tell you that I have no intention of hunting your father for revenge. That's just not me. Does that make you feel better?"

He gave me a long, thoughtful stare. Trying to read me, I guessed. I'd told him the truth, even if I hadn't exactly told him everything, and he seemed to read that in my face. He nodded and let out a little sigh.

"Thank you. That does."

He looked honestly relieved, like he'd been worried about Konstantin's safety. I knew there were all sorts of people out there, but I still had trouble understanding how someone could actually *care* about Konstantin. Fearful respect I could understand, but not affection. And yet I didn't think it was fear or respect driving Cyrus right now.

"Anderson told me Konstantin killed all his children before you," I said. "Why would you care so much about his safety? And what makes you think he won't kill you, too, someday?"

Cyrus shrugged. "He's my father, Nikki. I know he's not a nice person, and I know he doesn't have a good history with his children. But he's still the man who raised me, and I think we both learned a lot from what happened with the others. I've made it clear that I have no desire to take his place, and while he doesn't trust me completely, I think he at least for the most part believes me."

"Um, correct me if I'm wrong, but you *have* taken his place. Haven't you?"

He smiled blandly at me, and I understood.

"You've taken his place in name only," I said. I should have known someone like Konstantin would never voluntarily step down. "He's still pulling the strings." I frowned. "And he's okay with your decree that the Olympians not kill Descendant children anymore?"

It had always been the Olympian policy under Konstantin that when they discovered a family of Descendants, they would kill them all, except for children under the age of five, who would be raised to believe in the Olympian ideal—and would later be used as lethal weapons against other *Liberi*. That policy had been the first thing Cyrus had changed when he'd taken over.

Cyrus grinned wryly. "He doesn't love it," he admitted. "But since I don't actually *want* to lead the

Olympians, he had to make some concessions to get me to do it."

I didn't for a moment believe Konstantin had abandoned his quest to rid the world of all Descendants and *Liberi* who weren't under his thumb, and in his mind, that meant killing children too old to be controlled. If he was letting Cyrus put a stop to the practice, that meant he thought of his son's rule as nothing but a temporary inconvenience. I didn't like Cyrus's chances of surviving the regime change when Konstantin took back the reins.

"You keep playing with fire and you're going to get burned," I said, and Cyrus laughed like I'd made a particularly funny joke. I thought back on my words, but they were nothing more than a perfectly ordinary cliché, not funny at all. Whatever the joke was, I didn't get it.

Cyrus realized I didn't get it and raised his eyebrows at me. "Playing with fire?" he prompted. "Getting burned?"

Nope, that didn't clear things up a bit.

"You are aware that my father and I are descendants of Helios, the sun god, aren't you?"

Actually, I'd never bothered to ask. For some reason, I'd kind of assumed they were descendants of Zeus because he was king of the gods. I wouldn't have thought Konstantin, who puffed himself up with so much pomp and circumstance, would be the descendant of a god many people had never even heard of.

"I'll take that as a no," Cyrus said. He turned in

his chair and tugged down the collar of his shirt so I could see the glyph that marked his skin, right where his neck joined his shoulders. It was an iridescent sun with long, spidery rays. If he wore a shirt with no collar, some of those rays would be visible, though only to other *Liberi*. I myself had a glyph in the middle of my forehead, and no mortal had ever shown any sign that they could see it.

"I'm still kind of new at this game," I reminded Cyrus. "I tend not to think about who a person's descended from unless I can see their glyph. Out of sight, out of mind."

"Understandable," he said, turning back toward me. "I've known what my father was, what *I* was, for all my life. I can't imagine what it must be like to have all this thrust upon you all of a sudden."

There was real sympathy in his words, and I had to give myself another mental slap in the face to remind myself he was one of the bad guys. He was just more subtle and deceptive about it than the rest of the Olympians.

The waitress returned to our table, bringing our food. I tried not to stare at his *croque monsieur* with naked envy, but it was hard when the bread was a perfect toasty brown and glistened with butter. My soup and salad would make a perfectly nice lunch, but Cyrus's looked positively decadent.

To my surprise, Cyrus didn't even bother to glance at his food. Instead, he opened his wallet and pulled out a twenty-dollar bill.

"Lunch is my treat, since I barged in on you so

rudely," he said, laying the money on the table and pushing back his chair.

"You're not going to eat?"

He shook his head. "I've said what I needed to say. There's no reason for me to disturb you any further."

Then why did you order food? I wondered, but declined to ask.

"I'm sure they'd be willing to give you a to-go bag. Throwing away a *croque monsieur* is a crime against nature."

Cyrus grinned at me as he stood up. "I saw the way you looked at my food when the waitress brought it. I have a strong suspicion it won't go to waste. It's been a pleasure."

I watched him leave with what I was sure was a puzzled frown on my face. I'd been properly warned off, but I had the nagging suspicion that there'd been more going on during our conversation than met the eye. However, I couldn't figure out what it was. And the *croque monsieur* was getting cold.

Cyrus was right; his food didn't go to waste. It wasn't until I was almost halfway through the sandwich that I realized Cyrus had specifically come to talk to me here, nowhere near where I lived or worked. No one knew where I was. So how had he found me?

The only explanation I could come up with was that he had tracked me by my cell phone somehow. Not something a private citizen would ordinarily be able to do, but the Olympians had so much money to throw around they could buy just about any service known to mankind.

I resisted the urge to dig my phone out of my purse and remove the battery. Cyrus already knew where I was right this moment, so there was no point. But I added a new task to my to-do list: buy a disposable cell phone.

There are some people who can chow down on butter-soaked ham and cheese sandwiches for lunch every day without gaining an ounce. I am not one of them.

Considering the radical changes my life had undergone recently, I'd decided to step up my work-out regimen so I'd be in the best possible shape to fight off bad guys, and one of my favorite workouts was running in the woods. My overindulgence at lunch and the relatively mild weather meant this was a good day for a run.

I returned to the mansion and changed into my running clothes—nothing fancy, just a T-shirt and shorts. Sometimes my friend and fellow *Liberi*-in-residence Maggie went running with me, but after my meetings with Anderson and Cyrus, I needed some time to myself, so I didn't go looking for her.

Being a city girl, I have very little concept of how big an acre is, but I knew there were a lot of them on Anderson's property. Even just running up and back along the driveway was not an inconsiderable amount of exercise, but there were also tons of woods. Those weren't conveniently furnished with running trails, though Maggie had told me that during the warmer months, Anderson brought in a tree service on a regular basis to keep the weeds and underbrush tamed. The result was that we had all the beauty of nature, without any of the inconvenience.

I went up and down the driveway once as a warm-up, then plunged into the woods, just deep enough that I couldn't see the cleared land on which the house and its environs stood. Pine needles and leaves crunched pleasantly under my feet, and the air smelled of earth and evergreens. A brilliant red cardinal peeped from its perch on a branch above me, and I was far enough away from the road that I couldn't hear any car sounds. The knot of tension in my gut released as I drank in the peace and solitude.

I was in the zone, my breathing steady, my legs carrying me at a comfortable pace without any conscious control, and I felt like I could run ten miles without being overly winded. I couldn't, of course. Marathon running wasn't one of my supernatural powers. When I came out of the almost trancelike state I was in, I'd be breathing like a racehorse and the muscles in my legs would burn something fierce, but for a few perfect minutes, I was transported.

My footsteps faltered when I heard a sound that most definitely didn't belong out here in the woods of Maryland—a roar that sounded like it came from the throat of a big cat. The sound of that roar brought me back to myself, and I felt the brisk January air burning my throat and lungs as I panted heavily. My legs felt like a pair of tree trunks, rooted to the ground, and I bent over and put my hands on my knees, watching my breath steam as I slowly came to myself.

There was another roar, and I forced myself to stand up straight and look around. I have a very good, possibly supernatural, sense of direction, and even though there were no obvious landmarks around me, just trees, trees, and more trees, I knew exactly where I was.

In the woods behind the house, there was a large, grassy clearing. I wasn't sure what its original purpose had been, but some of Anderson's *Liberi* used it as a sort of practice field, where they could hone their powers without anyone seeing them. I had used the clearing for target practice, trying to learn the limits of my supernatural aim, which seemed to apply equally well to throwing and shooting.

I was currently about fifty yards from the clearing, and with the leafless trees and the lack of underbrush, I wouldn't have to go very far before I'd be able to see whatever was going on there. The feline roar ripped through the air again, and I knew any sensible person would turn tail and run as far away from that sound as possible. But I've rarely been accused of being sensible, so I started forward again, this time at a brisk walk.

I knew who and what was in the clearing, of course. It had to be Jamaal.

A descendant of the Hindu death goddess Kali, Jamaal possessed a terrifying kind of death magic that almost had a will of its own and *wanted* to be used.

The death magic had driven him half mad, though I suspected his temper had always been an issue, even before he'd become *Liberi*. Thanks to some info I'd gathered from serial killer Justin Kerner, Jamaal had learned to channel some of that magic into the form of a tiger. Summoning the great cat seemed to vent the death magic for him, so that he was no longer as volatile as he had once been. However, his control of the tiger was shaky, to say the least, which meant that when I heard the roar, I should have known better than to approach.

Curiosity was more likely to kill *me* than the cat under the circumstances, but I'd had the reluctant hots for Jamaal almost since we first met, and I couldn't resist my urge to investigate.

I eased my way through the trees toward the clearing. I hadn't heard any more roaring, so it was possible Jamaal had put the tiger to rest. I'd only seen the creature once before, during our final battle with Justin Kerner, and I'd been too distracted by my attempts to catch a killer to take a good look.

I caught a flash of movement out of the corner of my eye. I stopped in my tracks and turned slowly, noticing for the first time that the wind was at my back—carrying my scent straight to the clearing. Perhaps the tiger had been aware of me all along and its roars had been warnings I'd foolishly failed to heed.

It was peering at me through the trees, way too close for comfort. It was a beautiful creature, no doubt about it, with pumpkin-orange stripes and a magnificently muscled body. Paws the size of skillets sported claws that could rip a person open with one swipe, and the amber eyes practically glowed with intensity.

I stood still and swallowed hard. I had no doubt the tiger could outrun me in about two strides if it felt so inclined. I stared into those amber eyes, trying to guess what it was going to do. The tiger snarled, showing off an impressive set of teeth, and I quickly dropped my gaze. I knew dogs and primates took eye contact as a form of challenge, but I wasn't sure about tigers. Of course, if this one was the embodiment of Jamaal's rage and death magic, it probably didn't take much to provoke it.

"Jamaal?" I called softly, afraid yelling would spur the tiger into motion. "A little help here?"

I didn't know exactly where he was, but he had to be nearby. I just hoped he hadn't completely lost control of the animal.

The tiger stalked forward, moving with sensuous grace. I scanned the ground in search of a rock I could use as a weapon, while keeping the tiger in my peripheral vision. Even with my powers, I didn't think throwing a rock at it would even slow the tiger down, but anything was better than just standing there and being mauled. As far as I knew, the tiger couldn't do me any lasting harm, but it could hurt me, even kill me, in the short term. The magic of the *Liberi* would bring me back no matter what happened to my body, but I'd died once before and hadn't enjoyed the experience. I wasn't eager for a repeat performance.

"Jamaal?" I called again, louder this time.

The tiger was close enough now that I could probably have reached out and scratched behind its ears. If I had a death wish, that is. I was shaking with the effort of restraining my primal urge to run, but I was sure that was the one thing I could do to make the situation even worse.

"I don't think Sita likes you," Jamaal said from behind me.

I hadn't heard him approach, but then I'd been keeping my attention firmly fixed on the tiger, where it belonged.

"Sita?" I risked a glance over my shoulder, and saw Jamaal standing a few yards away, leaning casually against a tree.

"I thought a name from Indian mythology would suit her best," he said, and even propped against the tree as he was, he swayed a bit on his feet. I realized he wasn't leaning against the tree in an attempt to look casual—he was leaning on it for support. "The wife of the god Rama."

I couldn't have cared less about the origin of the tiger's name. Jamaal's face was gleaming with sweat, and his T-shirt clung wetly to his well-muscled chest. He looked like he was about to collapse at any moment. It was possible Sita would disappear if he passed out. It was also possible she wouldn't, which would be bad.

"The name suits her," I said, rather inanely. She wasn't creeping closer anymore, but she was still giving me the evil eye, and the tip of her tail was twitching. In a house cat, that wasn't a good sign. I didn't know what it meant in a tiger, but I tended to think it was bad. "She's truly magnificent," I continued, "but don't you think it's time for her to go away now?"

Sita's lips pulled back in a snarl, as if she'd understood me and been insulted. Maybe she had.

"Come here, Sita," he called, and she obeyed, though she kept me pinned with her eyes the entire way.

Jamaal pushed away from the tree when Sita was an arm's length away, and I saw his legs trembling. He was pushing himself too hard, and it was dangerous as hell. Sita might not be able to do me permanent harm, but if he passed out and left her to her own devices . . . We didn't have any close neighbors—that was part of the point of the mansion—but the tiger wouldn't have to go very far to find more vulnerable prey.

I bit my tongue to stop myself from editorializing. The last thing I wanted to do was get Jamaal's back up while he had a lethal carnivore under tenuous control. So instead of urging him to hurry the hell up and put Sita away, I stood there and held my breath.

Jamaal reached out toward the tiger with a shaking hand, and she finally dragged her attention away from me. She closed her eyes and pressed her head up against his hand in what looked like an affectionate gesture. She followed that gesture by butting her head against his hip. I couldn't say with any accuracy how big Sita was, but if I had to guess, I'd say she weighed around five hundred pounds, most of it muscle. Her gentle head-butt was too much for Jamaal's shaky legs, and he went down.

"Jamaal!" I cried, instinctively taking a step toward him.

Sita whirled on me with a roar that made my bones vibrate, putting herself between me and Jamaal and crouching menacingly. But she didn't pounce on me, and I had the feeling she was defending Jamaal, rather than attacking. I wasn't about to argue with her, and I stepped back slowly, trying to give her some space without making her want to chase me.

Luckily, Jamaal had only lost his balance, not passed out. While I stood there with my heart in my throat, he reached up and touched Sita's flank. She gave me one last snarl, then disappeared.

For a couple of minutes, neither one of us moved. Jamaal lay on his back on the ground, his eyes closed as the sweat evaporated from his skin. His breathing was deep and steady, and I might have thought he'd passed out after all if it weren't for his bent knees, which didn't flop to the side as they would if he were unconscious. For myself, I continued to stand still, willing the adrenaline to recede.

Unfortunately, when I didn't have the heady rush of adrenaline keeping me warm, I noticed that I was freezing. I was as sweaty as Jamaal from my run, and I was wearing even less clothing. It was a nice day for January, but it was still January. I shivered and crossed my arms in a vain attempt to keep warm.

"What are you doing here, Nikki?" Jamaal asked without opening his eyes.

"I was running," I answered, although surely he'd figured that out on his own based on how I was dressed. "Did you send Sita out to stalk me, or was that her own idea?" Jamaal wasn't what I'd call the mischievous sort, and I doubted he'd have used Sita to scare me like that, but I didn't much like the idea of a magical tiger with a mind of its own.

For a moment, I thought he wasn't going to answer me, which was answer enough in its own way. Then he opened his eyes and levered himself up into a sitting position with an obvious effort. I almost reached out and offered him a hand, but I knew better by now. Jamaal was not the type to graciously accept help of any kind.

"My guess is she heard you running and decided to investigate the potential threat," he said. "You might have noticed she's a little protective of me." He shook his head as if to clear it, and I noticed that the beads at the ends of his braids were a combination of orange, black, and white.

Jamaal was color coordinating with his tiger? I had to suppress a laugh at the idea, though I wondered if Jamaal was even conscious he'd done it. He had enough beads to wear a different color every day for a year; maybe it was just a coincidence that he'd chosen tiger colors.

"I can't blame her for that," I said, though I'd have been happier if he could teach her the distinction between the good guys and the bad guys. "But maybe you should go a little easy on your practice sessions. You know, stop before you're about to drop from fatigue?"

He gave me a sour look as he laboriously dragged himself to his feet. "Venting the death magic was *your* idea. Don't complain if you don't like the results."

Jamaal's temper was a lot more stable now that he'd learned how to summon Sita, but he was still a pro at being surly. I tried not to take it personally, though I suspected there *was* something personal about it. And maybe it was time we got whatever it was out into the open. Ordinarily, I wouldn't think to initiate a personal conversation when I was standing outside in January in a damp set of running clothes and Jamaal was so shaky on his feet he had to concentrate to stand up, but this might be my only chance to get him alone for a while.

"Are you still pissed at me for trying to leave?" I blurted, wincing a bit in anticipation of his response. At the time, I'd thought leaving was the only way I could protect both myself and Steph. Emma and Anderson had still been trying to make a go of it, and Emma had—for reasons that mystified me to this day—decided that I was after her husband. I'd been sure that Emma and I couldn't coexist in the mansion, and that if it came down to it, Anderson would choose her over me. And so I'd decided I should make myself disappear.

It had seemed like a good idea at the time, though I realized now that deciding to disappear without talking it over with anyone, or even saying good-bye, had been taking the coward's way out. And I was pretty sure I'd hurt Jamaal's feelings, though he'd never admit it.

Jamaal blinked, as if confused by the abrupt change of subject. "What are you talking about?"

I didn't for a moment believe he didn't know. He just didn't want to talk about it. Like most men I knew, he wasn't a big fan of talking about his feelings.

Actually, he wasn't a big fan of talking, period. He was the strong, silent type personified, but I didn't think that was particularly good for him. Even living in the mansion with seven other people, he managed to hold himself aloof, and I thought the isolation, self-imposed though it was, exacerbated his difficulties with the death magic.

"It was wrong of me to try to sneak away like that," I said. "I was afraid that if I let anyone know I was leaving, someone would try to talk me out of it." I'd been equally afraid of how I'd feel if someone *didn't* try to talk me out of it, but I wanted to talk about Jamaal's baggage, not my own. "And I was afraid I wouldn't be able to force myself to leave. I—"

Jamaal shook his head, making his beads click. "Don't make something out of nothing. I don't care whether you stay or go."

I couldn't help flinching at his words, my heart clenching unpleasantly in my chest. I shouldn't have let it get to me. I *knew* he cared, whether he admitted it or not. And yet the words still hurt.

Jamaal sighed and wiped some of the drying

sweat from his brow. "Sorry. Didn't mean it like that. Just meant it's your decision, not mine. Now I need a shower and a nap, and you need to get inside before you turn blue."

He didn't wait for my response, turning his back abruptly enough that he almost lost his balance again and heading toward the house with a ground-eating stride. I considered running after him, trying to get him to stop and talk, but I didn't like my chances of success. And yeah, I was still feeling pretty stung.

Trying to act as if none of what had happened had gotten to me, I resumed my run. I doubt I managed more than a couple hundred yards before I gave it up as a lost cause.

THREE

The phone call came at three thirty Saturday morning, startling me out of a deep sleep. For a moment after I opened my eyes, I just lay there and hoped the annoying ringing sound would go away, but of course it didn't. I sat up, groping for the phone and staring blearily at the illuminated numbers on my clock. I'd had a land line installed in my room, but I rarely used it. I picked up the receiver and crossed my fingers it would be a wrong number.

"Hello?" I croaked.

"Don't panic," Steph's voice answered, and it sounded like she'd been crying recently. "I'm all right. No one is hurt."

Well, *that* woke me up in a hurry. I yanked the chain on the bedside lamp, blinding myself with the glare, and rubbed at the crust on my eyes.

"What's wrong?" I asked, panicking despite Steph's orders not to. Anything bad enough for her to call me at this hour was going to suck even if no one was hurt.

Steph sniffled. "It's our house." Steph lived alone, so I could only assume that by "our" house, she meant the house we'd grown up in. My throat tightened. "There was a fire . . ." Her voice faded into more sniffles.

My own eyes burned with sympathetic tears as something cold and hard sank to the pit of my stomach. "How bad?"

Steph's more of a crier than I am, and it took her a while to get her tears under control enough to talk. "The worst," she finally said. "It's gone. Everything's . . . gone."

I tried to absorb the enormity of what had happened, but I couldn't quite wrap my brain around it. Maybe I wasn't fully capable of it. Until I'd moved in with the Glasses at the age of eleven, the concept of a "home" had been alien to me. Homes were just temporary way stations, interchangeable places to sleep. I'd resided in more houses and apartments than I could count. The Glasses' house meant more to me than all the rest of them put together, but I knew instinctively that it didn't mean as much to me as it did to Steph and her parents. After my childhood, I just didn't let myself grow attached to places the way normal people did.

That didn't mean I didn't feel the loss.

I'd spent the happiest years of my life in that house, after I'd finally come to accept that the Glasses were going to keep me no matter how badly I acted out. It was warm and beautiful, decorated with exquisite taste while still managing to look comfortable and inviting. It was the Glasses' history, Steph's childhood, and my safe haven, all rolled into one. I was going to miss it, but my adoptive family was going to *grieve* for it. And I was already grieving for them.

"What happened?" I asked. I wanted to say something comforting and sympathetic to Steph, but I knew better. Steph would expect me to be as devastated and heartsick as she was about the loss of our childhood home. Comforting her when I was supposed to be equally upset would make me sound aloof and distant. I *was* heartsick, but not for reasons she'd understand.

"They don't know yet," Steph said. "The fire's out, but they won't be able to investigate until daylight."

I hoped like hell it had been a freak accident of some sort, but I couldn't help wondering . . . Emma wasn't allowed to hurt me or my family because of the treaty between the Olympians and Anderson. But I doubted that protection applied to our *property*. What also gave me pause was the fact that this wasn't the first fire that had affected me in recent weeks. Earlier this month, the office building I was renting space in had had a fire, one that destroyed my office. It hadn't *started* in my office, and the fire investigator had determined that some idiot had left his space heater on by accident. Maybe it was completely unrelated, but it seemed like quite the coincidence.

"Have you called your folks yet?" I asked.

The Glasses were on an around-the-world cruise and had been gone for two and a half months already. They still had three more weeks left, and I hated the idea of spoiling it for them when there was nothing they could do.

"*Our* folks, Nikki," Steph said sharply.

Oops. I'd forgotten. It was about fourteen years too late, but I was trying to train myself to think of the Glasses as my parents. Despite all the warmth and love they'd shown me, I'd always managed to keep a little bit of distance between us. It wasn't like I was *trying* to do it. It just sort of happened. I didn't feel like I was really their daughter, no matter what the adoption papers said. I think my insistence on referring to them as Steph's parents had been bugging her for a long time, but it was out in the open now.

"Our folks," I repeated meekly. I wasn't sure I'd ever be able to get myself to call them Mom and Dad, but I could at least take a couple of baby steps. "Have you called them yet?"

"No," she said in a small voice, and I knew she was about to cry again. "I don't know how—" She couldn't finish the sentence, her voice breaking in a sob.

"I'll do it," I told her, though it was going to be hell. Who likes breaking that kind of news to people they loved? And I *did* love the Glasses, even if I didn't truly think of them as my parents. But I could give them the news without bursting into tears, and I doubted Steph could.

"You don't have to," Steph managed to choke out, but I heard the hope in her voice.

"I'll do it," I repeated. "You shouldn't have to make this phone call more than once."

"And you can stay calm, cool, and collected when you tell them."

I was pretty sure there was a hint of censure in those words, but I chose to ignore it. I was never going to be as open and demonstrative as Steph was, and I refused to apologize for it.

"Why don't you come over when we get off the phone," I suggested. "Neither one of us is going to get any more sleep tonight. We have several industrial-sized tubs of ice cream in the freezer. Maybe you and I can demolish one together."

Steph thought about it briefly, then let out a shuddering sigh. "Okay. I'll be there in about forty minutes."

Dreading what I had to do next, I hung up the phone.

The phone call with the Glasses was every bit as excruciating as I expected. My adoptive mother's heartbroken sobs would haunt me for a long time. I wished I could give her a hug, but she was halfway around the world, and I wouldn't be hugging her anytime soon. At least Mr. Glass was there so she could cry on his shoulder. He's the stereotypical stoic male, and though the news had to have hit him hard, he kept himself together. I hoped that when he and Mrs. Glass were alone together and he didn't feel like he had to put up a brave front for me, he would take comfort from her as well as give it.

"I don't know how soon we'll be able to get home," he said. There was just a hint of hoarseness in his voice, betraying the emotions he was trying to repress. "Even if we get on the next flight, it'll take a couple of days."

"There's no need for you to cut your trip short," I said, and my motives in saying so weren't entirely pure. No, I didn't want them to miss out on whatever exciting destinations were still on their itinerary, but I also hadn't yet figured out what the hell I was going to tell them about what was going on in my life. I'd talked to them a couple of times since I'd become *Liberi,* but I hadn't told them much of anything. How I was going to explain that I was now living in a mansion with seven other people was beyond me. Especially when I insisted on holding on to the condo the Glasses had bought for me. (They'd bought it for me as a gift, but I insisted on paying rent. My baggage made it hard for me to accept money or gifts from them.)

"Steph and I can take care of anything that needs doing until you get back," I continued, crossing my fingers that he'd find my argument sound.

Mr. Glass sighed heavily. "We're not going to be in any mood for sightseeing or even relaxing after this. We might as well come home."

I had to agree that I wouldn't feel much like being on vacation, either. However, that didn't mean I had to concede the point. "I know you're not in the mood, but it might be nice to have something to take your mind off your troubles for a while. As far as I know, there's nothing you have to do that can't wait until you get back." Not that I knew much of anything about what needed to be done. There would be insurance company wrangling for sure, and heaven only knew what would be involved in getting the ruins cleaned up and a new house built. Surely Steph and I could take care of *some* of that on their behalf.

"At least take a little time to think about it," I urged. "If you decide to stay on the cruise, you can always change your mind and come home, but vice versa doesn't work. Steph and I will find you a nice rental so you don't have to stay in a hotel or anything. And we'll start the ball rolling on insurance and stuff. There's no need to make a bad situation worse by losing out on the rest of your cruise."

He let out another heavy sigh. "When did you get so smart?"

I smiled at the affection in his tone. "Guess someone just raised me right."

"All right. Your mother and I will talk it over before we make any hasty decisions. But you call us if there are any updates, or if there's anything we need to do."

"I promise."

"We'll call you tomorrow to let you know what we've decided."

"Okay."

I suspected from the tone of his voice that he was still leaning toward coming home immediately, and I couldn't blame him. Probably I'd have done the same in his shoes. But at least I'd bought a little bit of time.

Of course, if I hadn't been able to figure out how to explain my current circumstances over the course of the last few weeks, a couple of extra days probably weren't going to help all that much.

For those of you who might be tempted, I wouldn't recommend downing a tub of chocolate ice cream at four in the morning, even if you have just learned your childhood home burned to the ground. Steph and I had had help—she'd called Blake while I was on the phone with the Glasses, and he'd met me at the bottom of the stairs when I went to let Steph in. I felt like the third wheel all of a sudden, but that didn't stop me from shoveling down the ice cream until my stomach felt queasy. The sugar high buoyed me for a while, but when the crash came, I decided it was safest to leave Steph and Blake to their own devices. I felt sick enough from overeating without getting myself all worked up about their relationship.

I excused myself and went back to my suite to brood in quiet solitude. I was trying to hold on to hope that the fire had been the result of faulty wiring or some other legitimate accidental cause. I'd brought enough hardship down on my adoptive family since the fateful day my car had slammed into Emmitt Cartwright and killed him, making me a *Liberi*. The last thing I wanted to do was be the cause of more pain and heartache.

I might have lived on in blissful ignorance for at least another few hours if I hadn't decided to check my email.

I wasn't getting a whole lot of email lately, not since I'd temporarily closed up my business as a private investigator. There was never anything important in my in-box, so mostly when I checked email, it was to delete the spam that had gotten through the filter. I was happily deleting away when my cursor hit a message that chilled my blood.

THIS IS JUST THE BEGINNING, screamed the subject line, and the name in the From column said Konstantin.

Dreading what I would see, I opened the email and held my breath.

Dear Nikki,

I hope this letter finds you well.

Actually, no, I don't. I hope it finds you miserable and guilt stricken.

I've put a lot of time and thought into my current situation. I have been forced to step down as king of the Olympians, a position I've held for several centuries and to which I had become accustomed. I have been exiled from my people, forced to live in hiding for fear that the more predatory amongst them might want to ensure my permanent removal. I have been forced to abandon a magnificent home and watch as my worthless son attempts to destroy from within everything I've built over my long, long life.

All of these indignities I've been forced to face, I can trace back to one person: you.

If you had joined the Olympians when I invited you, none of this would have happened. You and I could have lived harmoniously together, and we could have hunted down Justin Kerner without all the fuss and fireworks. Maybe if I hadn't had to ask for Anderson's help to stop Kerner, we could have captured and neutralized him before he killed Phoebe. Certainly we could have taken care of him quietly, in such a way that no one untrustworthy had to know about my lapse in judgment.

But you *didn't* join us. Instead, you set yourself up in opposition, and you went out of your way to reveal every detail of what had happened. You cost me everything I hold dear, and I plan to pay you back in kind.

This morning's little surprise was nothing more than a warning shot across the bow. I have much, much more in store for you. I know you'll be hunting for me, and maybe you think you'll catch me before I can fully realize my revenge. But I didn't manage to become king of the Olympians and lead them for centuries without having an impressive bag of tricks at hand. I'm betting I can break you before you get to me. And if you think you can invoke your silly little treaty and get Cyrus to control me, you are gravely mistaken. I will do nothing to harm you or your family. Nothing that will officially break the treaty. Hurting you without breaking the treaty will be quite the enjoyable test to my creativity. And believe me, I am highly creative.

Be afraid, Nikki Glass. I am coming for you.

Yours, Konstantin

I read the email twice, hardly believing what I was reading. Konstantin blamed *me* for all his troubles? That was nuts.

I'll admit, I'd certainly had a hand in his downfall. It was I who'd unraveled the mystery and found out why Justin Kerner was hunting the D.C. area. I'd discovered that his death magic combined with the taint of supernatural madness made him capable of killing *Liberi,* and that he wanted to kill them all—starting with Konstantin—for having forced him to take the tainted seed in the first place. I'd uncovered the fact that all of the Olympians could have been killed because Konstantin made a mistake, and that was what caused him to lose power. But that didn't mean it was my *fault*.

I rubbed my eyes, which ached with a combination of weariness and lingering grief over my family's pain. Why did every *Liberi* blame *me* when things went wrong in their lives? Jamaal had originally blamed me for killing Emmitt. Emma blamed me for the dissolution of her marriage, which I believed she was 100 percent responsible for herself. And now Konstantin was blaming me for his own screwup.

I had only met Konstantin once, and though he'd chilled me to the bone with his coldness and malice, I had never once suspected he was *insane*. But a vendetta of this magnitude did not speak of a man of sound mind. Maybe losing his place at the top of the totem pole had cost him his sanity as well as his power.

Whatever the reason, he was one hell of a dangerous enemy. And if he was coming after me, my life was going to get a lot more difficult very soon.

Four

It was still oh-God o'clock, and the sun hadn't even begun to peek up over the horizon yet, but I was so wired on stress and chocolate ice cream that I didn't put much consideration into other people's comfort and routine.

I forwarded the threatening email to Leo, our resident computer expert. He was a descendant of Hermes, and had a Midas touch where money was concerned. He'd first started learning about computers so he could keep in constant touch with the stock market, but he'd taken to them like a duck to water, and his hacking skills were sometimes downright scary.

Leo's rooms were down the hall from mine, and after I hit send, I scurried to his door and knocked. I figured the email I just forwarded needed an explanation, and it wasn't until I'd knocked a second time without an answer that I realized what time it was, and that I was probably the only person in the house awake at this hour, other than Blake and Steph, if they were still up. I was badly rattled and wanted to get a start on finding Konstantin *now,* but as urgent as it felt to me, I knew it wasn't reasonable to be waking anybody up before six. Whatever Konstantin had planned for me, it would take days, weeks, maybe even months to develop, and letting Leo get another couple hours of sleep wouldn't endanger anyone.

I was just turning to go back to my room when the door behind me opened.

When I first caught sight of Leo, I was sure I'd routed him out of bed. He was wearing a fluffy white bathrobe over blue and white striped pajamas. A second glance showed me that his mousy brown hair was slightly damp and his cheeks were freshly shaven. He smelled of drugstore aftershave and Listerine, and I came to the inevitable conclusion that I hadn't woken him up after all. His eyes widened when he saw me.

"Nikki?" he said. "What are you doing here?" He reached into the pocket of his robe and pulled out a pair of wire-rimmed glasses, shoving them onto his face in a gesture that looked almost nervous. I realized I'd never seen him without the glasses before.

I think Leo has a good heart, or he wouldn't be working for Anderson, but he's about as socially awkward an individual as I've ever met. He has an obvious aversion to eye contact, and he always seems a bit nervous and distracted, like only a fraction of his attention is actually focused on whoever he's talking to. I suspect when he heard the knock on his door, he assumed it was Anderson, and finding me there threw him for a bit of a loop. His shoulders hunched as if he were expecting a blow, and his gaze dropped to the floor.

He was nervous with everyone, but more so with me, the newcomer to the house. I wondered if I should have explained what was going on via email instead of coming to his suite, but it was too late now.

"Hi, Leo. I'm sorry to bother you so early in the morning. I hope I didn't wake you." I knew I hadn't, but it seemed like the polite thing to say, and I found Leo's nerves and awkwardness contagious.

"I was awake," he told my left shoulder. "The European markets start opening at four."

Geez, and I'd thought *I* was an early riser. I'd never known anyone else in the house was up at this hour, which I guessed meant Leo didn't venture out of his rooms in the morning. Actually, Leo didn't venture out of his rooms much at all. Sometimes he had to be reminded to step away from his computers and eat. It didn't seem like much of a life to me, but what do I know?

With anyone else, I probably would have tried a little small talk before launching into my request, but I figured Leo wouldn't blame me—hell, he probably wouldn't even notice—if I skipped the social niceties.

"I forwarded you an email," I told him. "It's supposedly from Konstantin. I wonder if you'd be able to trace it or something." I honestly didn't think Konstantin was stupid enough to send me a trail of bread crumbs that would lead right to him, but I figured it would be foolish not to at least check it out. Not to mention that Konstantin was centuries old and might not be as computer literate as a modern man.

"I'll see what I can do."

Leo didn't beckon me to follow as he retreated into his room, but he didn't close the door, either. I assumed that was an invitation to come in, so I stepped inside.

All of the suites Anderson's *Liberi* inhabited consisted of two rooms. For most of us, one of those rooms was the bedroom, and one was some version of a sitting room. I supposed with his fanatical attachment to the stock market and his lack of socialization, a sitting room would have been useless for Leo. Instead, the first room of his two-room suite was what I imagined the inside of a NASA control room might look like, only less tidy.

A huge L-shaped desk took up about half the room, and practically every inch of that desk was covered with computer equipment, bristling with tangled cords and surge protectors. I saw laptops and desktops, Macs and PCs, shiny new machines and old clunkers that looked like they were held together by duct tape. There were monitors sprinkled here and there on the desk, but there was also a bank of them mounted on the wall. Disassembled units spewing spare parts were tucked under the desk and pushed up against the other walls, and a freestanding air conditioner blasted cold air into the room even though it was January.

Leo must have noticed me staring at the air conditioner.

"The computers generate a lot of heat," he explained. "If I didn't keep the air conditioner going, my equipment would overheat."

He plopped down into a rolling chair and used the edge of the desk to pull himself over in front of one of the computers. His fingers moved lightning fast over the keyboard. Whatever he was using as an email reader wasn't anything I'd seen before, and I wondered if it was something Leo had created himself. There were no pretty icons or neatly labeled buttons, and instead of tooling around with a mouse or track pad, Leo was typing into a command window. He paused practically midkeystroke and glanced over at one of the other monitors. He frowned and wheeled himself over, hit a couple of keys, then returned to the email.

"You're really into multitasking, aren't you?" I murmured.

"Have to be," he answered without turning his attention away from the computers. "Sometimes all the markets are open at the same time. Don't want to miss anything."

I was tempted to ask him what he did for fun, but I already knew the answer. Maybe he wasn't just socially awkward. Maybe he actually bordered on autistic, though he was obviously high functioning. I wondered if he'd always been like that, or if becoming *Liberi* had changed him. Then I wondered how someone as mild mannered and aloof as Leo could have become *Liberi* in the first place. Unless he was one of the original *Liberi*—the *son* of a god, rather than just a descendant of one—he had to have killed someone to become immortal. I had a hard time imagining him doing that.

"I like numbers more than I like people," he said without looking up, as if he could guess the direction of my thoughts. His fingers kept zipping across the keyboard. There was an edge of defensiveness in his voice. "Whenever someone new comes along, they feel sorry for me and try to draw me out, but I'm not like the rest of you. I'm happy like this."

Maybe that was why he was so nervous around me—he was waiting for me to try to "save" him. If he were an ordinary human being, I might have thought him desperately in need of human contact. I might have thought he couldn't possibly be living a good life shut up in his room with his computers all the time. But he wasn't an ordinary human being—he was a *Liberi*. Immortality, and the powers that were awakened in a *Liberi* when he or she became immortal, changed people, made them something other than human. When Leo said he was happy with his life as it was, I believed him.

"I don't feel sorry for you," I said, though maybe that wasn't strictly true. It seemed sad to me that Leo would spend so much of his time so completely alone, but I knew I was imposing my own likes and dislikes on him. "I wouldn't want to live like this, but if it works for you, that's all that matters."

He paused for a moment in his typing, looking

over his shoulder at me, though he still didn't meet my eyes. "Thank you."

"No problem."

He turned back to his computer and tapped a few more keys. Then he nodded sagely and spoke without turning around.

"The email was sent from a computer at the FedEx Print and Ship on K Street at 4:02 A.M. The email account was created at 3:46 A.M. and deleted at 4:03. Sending that email is the only activity associated with the account, and the user registered as John Smith."

"Creative," I muttered under my breath. I'd have to swing by and see if anyone there remembered seeing Konstantin, though even if they did, I didn't think it would be much help. I needed to know where he was *now,* not where he'd been at 4 A.M.

Leo shrugged apologetically. "Sorry that's all I could get."

I almost laughed. "You got everything there was, and in about five minutes. I couldn't have asked for more."

He didn't respond, instead zipping his chair over to another computer and typing at high speed. But even so, I didn't miss the pleased little smile on his lips.

I'm not particularly fond of admitting I'm wrong—who is?—but it seemed like the logical conclusion, given the evidence. Trying to catch Konstantin all by myself would be flat-out stupid, and it wasn't like I could do anything to him if I caught him. Which meant I had to swallow my pride and tell Anderson I'd changed my mind about the hunt.

I was in a foul mood when I stepped into his study after a late breakfast I'd forced myself to eat in an attempt to counteract the ice-cream binge. I desperately wanted to catch Konstantin before his next attack, whatever that would be, but I wasn't overly optimistic about my chances. I didn't have much to go on, and since Konstantin knew he'd have a descendant of Artemis on his tail, he was no doubt going to be extra paranoid and careful about keeping himself hidden.

The icing on my grumpy-pants cake was the sympathy the rest of Anderson's *Liberi* had thrown my way. Blake had apparently spread the word after Steph's visit, and my friends/coworkers had paraded through my suite to offer their condolences. I had to endure a long, motherly hug from Maggie, who was so sweet my misfortune brought a sheen of tears to her eyes; an awkward visit from Logan, who was too much of a manly man to know how to express his sympathies comfortably; and an even more awkward visit from Jack, who, with his trickster heritage, had trouble being serious for more than two minutes in a row.

Only Jamaal failed to put in an appearance, and that hurt me though it probably shouldn't have. He was even less comfortable with expressing feelings than Logan. But I couldn't help taking it as even more evidence that whatever friendship we had started to build together had been destroyed, either by my willingness to leave, or by our tentative foray into romance. I wished I knew which.

Anderson was sitting at his desk when I ventured through the open door of his study. I had the immediate impression he'd been waiting for me, though perhaps that was egocentric of me. He spent a lot of time in his study, and it was always the first place to check when I wanted to look for him.

I didn't know what Anderson generally did all day while he was sitting around in his study, but this morning, he was reading the newspaper. I hadn't read a real, printed newspaper since I was a kid clamoring for the Sunday comics, but Anderson was a bit of a traditionalist. Not surprising for a god who'd been around since the dawn of time, I suppose.

He folded the paper when I came in and laid it down on his desk. His fingertips were stained gray from handling newsprint. He was badly in need of a haircut, and I wished he'd either learn how to iron or start buying no-iron shirts. But looking like an unprepossessing slob is part of his disguise, part of how he hides the enormous power that lies just beneath his surface.

"I'm sorry to hear about your house," he said, beckoning me to one of the chairs in front of his desk. There was no hint of "I told you so" in his voice, and he looked genuinely sorry.

If one more person told me how sorry they were, I was going to scream. *Unless that person is Jamaal,* I mentally amended.

The sympathy—I refused to think of it as pity—sat heavily on my shoulders, and I practically collapsed into the chair. I wanted to maintain some semblance of dignity, but the weight of it all was getting to me, and my throat tightened like I was going to cry.

It was just a house, dammit. A thing, an object. Something that could be rebuilt. It had been empty when it burned down, and no one was hurt. That was all that mattered. I swallowed hard, trying to push the irrational grief back down inside. The Glasses and Steph had a right to grieve over the loss of their home, but it had never really been mine to begin with. So why did I suddenly feel like someone had just died?

Anderson rolled one of his desk drawers open and pulled out a little pop-up box of tissues, setting them on the edge of the desk within easy reach. "Just in case," he said with a small, sad smile.

I was *not* going to cry about this. I was not going to make it that easy for Konstantin to hurt me.

"I'm fine," I said, more to convince myself than to convince Anderson. "And you win: I will hunt Konstantin to the ends of the earth if that's what I have to do to keep him from hurting my family anymore."

I had the brief, unworthy thought that it was convenient for Anderson that the very week when he'd pinned me down and forced me to listen to—and refuse—his request, my adoptive parents' house should burn down and Konstantin should taunt me with that email.

"I knew he'd lash out eventually," Anderson said. "But it never occurred to me that he'd come after *you*. *I'm* his true enemy here, not you."

"Yes," I agreed, "but you're a lot harder to hurt. Plus, he's scared of you, though I don't suppose he'd admit it."

To tell you the truth, despite Anderson's dire predictions, I was actually kind of surprised that Konstantin had decided to go on the warpath. If he'd kept his head down and hadn't bothered anyone, I wouldn't have been motivated to hunt him down for Anderson to kill. Though perhaps he didn't know that. Perhaps he was incapable of understanding my reluctance to commit murder for revenge. Even Anderson hadn't understood, and he had a much firmer grasp of the concept of morality than Konstantin did.

"Good point," Anderson said. "Though I expect he will eventually scrape up his courage. I already want him dead, and he knows that. It's not like provoking me would change anything."

No, but provoking *me* had had a definite effect, spurring me into the hunt. Maybe Konstantin hadn't realized I wasn't planning to hunt him—or maybe someone who really, really wanted Konstantin dead had thought it a good idea to provide me a little motivation.

I stared at Anderson across the desk, wondering if he was ruthless enough to do something like that. He'd wanted his revenge badly enough that he'd neglected to tell anyone that Konstantin was still under the Olympians' protection. But still, burning down my parents' home . . . As ruthless and manipulative as I suspected Anderson could be, I couldn't see him doing something like that to innocent bystanders. However, I didn't have much trouble coming up with another suspect.

"What if someone knew I wasn't going to hunt him for you?" I asked, watching Anderson's face carefully. I suspected I was about to piss him off. "And what if that someone wanted him dead and would get a real kick out of hurting me in the process?"

Anderson froze in his seat, his face going so still he looked like a statue. He didn't breathe or blink, and I had the feeling something dangerous was brewing inside him. I half expected him to leap over the desk and seize me by the throat, and I mentally mapped out my escape route. Then he blinked, and the life returned to his face.

"You mean Emma," he said, as if there could be any doubt who I was talking about. His voice was even and his expression bland, but he had never taken well to accusations about Emma, and I didn't expect that to change now.

"Yeah. She'd love to be able to hurt me without breaking the treaty. And she knows my family is my weak spot. And the only person she hates more than me is Konstantin."

"I understand why you suspect her," Anderson said carefully, then paused.

"But . . . ?"

"She was . . . damaged by what Konstantin and Alexis did to her. I know that for a long time I tried to ignore that damage, and that makes my judgment where she's concerned questionable in your mind. But no matter how damaged she is, she's still the same woman I married, beneath it all. She's joined the Olympians to spite me, but just because she's joined them doesn't mean she *is* one at heart."

I clenched my jaws to hold back my protest. His judgment was more than just questionable where Emma was concerned, and I had absolutely no doubt she was capable of burning down my parents' house if she thought that would get her what she wanted. What I *did* doubt was that any force on earth could make Anderson believe that without some pretty overwhelming evidence to support the theory.

Anderson shook his head, having thoroughly talked himself into discounting my suggestion. "Emma didn't do it," he said firmly. "I told you Konstantin would strike out, and he has. Let's not go looking for complex explanations when a very obvious and simple one exists."

That clanking sound I heard was the doors of his mind slamming shut. I would have argued with him more if I thought there was a chance I could convince him, and if I thought for sure Emma really was the culprit. I was certainly willing to entertain the possibility, but I had to admit that for the moment, Konstantin had to take center stage as the prime suspect.

"I don't have any clue how I'll find him," I said,

cursing my annoyingly mercurial power. My ability to find people is based on supernaturally fueled hunches, but it's hard to tell the difference between an honest-to-goodness hunch, wishful thinking, and random stray thoughts. "But I'll get right on it. I still have that list of Olympian properties from when I was searching for Emma. I doubt he'll be on one, but I'll start cruising by them one-by-one tonight."

For the most part, I didn't truly understand how my powers worked. It would probably take years of trial and error before I had any real confidence in them. But it did seem they worked better in the moonlight, which made sense because Artemis was a moon goddess as well as a huntress.

"The question then becomes, what do we do if I find him?" I gave Anderson a hard look. "I ran into Cyrus the other day, and he informed me that his father is still an Olympian and under their protection. He said he'd talked to you about it and you'd agreed to leave Konstantin alone."

Anderson didn't bother trying to act like he felt guilty about his tacit deception. "I gave him that impression, it's true. And if there's any way we can eliminate Konstantin without Cyrus having to know we're responsible, that's how we'll do it."

I shook my head. "If you kill him and he disappears off the face of the earth, everyone's going to know you were behind it."

"Not true. Only you know what I can do. As far as anyone else is concerned, I can't kill Konstantin unless I have a Descendant around to do my dirty work, and I don't. As long as we leave no evidence that can be traced back to us, Cyrus will have to assume that one of Konstantin's other enemies got to him. An Olympian enemy, because, believe me, those exist."

I did believe him about Konstantin having enemies within the Olympians. There were probably plenty of them who'd chafed under his rule over the years. But I didn't buy the idea that Anderson wouldn't be suspect number one.

"Look," Anderson said, leaning forward and clasping his hands on the desk, "Cyrus isn't going to start a war unless he's certain I've broken our treaty. Unlike Konstantin, he actually values people and would care if someone close to him got killed. It's not something he's going to risk unless he has to."

I reluctantly had to admit that Anderson had a point. I knew Cyrus wasn't as nice a guy as he pretended to be, but he wasn't *evil*. After all, he was protecting his father out of loyalty—misguided though it might be—and that proved he cared about something other than himself. I didn't know who else among the Olympians Cyrus cared about, but I did know he cared about Blake. And Blake could very easily get killed if we went to war.

"So what you're saying is if I find Konstantin, I should keep my mouth shut to everyone else and only tell you. Right?"

Anderson nodded. "Exactly. I don't mind everyone knowing you're hunting him, because no one would believe you weren't, after what happened. But if you find him, that has to be our secret. And I'll take care of what needs to be done."

I still didn't like it, not one bit. But I'd gotten as much concession out of Anderson as I was going to, and I had to be satisfied with it.

FIVE

The rest of the day didn't go a whole lot better than the beginning of it had. Steph called me to say the fire investigator had already declared the incident was arson. Whoever had set it had made no attempt to be subtle or try to hide the crime. Which made sense, considering the whole point of it was for me to know it was the start of Konstantin's path to revenge.

Steph was brisk and businesslike when we talked, telling me the facts without falling apart or betraying any emotion whatsoever. She was in problem-solver mode, and she'd distanced herself from her own pain. Considering how much charity work she did, and how often she ended up in charge of the charity functions she worked on, she was better suited for the job than I was. She'd already been in touch with the insurance company and had even tracked down the builder who'd designed and constructed the house more than twenty years ago.

Not once did Steph hint that she blamed me for what had happened, but I didn't know how she could *not*. I had already brought so much misery into her life. She'd been attacked by Alexis because of me, and now her childhood home had been destroyed. She didn't need me to tell her the fire had something to do with me, not after it was declared arson. Guilt pounded at me relentlessly, and I didn't know what to do with it. Big Sister Steph was the one I leaned on when I needed emotional support, but that wasn't an option this time.

I tried burying myself in work, digging up my previous list of Olympian properties in the D.C. area and then doing some research to see if they'd bought anything else since last I'd checked. Let me tell you, the Olympians own a lot of property, both commercial and residential, and I doubted I'd identified all of it despite my research. They knew how to use shell corporations and offshore bank accounts and out-and-out bribery to hide their assets. And let's not even talk about their worldwide holdings.

My gut told me Konstantin would not have left town, and the fact that he'd sent that email from a local FedEx seemed to support the theory. My ever-present voice of self-doubt pointed out that Konstantin could easily have hired someone to do the dirty work from afar. Maybe he was living like the king he thought himself to be in Monte Carlo or somewhere else far away from here. But if I had to search the whole world for him, I was in deep trouble.

I mapped out a driving route that would take me

past many of the Olympian properties that I deemed likely candidates. It would take several nights to do a drive-by on every one, especially if I wanted to actually get some sleep once in a while. For the time being, I was skipping the places that were directly owned by known Olympians, figuring those were just too obvious, but that still left me with a daunting list of possibilities. Yet I had to start somewhere.

I got so caught up in what I was doing that I forgot to eat lunch, and when I finally was satisfied with my itinerary for the first night, the sun was on its way down and I was ravenous. I ventured downstairs into the kitchen, hoping someone was cooking a communal dinner.

It was something of a frail hope, as only Maggie and Logan did much in the way of cooking, and they usually let everyone know when they were doing it. Anderson made a vat of chili every once in a while, and Jack had once made some kind of stew that no one in the house had been willing to touch. Maybe he'd thought he'd fool me into tasting it, seeing as I was the new person, but I wasn't stupid enough to eat something a trickster prepared.

There were no enticing aromas drifting from the kitchen, and I figured it would be a Lean Cuisine night for me. However, I was in luck after all. There were no enticing smells, but Logan was hard at work on some kind of cold noodle dish. A huge salad bowl filled with noodles in brown sauce sat on the counter, and Logan was shredding a head of bok choy with the ease and quickness of a professional.

"Need a sous chef?" I asked as he tossed the shredded bok choy in with the noodles.

Logan looked at me doubtfully as he sliced a red pepper into ribbons. If it had been me wielding the knife, I'd probably have sliced my own fingers off, even if I *was* looking at what I was doing. He jerked his chin toward the salad bowl.

"You can toss all of that together, if you'd like. I'm almost done with the knife-work."

I was just as happy not to be put to work slicing veggies, as it would take me at least four times as long as it was taking him. The man was almost as fast and efficient as a Cuisinart. He was a descendant of Tyr, a Germanic war god, and apparently his supernatural skills with weapons carried over to the kitchen.

I grabbed the salad tongs and began gingerly tossing the noodles and veggies with the sauce. I was afraid to do it too vigorously, or I'd spill stuff all over the place. Close up, I could smell soy sauce and ginger, and now the aromatic tang of red pepper. Leave it to Logan to make a cold salad into an enticing meal.

Logan finished his chopping and shredding, then nudged me aside to take over tossing the noodles. I don't think he'd really wanted my help in the first place.

I drifted into the breakfast nook, which is like a mini-sunroom with three walls of glass looking out over the back lawn. Sunset tinged the scattered clouds with hints of peach and pink, and the woods beyond the lawn created the illusion that we were miles from civilization.

It was a nice view, until I saw the familiar orange and black stripes through a break in the trees. Moments later, Sita emerged onto the lawn, ambling along like she was taking a leisurely tour. I didn't think it was smart of Jamaal to bring her this close to the house, particularly when she didn't seem to differentiate friend from foe. Then again, I didn't see Jamaal anywhere, so Sita might have decided to go on a walkabout all by herself, which did not speak well of his ability to control her.

"What are you looking at?" Logan asked as he set a couple of bowls of noodles down on the table.

Mutely, I pointed.

"Oh." Logan sounded about as thrilled to see her as I was. There had been an . . . incident with Logan and Sita before and he'd almost gotten mauled before Jamaal was able to reel her in. I think he held a bit of a grudge. "Where the hell is Jamaal?" he muttered, and it was a good question.

If Sita were to leave the edge of the property, that would be bad. I didn't want to think about how the humans around us would react if she toured the neighborhood, nor did I want to think about what Sita would do if she took exception to the reactions.

"We can't just let her wander around loose," I said.

"I know," Logan replied grimly, then headed back into the main part of the kitchen and grabbed the chef's knife he'd been using. "I'll keep the damn cat busy, and you use your mojo to find Jamaal and drag his ass over here to corral her."

This did not sound like the world's greatest plan to me. Logan might be a war god descendant and really good with a knife, but I doubted he was a match for a full-grown tiger. Especially a supernatural one that might have powers we were as yet unaware of. However, he and I could survive being mauled if it came to that; our human neighbors could not. I hoped Jamaal wasn't passed out somewhere.

Logan strode out the back door with me following close on his heels. Sita caught sight of us immediately and went eerily still. Her lips pulled back in a snarl.

"I am going to kick Jamaal's ass," Logan muttered, then started toward Sita with a resigned sigh.

I began edging my way toward the woods, keeping a wary eye on the tiger. She *should* have been focused on Logan, who was coming directly toward her, but to my dismay, she was looking straight at me.

"Here, kitty, kitty," Logan called, and I had to admit I was impressed with his bravery. He was acting like initiating hand-to-claw fighting with a supernatural tiger was nothing more than an annoying inconvenience.

Sita flicked a glance at Logan, flattening her ears, and I thought our plan, such as it was, was working. I sped up, making sure not to get any closer to her on my way to the woods. Unfortunately, Sita dismissed Logan after that single glance, fixing her gaze on me once more and stalking toward me. I'm no expert at reading tiger body language, but the predatory glide of her movement suggested she wasn't heading over to give me an affectionate head-butt like she'd given Jamaal. I'd thought Jamaal was being a smartass when he said Sita didn't like me, but I was beginning to think he'd meant it literally.

"Oh, come on, you dumb animal," Logan said, moving to put himself between me and the tiger. "She's no threat. *I'm* the one you have to worry about."

Sita roared, and I didn't know if she was pissed off because Logan had gotten between her and her prey, or if she was smarter than your average tiger and was insulted by the "dumb animal" comment. Logan crouched, ready for the tiger's attack, but Sita decided that was a good time to remind us that she wasn't really a tiger and was in fact a supernatural being. Instead of attacking Logan to get him out of the way, she merely leapt over him, her ridiculously powerful haunches lifting her so high that she sailed over the point of Logan's knife as he tried to strike at her.

"Shit!" I yelled succinctly, and though I knew running would only stimulate her predatory instincts, I didn't have a choice.

I bolted for the door as Logan yelled again, trying in vain to distract Sita. I could have sworn I felt the vibration of her footsteps as she thundered after me, but that was probably just my imagination. I knew better than to look over my shoulder, because the last thing I needed was to lose speed.

I made it to the door and shoved it open, skidding over the threshold and practically falling flat on my face. I turned to push the door closed, and saw that Sita was almost upon me. I pushed with all my might, and this time I really did knock myself down. But the door closed before Sita made it through, and for a moment, I lay there on the floor and tried to regain my breath and slow down my frantic heart.

Until Sita gave me another nasty reminder that she wasn't a natural tiger and passed right through the door.

There was nothing I could do to defend myself. I was lying on my back on the floor, gasping for breath, and she was practically on top of me. She roared directly in my face, so close I could feel the heat and dampness of her breath. I closed my eyes and tried to brace myself for the pain I was about to suffer, and the horrifying ordeal of death that would come shortly after.

She roared again, nowhere near as close to my face, and I opened my eyes to see that Logan stood in the doorway and had grabbed her tail with his left hand. That finally got her attention, and she turned to swat at him with one massive paw. He let go of her tail and jumped backward, moving faster than should have been possible, and she just missed him. I could almost see her moment of indecision, as she tried to decide which of us she wanted to kill first.

"Sita, stop it!"

Jamaal's voice was about the most welcome thing I'd ever heard. Sita gave a snarl that sounded almost surly. I didn't want to attract her attention by moving while she was still in easy swatting range, but I didn't much like lying flat on my back on the floor, so I cautiously pushed myself up into a sitting position.

Between Sita and Logan, my vision was well and truly blocked, and I couldn't see Jamaal.

Logan couldn't see Jamaal, either, because he was still focused on Sita, his knife at the ready. "I am going to kick your ass six ways from Sunday," he said with feeling, and he wasn't talking to the tiger.

Sita roared out another challenge, this one directed at Logan, not me.

"No!" Jamaal yelled, and his hand clamped down on Logan's shoulder and pulled him back out of the doorway. "He didn't mean it!" Jamaal said to Sita. "It was a figure of speech."

I blinked at him. He looked terrible, his clothes drenched with sweat, his eyes bloodshot, but at least he wasn't passed out somewhere.

"Does she understand you?" I asked.

Jamaal nodded. "I'm not sure exactly how *much* she understands, but yeah, she definitely understood that."

Yet another reminder that she wasn't a normal tiger. "Well, maybe you could have a talk with her about the difference between the good guys and the bad guys."

Sita snorted, and flicked her tail across my face. I took that as an insult, though if she had to hit me with something, I definitely preferred her tail to her paws.

"Enough excitement for one day, sweetheart," Jamaal said, smiling fondly at the creature that had just almost eaten Logan and me for dinner. He reached out and scratched behind her ears. She turned to look at me once more, and I could swear the expression on her face was *smug*. Then, she disappeared.

Jamaal sagged against the door frame, his head lowering in obvious exhaustion. He was shivering in the cold, and there was dirt ground into the knees of his jeans. I was pretty sure this meant he had collapsed during his practice session with Sita and that was why she'd been free to wander around the property on her own.

"Get inside and sit down before you fall down," Logan said curtly, then gave Jamaal a little shove to get him moving.

Jamaal wasn't up to handling a shove in the back, and he pitched forward just as I was getting up off the floor. I held out my hands, both to steady him and to avoid being crushed, while Logan stepped inside and closed the door behind him with more force than necessary. I had to admit, he had reason to be pissed off, but now wasn't the time to express it. I gave him a dirty look as I looped Jamaal's arm over my shoulders and braced myself against his not-inconsiderable weight. It says something about the shape he was in that when he tried to pull away from me, he couldn't.

"Come on," I said, taking a step toward the breakfast nook, which was the closest place to find a chair, and hoping Jamaal would move along with me. After a moment's hesitation, he did. He was still shivering, and I didn't think his sweat-soaked shirt was helping the situation.

I helped Jamaal to one of the chairs, which he practically fell into. Logan was still behind me, and I knew without looking that he was giving Jamaal the evil eye. Jamaal tried to take a deep breath, but he was shivering too hard.

"Will you let me get you a dry shirt?" I asked.

"I'm fine," he said with a shake of his head that rattled his beads. It would have been more convincing if his teeth weren't chattering.

I knew without needing to be told that Jamaal had never taken his shirt off around his fellow *Liberi*. He was more than a little self-conscious about the wealth of scars that riddled his chest and back, a consequence of his mortal life, in which he'd been a slave. He had never told anyone but me about his background, and Anderson and the rest of his *Liberi* were under the impression that Jamaal was only about fifty years old.

"You are *not* fine," Logan snapped, and to my surprise, he pulled off his own long-sleeved tee and threw it at Jamaal. "Put that on!"

Jamaal had never been too good at taking orders, and he gave Logan a snarl that would have done Sita proud. "I'm not wearing your fucking shirt," he said, and threw the shirt back at Logan. Which would have worked better if he weren't weak as a kitten. The shirt fluttered to the floor well short of its goal.

Logan snatched the shirt from the floor and held it out to Jamaal. "Put it on yourself, or I'm putting it on you. You're in no shape to fight me."

Jamaal growled, but Logan was right and he

didn't have the strength to put up a fight. He took the shirt with obvious reluctance and went to pull it on over his head.

Logan rolled his eyes. "Take the wet shirt off first, dimwit."

Jamaal froze, a look of near panic on his face. He gave me a pleading look, and it shows just how shaken he was that he was willing to reach out to me for help.

"You think I don't know you have scars?" Logan asked, his voice suddenly gentling.

Jamaal's eyes went even wider, and he gaped at Logan. "How can you know?" he asked.

"I tended your body after the executions, man. I know you have a shitload of scars. You don't want to talk about them, that's fine with me. Just change out of that wet shirt before someone else comes in looking for dinner."

Still shivering, Jamaal reluctantly peeled off his shirt, his shoulders hunched in a protective posture. He pulled Logan's shirt on so fast it was a wonder he didn't rip it, especially since he was at least a size larger than Logan.

"I'm going to run up and get a new shirt," Logan said, "and when I get back down, we're going to talk about what just happened."

"That's what you think," Jamaal muttered under his breath, but Logan hadn't waited to hear his answer and was already on his way out the door.

Jamaal's head was bowed, maybe in exhaustion, maybe in shame. He'd always seemed ashamed of himself when the death magic made his temper crack, but from my point of view, he had nothing to be ashamed of. It wasn't like the death magic was a character flaw; he'd never asked for it. But I knew he wouldn't appreciate it if I voiced the sentiment, especially when he seemed to be studiously avoiding my gaze. I decided acting as if nothing had happened might be the wisest course of action.

"Do you want some coffee?" I asked. "Or some food? Logan made some kind of cold noodle dish that looks delicious."

"I'm sorry Sita went after you," he said, ignoring my question and still not looking at me.

I sighed and pulled out a chair so I could sit closer to his eye level. He met my gaze for about a millisecond before glancing away again.

"Please talk to me," I said. "I can't help thinking Sita's aversion to me may have something to do with how *you* feel about me." It made sense to me that if Jamaal was still pissed at me for my attempted abandonment, Sita would pick up on it and hold it against me.

"I'm not the sharing-my-feelings type." He shoved to his feet, his balance still unsteady.

I reached out to help him, but he neatly avoided my grasp.

"I don't need your help."

"Jamaal—"

"Leave me alone, Nikki."

He turned his back on me and staggered out of the kitchen. I wanted to follow him, to try again, but

I knew better. He had shut himself off from me—and from the rest of Anderson's *Liberi*. Everyone was relieved that his temper was so much better controlled these days. So relieved I doubted anyone but me had seen the downside yet. Sure, he was easier to live with this way, but I didn't think the isolation was good for him. Leo might be genuinely happy to live ensconced in his room with his computers and minimal human contact, but Jamaal needed people, whether he liked to admit it or not.

Someone was going to have to chip away at the barriers he'd built around himself. I had a feeling the only someone who'd even be willing to try was me.

Six

My appetite had fled after all the excitement, but I sat down and ate the bowl of noodles Logan had dished out for me anyway. Logan didn't return to the kitchen, and I wondered if he and Jamaal had bumped into each other on the stairway. Logan had seemed pretty determined to give Jamaal a talking to, and Jamaal had been equally determined to avoid it. I hadn't heard any sounds of battle, so I assumed either it was something else that distracted Logan, or he and Jamaal were talking things out like civilized adults.

I put the rest of the noodles in the fridge, then picked up the soggy shirt Jamaal had considerately left in a heap on the floor. I draped it over the back of one of the chairs to dry, then retrieved my purse and my planned itinerary for the night from my room. I thought long and hard about whether to bring my .38 Special with me. I would be within the D.C. city limits for some of the drive, and it would be illegal to carry a loaded gun when I was. I could have locked the gun in the trunk, unloaded, but that would defeat the purpose of having it with me.

In the end, as I had so many times in recent weeks, I decided to risk carrying it. I was probably in no danger just driving by Olympian properties, but I had too many enemies to feel comfortable going anywhere near them unarmed. I would have to be doubly careful to obey all traffic laws while I was out.

I got into my Mini and started the long and tedious journey. There were scattered clouds in the sky, and the moon was only a crescent when it was visible. I didn't know how much moonlight my powers needed to be juiced up to the max—hell, I wasn't even certain moonlight had any effect. If the moon was covered by clouds when I neared one of the properties of interest, I tried to find a way to hang around inconspicuously until it broke through. I spent a lot of time by the side of the road with my map unfurled as camouflage, but whether the moon was peeking through or not, I didn't feel any special interest in anyplace I passed.

I didn't have a huge amount of time until the moon set at a little before ten, but I was determined to use every glimmer of moonlight I could, methodically going through my itinerary. I was using the Beltway to carry me between locations, and the traffic was for once cooperating without any snarls or major slowdowns. The steady movement, and the sound of my tires on the asphalt, lulled me, and I went into autopilot—that state of mind where you arrive at point B and realize you have no memory of the turns and exits you took on your way from point A.

I came back to myself as I was hanging a right off the exit ramp, and I honestly had no idea what exit I had taken. I glanced at the dashboard clock and knew for sure that wherever I was, it wasn't the exit I'd been aiming for, or I would have been there ten minutes ago. A bolt of adrenaline shot through me, banishing the cobwebs in my brain and making me feel awake and alert again. If I'd just been driving on normal autopilot, I would have gotten off at a familiar exit, but I had to consult my map to figure out where I was, which likely meant that my supernatural hunting sense had taken over.

There were no known Olympian properties anywhere close, and now that I was alert again, I felt no particular pull to go one way or the other. I tried to send myself into autopilot again, but that's hard to do when you're driving unfamiliar streets. I also tried pulling over and closing my eyes, attempting to tuck my conscious mind away so my subconscious could feed me some clues, but it's almost impossible to get your mind to drift on command.

Frustration beat at me. I *knew* I'd been going in the right direction to get to Konstantin when I'd pulled off the Beltway, but now I had nothing. I slapped the steering wheel and uttered a few choice words as I reluctantly turned back toward the Beltway. Whatever had led me here was now refusing to cooperate, and the moon had set for the night.

Playing a long shot, I stopped by the FedEx store Konstantin had used when sending his nasty email. I luckily found an employee who'd been at work at the time Konstantin had been there. When I described Konstantin to her, she shrugged and said she didn't remember seeing anyone meeting that description. However, she also said she could barely remember her own name when she worked the graveyard shift, so I had no way of being sure whether Konstantin had been there or not.

Disappointed but unsurprised by the dead end, I headed back to the mansion.

I slept in on Sunday morning, though I was still up earlier than anyone else in the house—with the exception of Leo. I had developed a morning ritual very similar to the one I had had when I'd been living blissfully alone in my condo. I still missed the place, and I tried to stop by on a regular basis to have some time to myself and to remind myself that I had a home to go back to if and when I could ever extricate myself from these messes with Konstantin and Emma. But every time I left the condo, I found myself taking something else back to the mansion with me, moving in little by little, growing ever deeper roots.

In my condo, my morning ritual was to make a pot of coffee and a couple slices of toast, then sit on the couch in my bathrobe with my laptop on my lap and read, or at least skim, my favorite news sites. Having brought over my toaster and coffeemaker,

I was now able to re-create the ritual in my suite, though I'd gotten away from it when I'd been trying so hard to avoid Anderson.

I was enjoying the leisure of my "new normal" when my cell phone rang. My gut clenched in anxiety because I feared it was the Glasses calling to tell me they had decided to come home. But when I picked up the phone, the caller ID said Cyrus Galanos. I knew Cyrus and Konstantin by first name only— very kingly of them—but I suppose it would have been legally inconvenient to go by only one name.

I stared at the phone for a good long time, wondering what he could possibly want and if it would be better to let him go straight to voice mail. But until I got around to getting a disposable phone, he could probably find me and waylay me somewhere if I played hard to get. With a sigh, I answered the phone.

"Hello?" I said, sounding tentative. Showing weakness of any kind probably wasn't the wisest idea, but I doubted he was calling for anything good.

"Hello, Nikki," Cyrus said, his voice warm and friendly as always. "I hope I didn't wake you."

"No, I was up."

"I thought maybe you were sleeping in after your late night."

Oh. That was what this was about. My drive-bys last night must not have been as subtle as I'd hoped. Taking the Mini had been a mistake. I should have rented a nondescript sedan that no one would notice.

"What, no clever comebacks?" Cyrus mocked,

sounding considerably less friendly. "No elegant denials?"

I shook my head. "What do you want, Cyrus?"

"I think I made that quite clear the other day: leave my father alone."

"I'd have been happy to do that, if he'd left *me* alone."

"Huh?"

I did a mental double take, because he sounded genuinely puzzled. I supposed Daddy Dearest hadn't run his little vendetta idea by Cyrus before acting on it.

"He burned down my parents' house, Cyrus," I said, letting my own anger rise to the surface and color my voice. "Then he sent me an email telling me how creative he was going to be in making my life miserable without formally breaking the treaty. If you think I'm just going to sit here and take it—"

"He didn't do it."

There was no hint of doubt or uncertainty in Cyrus's voice, but I had to wonder how well Cyrus really knew his father. He seemed like such a decent guy himself, it was hard to believe he could condone the kinds of things Konstantin did. Maybe his mind just didn't work the same way and he couldn't fully grasp his father's evil.

"He claimed responsibility for it," I argued, despite my own doubts.

"Really. Via *email*. Anyone can write an email. Ask yourself who has the most to gain from threatening you. It sure as hell isn't Konstantin."

"Oh, come on—Anderson wouldn't do that," I

said, because there was no doubt in my mind who Cyrus meant. I sounded 100 percent certain, but that was only because I was pretty good at acting. I had mostly convinced myself that Anderson wasn't behind it, but there remained a touch of doubt.

"You've known Anderson, what, a couple of months? I'm telling you he's not the saint he pretends to be. He's a world-class manipulator, and like all old *Liberi,* he's deeply selfish at heart. It's impossible not to be when you've lived for centuries."

I snorted. "And how old are *you*?"

Cyrus laughed. "I'm selfish, too, and I'm not afraid to admit it. Just ask Blake. But my point is that Anderson might seem like he's too good and moral to do something like that, but he isn't. He'll do whatever it takes to get what he wants, and what he wants is you hunting Konstantin."

I'd have been able to put up a better protest if I hadn't had the same thoughts myself. Instead of defending Anderson and perhaps letting Cyrus see the seed of doubt, I changed tactics.

"As far as I'm concerned, the top suspects are Konstantin . . . and Emma. She hates both of us, so she'd be happy to hurt me while pushing me into hunting Konstantin."

There was a moment of silence as Cyrus thought that over, but he soon rejected it. "It's not Emma. It's true that she hates you and my father, but the person she wants to hurt most right now is Anderson. I don't know exactly what happened between the two of them, but it was obviously a very nasty breakup."

It certainly had been. However . . . "Emma blames me for it, though I *still* don't understand why. She may complain about Anderson, but it's *me* she wants to hurt."

"I hate to contradict you, but I can guarantee you it's Anderson she's after. And she's already taken her revenge."

"Huh?" Even not knowing what he was talking about, I felt a chill.

Cyrus sighed. "I believe she's planning to visit to explain later today."

"Explain what? Cyrus, what are you talking about?"

"You'll find out soon enough. Having seen her in action, I know I don't want to get on Emma's bad side, and she wouldn't want me spoiling the surprise."

"Bastard."

"Sorry. I shouldn't have brought it up in the first place. Suffice it to say that she's made it clear to me that you're not her target. And what I said about Konstantin still stands. If you or any of your people harm him, it'll be a declaration of war."

I was too sick with dread to keep talking. "I understand," I said, and hung up the phone.

It was hard to go back to my morning routine when I got off the phone with Cyrus, but I gave it my best shot. I drank my coffee and scrolled listlessly through the news, not really reading anything, just sort of skimming and making a show of it. As if by going through the motions of acting normal, I could actually *be* normal. But it was damn hard not to obsess, both about who was responsible for the fire, and about what hell Emma was going to release on Anderson in the near future.

When something finally *did* capture my full attention, it was an ad, of all things. There was a new exhibition opening at the Sackler Gallery next weekend. I'm not a huge fan of museums—thanks to umpteen million school trips in this museum-filled metropolis, and aided by the necessity of taking every visiting relative and friend of the family on museum tours—and normally, I wouldn't even notice an ad like that, or care what exhibitions were in town. But since I'd set my sights on mending my fences with Jamaal . . .

You wouldn't think to look at him that Jamaal was into museums, not with the testosterone that fairly oozed from his pores. Ask your average manly man if he'd like to go to a museum, and he'll look at you like you suggested he wear a tutu in public. But there was nothing average about Jamaal, and the one and only time I'd been in his suite I'd noticed an impressive collection of museum catalogs displayed on his bookshelves. Not to mention the crowning glory of his sitting room, which was a tiny Indian painting of the goddess Kali, from whom he was descended. It was a bona fide work of fine art, dating from the seventeenth century.

The new exhibition opening at the museum was of Indian art, and I'd bet anything Jamaal would want to go. Maybe I should tell him I was planning a visit and invite him to come along.

Yeah, like Jamaal would make it that easy.

I had about a half hour to make and reject a number of plans to coax Jamaal out of his shell before Emma and her malice drove every other thought out of my head.

SEVEN

The window of my sitting room looks out over the front of the house, so when a candy-apple-red sports car wended its way down the long and twisty driveway, it caught my eye. I'm not enough of a car nut to guess what it was, except that it was probably something Italian and obscenely expensive. No one in this house drove anything so ostentatious, and I made an educated guess that Emma was behind the wheel, dropping by for the visit Cyrus had warned about.

I told myself it was none of my business, and that I should stay up in my suite, as far away from the impending fireworks as possible. But after Cyrus's advance warning, my stomach was tied up in knots wondering what terrible thing Emma had done. Whatever it was, whatever Anderson's faults, I was sure he didn't deserve it, not from her. He'd done everything he could to take care of her after we'd rescued her, had made excuses for her and forgiven her outbursts well past the point of being reasonable. *She* was the one who'd walked out.

My feet carried me to the door before I'd consciously made the decision to go downstairs. I was probably being stupid. My presence was likely to throw gasoline on the fire, and though I considered Anderson a friend, of sorts, we weren't close enough to justify me sticking my nose into his marital difficulties. But of course I kept heading downstairs anyway.

Anderson was waiting in the foyer when I reached the landing above the first floor. He was standing straight and tall, his arms crossed over his chest and his gaze focused on the front door. Emma had to have called him to let him know she was coming, or she'd never have gotten past the front gate. Anderson had changed its code the day after she'd left.

"Go back upstairs, Nikki," Anderson said without looking up.

I stopped on the landing and blinked in surprise. "How did you know it was me?" I wasn't surprised he'd known *someone* was coming, considering we had a few creaky steps, but unless he had eyes in the back of his head . . .

He glanced up over his shoulder at me, and his expression was inscrutable. "Because you're the only private investigator in this house, and the only one nosy enough to try to eavesdrop."

"I wasn't eavesdropping!" I said in outrage, but the doorbell rang, and I no longer had his attention.

I stood hesitating on the landing as Anderson opened the door. It was hard to interpret his words as anything but a direct order, and yet I was reluctant to leave him alone to face Emma. Which was ridiculous, of course. He wasn't a man, he was a *god*. He could probably handle whatever Emma was about to dish out.

I was still debating what to do when Emma swept into the room, followed by another woman I didn't know. Both women wore full-length fur coats, and diamonds sparkled from their earlobes and fingers. Clearly, Emma had embraced the Olympian way of life, where ostentation was considered a good thing.

I decided too late that I had made a foolish decision in coming downstairs. I turned to leave, but Emma had already spotted me.

"Nikki!" she cried in feigned delight, and I had to suppress the instinct to cringe. "How lovely to see you."

Anderson shot me a steely look. "Upstairs. Now."

"Yup, I'm going," I assured him, holding up my hands in surrender.

"Oh, please, *do* stay," Emma said, smiling up at me as malice glittered in her eyes. "What I have to say concerns you, too."

I looked at Anderson for a verdict, and if he had told me to leave, I'd have been out of there.

"Very well," he said. "Come on down."

"Aren't you going to invite us in to somewhere more comfortable?" Emma asked as I descended the last flight of stairs.

"If it weren't so cold out, we'd be having this meeting on the front porch." Surely Anderson was battling a severe case of mixed emotions, but he sure as hell wasn't letting it show in his face or voice. He spoke to Emma as he would speak to any other Olympian, with no pretense of courtesy.

Emma's eyes narrowed at Anderson's response, whether from pain or from anger, I wasn't sure. Maybe both. I didn't understand what gave her the idea that Anderson's interest had strayed to me, but I was sure she actually believed it, and that his imaginary betrayal hurt her. If she weren't such a crazy bitch, I might even have felt a tad sorry for her.

I descended the last few steps, getting a closer look at Emma as she opened her coat. She was as beautiful as ever, but I could tell she'd lost weight. Her cheekbones looked sharper, her eyes almost sunken, and her hair seemed to have lost a little of its luster. She stroked the fur of her coat absently, and I saw that her fingernails were chewed down to nubs, a fact her glossy red nail lacquer accentuated more than it hid.

The smile on her face was cruel, and the glint in her eyes held both confidence and spite, but her body told a different story. She was *not* flourishing as an Olympian, no matter what she wanted Anderson to think. But leaving him to join them had been her choice, and she now had to live with it.

Emma's companion looked far more comfortable in her own skin. She wore a skintight black miniskirt displaying legs about a mile long. Personally, I thought she was too skinny to pull off the look, and her legs looked like matchsticks tucked into expensive designer pumps. A crescent moon glyph glowed on her cheek, and her gray-blue eyes glittered with what looked to me like anticipation.

Shrugging as if Anderson's rebuff meant nothing to her, Emma turned to me. Her gleeful self-assurance might be an act, but her hatred of me was definitely not. "Come meet Christina," she said, beckoning. "You two have a lot in common. She's a descendant of Selene, who's also a moon goddess."

I was sure that was about the *only* thing we had in common. "Charmed," I said with a curl of my lip and went to stand by Anderson.

"I don't remember giving you permission to bring a guest," Anderson said coldly.

The calculating gleam in Emma's eyes sharpened. "Oh, but I just *knew* you'd want to meet Christina."

Christina just stood there smiling, a prop rather than a person.

"Whatever it is you have to say, just say it and get the hell out," Anderson said.

Emma pouted. "You never did have a sense of drama, did you?"

"I'm in no mood for banter. I let you come here because you said it was important, but I'd be happy to throw you and your lovely companion out on your asses. So talk."

The look on Emma's face said she was genuinely disappointed Anderson didn't want to play word games with her. She was purposely drawing out the encounter as much as she could, letting the suspense build. I wondered if Anderson knew she was here to unveil her revenge, or whether he thought something more mundane was going on.

"Fine," Emma said with a resigned sigh. "I'll get to the point." She turned to me. "You remember when Kerner's jackal bit you and you came down with rabies?"

I tried not to shudder at the memory. The supernaturally enhanced rabies would have killed me permanently if it had been allowed to run its course. Instead, Anderson had killed me himself and burned my body, and the seed of immortality had generated a brand-new, virus-free body for me. It was something I'd have loved to forget.

"It rings a bell," I said, hoping I sounded dry and casual despite the chill the reminder had given me. "What does that have to do with anything?" I glanced over at Christina, and the lump of dread in my stomach grew tighter and colder as my mind began rapidly connecting the dots.

"Anderson was so very concerned about you that he called a *Liberi* who had refused to join his merry band and was living in quiet anonymity out in the countryside. He needed a descendant of Apollo to examine you and figure out what was wrong with you, and she was the only one he knew who might actually help."

I started to shake my head, as if I could somehow stop her from finishing her thought.

"What have you done?" Anderson asked in

a horrified whisper, but we were both looking at Christina now, and I think we both knew what was coming.

"I never liked Erin," Emma said to him. "And not just because she was your lover before me. She was so bitter about you dumping her it made her quite unpleasant to be around. I'm sure it was the bitterness that made her choose not to live under your roof, where she would be off-limits to Olympians."

Anderson stood frozen in shock and horror beside me. Frankly, I wasn't doing much better myself, and I shared Emma's opinion about Erin's likability.

Emma drank in Anderson's pain, then turned to me with another of her vicious smiles. "I have you to thank for making this so easy for me. I don't know if I could possibly have hunted her down if she hadn't come out of hiding to treat you. When she left, I followed her home so I knew where I could get to her if I ever had a need."

I guess I was supposed to feel guilty about that, but there was no way I was going to accept it as my fault. Although perhaps I should have thought of it when Emma left us to join the Olympians. Maybe I should have anticipated the animosity between Anderson's ex-girlfriend and his ex-wife and constructed a new cover identity for Erin.

"I told Cyrus where she was hiding," Emma continued, "and he sent a squad to harvest her seed. Of all the mortal Descendants in our service, Cyrus thought Christina the most deserving of elevation, so he had her do the honors."

By which Emma meant Christina had killed Erin, thereby stealing Erin's seed for herself. She was no longer a Descendant, but had joined the ranks of the *Liberi*. With an act of deliberate murder.

I swallowed hard, horrified by what Emma had done—and by the reminder that Cyrus wasn't really a nice guy, no matter what he liked to pretend. And then I sneaked a peek at Anderson and practically stopped breathing.

He was still firmly in his mortal disguise. There was no white light leaking from his eyes, nor was any glow coming from his hands, and yet he was still incandescent with fury. Enough so that Christina had taken a step backward, and even Emma looked just a touch less sure of herself. She glanced quickly down at his hand, and I knew she was wondering if she'd pushed him too far, if he was actually pissed off enough to use his Hand of Doom against her. Not that she knew what that hand could do if Anderson set his mind to it. Anderson took a step closer to Emma, his hand rising from his side. Her breathing quickened, but she held her ground.

"Do you want to go to war against all of the Olympians?" she asked. "Because if you hurt me, it will break your treaty with Cyrus, and he will destroy you and all of your people. Except for Nikki, of course." She smiled her malicious smile again. "We'd have other uses for your new girlfriend."

Even in the midst of the crisis, I couldn't help rolling my eyes. Emma was descended from Nyx, the goddess of night, but if there was a goddess of jealousy—and I was sure there was, even if I couldn't name her off the top of my head—I would swear Emma was at least her kissing cousin.

Anderson looked like he was about to choke on his rage. He was a god of vengeance, and it had to be killing him to restrain his need to strike out. I think everyone in the house was damn lucky he was rational enough to care about the consequences of unleashing his inner Fury. "I will not start a war," he said in a low and dangerous voice. "You and your companion may leave this house unscathed. I was a fool not to see this coming and move Erin to a new location."

It took everything I had not to burst out with something scathingly unwise. Even after all the crap Emma had pulled, Anderson was still willing to take some of the blame and put it on his own shoulders.

"But I warn you, Emma," Anderson continued, letting more of his anger creep into his voice, "you had better not try me again. I am better at vengeance than you are, and you would not be the first ex-wife to learn that the hard way."

Being the son of a Fury, Anderson most definitely was an expert in the vengeance business. *I* sure as hell wouldn't want to mess with him. Emma was crazy, but only if she was *stupid* and crazy would she take another shot at Anderson after this warning. There was a sense of . . . portentousness in the air, like Anderson's words might be more than just words. But maybe that was just my imagination running away with me because of what I knew about him.

Emma had lost her gloating smile, and I think that under her calm facade, she was actually afraid of Anderson for the first time. I *know* Christina was afraid, because her face was ghostly pale and her eyes too wide. I bet she'd have run screaming out the door if Anderson had said boo.

"I've done nothing wrong," Emma said, and I think she actually believed it. "I haven't broken the treaty, and it was your own fault Erin was vulnerable."

"Get out. Now."

I think Emma would have liked to have hung around and looked for more chances to gloat. This was probably the end of her revenge—Cyrus was right, and I couldn't see her settling for burning down empty houses when she had this rabbit already in her hat—and she wanted to savor it. But she also knew when Anderson had been pushed as far as it was safe to push him, and that was the case now.

"Well, it was lovely seeing you both again," Emma said, then turned her back on Anderson and walked with affected nonchalance toward the door. Christina, who truly had been there as nothing but a prop for Emma's revenge, was in such a hurry to get out she practically bowled Emma over on the way.

The door closed behind them, and seconds later the car revved its engine and pulled away. Leaving me alone in the foyer with an enraged god of death and vengeance who might be on the verge of exploding.

EIGHT

I was afraid to move. Afraid to even breathe. I felt like I was standing on a land mine, and one false step would blow me to smithereens. Should I try to say something sympathetic and comforting to Anderson? Should I apologize for my role in Emma's revenge, even while refusing to accept any blame? Or should I try to slink away without bothering him?

Sometimes it really sucked knowing the truth about him. Even having witnessed his Hand of Doom in action, I doubt I'd have felt this level of dread if I thought he were merely another *Liberi*. But I *did* know the truth, and I wasn't sure what would happen if Anderson reached his breaking point.

"Don't stop breathing on my account," he said. His voice sounded almost normal, but there was still something about him that *felt* dangerous.

"I've seen you lose it before," I replied quietly, thinking about what had happened when we'd trespassed on Alexis's property to rescue Emma from the depths of his pond. Alexis had taunted Anderson with what he and Konstantin had done to Emma while she was in their custody, and Anderson had dispensed with his mortal disguise and turned into a humanoid pillar of fire. "I don't want to see it again."

"I didn't 'lose it,'" he said, sounding affronted.

"I saw you turn into—"

"I know what you saw." He turned and looked me squarely in the face. "I was entirely in control of myself, Nikki. I had always planned to . . ." He looked around, as if just noticing we were standing in the foyer, where anyone could overhear. "What I did then was calculated. Trust me: you don't want to be near me if I ever really do 'lose it.'"

Oh, I trusted him about that all right. I might not know the details of what would happen, but it would be ugly, and there was likely to be collateral damage.

"I'm . . . sorry about Erin," I said, because I couldn't walk away without saying it.

"Me, too." He was almost eerily calm now, his face showing no emotion, his voice flat. "I need to be alone right now."

He turned from me without another word, climbing the stairs, no doubt heading for the east wing, which was his private domain within the mansion. My throat was tight, and my heart hurt for him. I'd had very little contact with Erin, and my memories of the time were a little hazy, but I remembered how she and Anderson had sniped at each other as ex-lovers often do. Yet Anderson had loved her once, and to have Emma bring about her death was a devastating blow. I wished he had someone to turn to, someone to give him support and companionship to help him through.

But Anderson was a god in hiding, and that meant he had to be used to dealing with the hardships of life alone. My heart might ache for him, but there was nothing I could do.

After Emma left, I tried to forget all about her nasty visit. I had enough crap on my plate that it wasn't too hard.

Despite Cyrus's unequivocal warning that I was to back off Konstantin, I had no intention of doing so, especially now that I'd crossed Emma off my suspects list. It was still possible Anderson was behind it, that he'd done it to light a fire under my ass, so to speak, but Konstantin was the more likely suspect. It might have been smarter for him to leave me alone, but being deposed from his position as "king" of the Olympians, he might be angry enough to act on emotion rather than logic.

I wasn't breaking the treaty by merely driving around the city looking for Konstantin, but just in case Cyrus didn't see it that way, I rented a sedan that would blend in with the city's traffic. Last night had revealed the pitfalls of cruising around by myself and trying to follow my instincts. I needed to be able to let my conscious mind drift, which was hard to do—and potentially dangerous—while driving. I'd be much better off if I could get someone else to do the driving for me.

There were only three people in the house I was willing to spend that many hours shut up in a car with. My first choice, naturally, was Jamaal, but he turned me down with some lame excuse about being too tired after having worked so much with Sita during the day. He didn't *look* tired when I cornered him. More like sullen and . . . distant. He was drifting further away, and I might be the only one in the house who saw it happening.

My second choice was Maggie, but I couldn't find her, and she didn't answer her cell. My third and last choice was Logan, but he informed me he already had plans for the evening. I was tempted to ask him what he was up to—for the most part, Anderson's *Liberi* didn't seem to have much of a social life—but it was none of my business, and he hadn't seemed like he wanted to share.

I tried Maggie one more time, but no dice. She was off the grid, and I was on my own.

That is, I was on my own if I insisted my driver be one of the *Liberi*. I hesitated to ask Steph to do anything that might be even remotely dangerous, but I couldn't see any problem with her driving me around. We'd be in a rented vehicle no one recognized, and I would not make the mistake of loitering around if the moon hid behind the clouds at inconvenient times. No one was going to notice a nondescript car that drove by without stopping or slowing.

My decision to ask Steph was reaffirmed when I

got a call from the Glasses. They had decided to come home early after all, although they hadn't been able to get a flight until Wednesday. That meant I could no longer put off trying to come up with a plausible explanation for why I was living in the mansion, and I'd need Steph's help to corroborate it. Driving around with her tonight would give me the opportunity to kill two birds with one stone.

It was getting uncomfortably late by the time I reached the decision to ask Steph to drive me, the sun already starting to set. Moonset wasn't until almost eleven, but a quick check on the weather had shown me rain was heading our way. The skies were still clear, but who knew how long it would last? I stood by my window and watched the sky anxiously as I called Steph. There was no urgent reason why I should have to go out hunting tonight, specifically, except for my fear that Konstantin wasn't going to wait very long before he struck again.

The phone call started off poorly, because Steph was planning to meet Blake for dinner. If the rain weren't moving in, I'd have said we could go on our hunting expedition afterward, but it didn't look like we were going to have a whole lot of time tonight. Steph reluctantly agreed she could reschedule her date for the next day.

The good news was that since she'd been planning to meet Blake, Steph was already on her way to the mansion when I called, and she arrived about fifteen minutes later. I waited for her on the front porch, my rental car parked along the mansion's circular drive. Steph pulled up behind the rental, and I took a deep breath before starting down the stairs toward her. Silly of me to feel nervous about seeing my own sister, but I was still swimming in guilt about the hell I'd brought on our family, and I knew she wasn't happy with me for interrupting her planned evening with Blake.

Our eyes met over the hood of her car as Steph got out, and maybe I was reading things into her expression that weren't there, but I thought I detected a hint of coolness. I wondered if asking her to do the driving tonight was a bad idea, but it was too late to change my mind now. I dug the keys to the rental out of my coat pocket and took a quick glance at the darkening sky. So far, there were only wispy clouds, and the moon was easily visible. It was a good night for a hunt.

"Thanks for helping me out," I said to Steph as I handed her the keys.

She certainly didn't need to dress up for a date with Blake, who would find her beautiful and alluring even in ratty sweats, but either they'd been planning to go somewhere fancy, or she'd dressed up because she felt like it. Her red wool swing coat covered most of the outfit, but her black pencil skirt and stiletto-heeled pumps gave her away. Not the kind of outfit she'd have worn if she'd known how she'd be spending the next few hours.

I guess my visual assessment of her outfit wasn't terribly subtle, because Steph looked down at herself and chuckled. "I'll be the best-dressed assistant private eye out there."

"I'm sorry—" I started, but Steph cut me off.

"I have even more reason than you to want Konstantin caught," Steph said, all hints of humor banished. "I'm not doing this as some kind of favor."

I knew that was the truth, but that didn't stop me from wanting to apologize. I refrained, because I knew Steph wouldn't appreciate it. "Am I allowed to thank you at least?"

She sighed dramatically. "I suppose so," she said in a tone of long-suffering patience.

My lips twitched with a smile. Maybe I really *had* been imagining the hint of coolness I'd thought I'd seen when she first got out of the car. She seemed like her usual self, full of warmth and good humor.

"Thank you," I said again, and then I gave her an impulsive hug. She was more than just my big sister; she was also my best friend, and a truly nice person at heart. Maybe somewhere deep down inside she was angry about all the chaos I'd brought into her life, but she would be ashamed of those feelings and would do her best not to show them. That was all I could ask for, and maybe more than I deserved.

"All righty then," Steph said when I released her from the hug, "let's get this show on the road."

I smiled at the stupid pun, and Steph and I piled into the rental. I'd thought about planning out an elaborate route that would take us by more Olympian properties, but I hadn't been near any of those properties when I'd spaced out last night, so I saw no reason to keep operating under the hopes that Konstantin was hiding somewhere I could find him by logic.

"So what's the plan?" Steph asked as she adjusted the seat and mirrors, then started the car.

"It's a pretty lame one," I admitted. "But I think we should just get on the Beltway and see what happens."

The Beltway circles all the way around the city, and driving on it is easily tedious enough to put anyone on autopilot. Unless you hit traffic or there's an accident, in which case it's more suited to road rage, but I was going to pretend those possibilities didn't exist.

Steph's sidelong glance told me how enamored she was of my plan, but she didn't argue. "Do you care which way I go when I get to the Beltway?"

"I don't think it matters. Take whichever way seems to be moving fastest. Once we get on the Beltway, I'll need you not to talk to me anymore. Just let me zone out."

"If you're zoned out, how are you going to tell me which way to go?"

I made a face. "I don't know," I admitted. "This is really just an experiment. I have no idea if it'll work. It might be a waste of time."

Steph shrugged. "Okay then. Only one way to find out."

During the ride to the Beltway, Steph and I tried to concoct a plausible story about why I was living in the mansion. Preferably one that didn't cause her parents—*our* parents—to ask too many questions. We didn't have a whole lot of luck. Let's face it, the situation was hard to explain. I could tell the Glasses I was working for Anderson, and they might almost believe that I'd spend a night or two there if I was working late for some reason. However, being there *every* night, as well as me moving an awful lot of my stuff from the condo to the mansion, was a lot harder. I was almost glad when we hit the Beltway and it was time to invoke radio silence, because thinking about it was making my head hurt.

It was full dark when we got to the Beltway, and there wasn't any sign of the upcoming storm yet. The moon's light was bright and clear even with the city lights doing their best to drown it out. I checked with my gut to see if I had any compulsion to go one way or another on the Beltway, but I felt nothing. There seemed to be a lot of brake lights going east, so Steph chose to go west, and I tried to let my mind drift.

As I'd already established numerous times, it's hard to get your mind to drift on command, especially when a sense of urgency is riding you. I found myself overanalyzing every minute sensation, every stray thought, every person, place, or thing that caught my eye. My mind bounced around like a hyperactive toddler on a sugar high, and the more annoyed I got at myself for not being able to knuckle down and concentrate, the harder it got for me to knuckle down and concentrate. Or *not* concentrate. Whatever.

After a fruitless half hour of driving in silence, I was climbing the walls and squirming in my seat with frustration. And that was when we hit the traffic.

I didn't know whether refraining from talking was necessary, especially since the silence didn't seem to be helping me, but I bit back a couple of curse words as I caught sight of the brake lights ahead and our car slowed first to a crawl, then to a stop. It was six thirty on a Sunday night, but I'd run into traffic snarls on the Beltway at two in the morning, so I wasn't entirely surprised. Irritated, yes, but not surprised.

Steph glanced over at me as the traffic eased forward about six inches before coming to a stop again. "Anything?"

I shook my head and wondered if we should just give up. We weren't getting anywhere—literally or figuratively—and being stuck in stop-and-go traffic is about as much fun as having a root canal.

"Maybe we should just take the next exit and call it a night," I said. To hell with my vow of silence.

Steph gave me a withering older-sister look. "You aren't seriously planning to give up after a half hour on the road, are you?"

We'd actually been on the road almost an hour, because the mansion wasn't particularly close to the Beltway, but I supposed that wasn't really very long in the grand scheme of things. Both Steph and I had understood that this would be a long, tedious night.

I shook my head. "Sorry. That was frustration talking. I can't seem to get my mind to shut up so I can zone out."

Steph shot me a droll smile as she propped her elbow against the window and laid her head down on her hand, waiting for the next opportunity to inch forward. "If anything can make your eyes glaze over, it'll be this traffic. Now hush and get back to work."

I hushed as ordered, and tried once again to let my mind wander. I spent more time than I care to admit mentally cussing out the traffic, wondering what the holdup was. My guess was an accident with rubberneckers, but if I was right, it was far enough away that we couldn't see any flashing lights yet.

Roll forward. Stop. Roll forward. Stop. Roll forward . . .

I can get pretty damned keyed up sometimes, particularly when I've been dipping into the coffee too much, but eventually the monotony of the drive got to me. My mind drifted a couple of times, but I unfortunately *noticed* it drifting, which yanked me back into full alertness. But it took me less time to start drifting, and I figured I was going to either get myself into the zone or fall asleep.

I blinked, and saw that not only were we not stuck in traffic anymore, we weren't even on the Beltway. I shook my head to clear the cobwebs.

I remembered thinking—dreaming?—that I was in a hedge maze, trying to find my way to the center. I'd mumbled to myself each time I got to an intersection and had to decide which way to go. I remembered a sense of urgency pressing on me, telling me to hurry. I'd started out walking, then switched to jogging, then to an all-out run. It was . . . clearer and more coherent than an ordinary dream, but fuzzier than just a flight of imagination. I honestly had no idea if I'd been awake or asleep.

The car came to a stop at a red light, and Steph turned to me with an inquiring raise of her brow. A couple of raindrops spattered on the windshield, and the trees swayed in a gust of wind. I leaned forward, staring up at the sky, but I saw no hint of the moon or of stars. The light turned green, and Steph drove through the intersection, continuing on straight, probably because I hadn't told her to turn.

"Umm . . . Have I been giving you directions?" I asked.

Steph glanced over at me again. More raindrops spattered down, and she was forced to turn on the windshield wipers.

"Yeah," she confirmed. "You've been kind of mumbling to yourself for a while. I thought you'd fallen asleep, only your eyes were open. Don't you remember?"

I rubbed my eyes, but I knew I hadn't been asleep. "I remember daydreaming, or something, about being in a hedge maze."

I ran my hand through my hair in frustration. "Let me guess: the clouds rolled in, and that's when I stopped giving you directions." The rain came down harder as if to emphasize the point that I wouldn't be getting any more moon-fueled hunches tonight.

"Yeah."

I was so frustrated I wanted to kick something. If I'd been able to get into the zone before the rain had started . . .

"We wouldn't have gotten here any faster if you'd started directing me earlier," Steph said, guessing my line of thought. "We were stuck in traffic, remember?"

I made a sound of grudging acceptance. I knew she was right, but it didn't make me any less frustrated. Two nights in a row, I'd been on Konstantin's scent, and two nights in a row, I'd failed to find him. I was not the happiest of campers.

Steph and I drove around the area a little while longer, just to be thorough, but the rain had settled in to stay, and the moon wouldn't be giving me any more help tonight. Our meanderings had taken us deep into the heart of D.C., and the most convenient way to get back to Arlington was to take Independence Avenue to the Arlington Memorial Bridge. I was staring out the rain-speckled side window, brooding about what a total failure this expedition had turned out to be. It wasn't until we passed the Sackler Gallery that I snapped out of my funk and directed my mind toward another of the many problems on my plate.

To be fair, I shouldn't have been thinking of Jamaal as one of my problems. I wasn't his girlfriend, was barely even his friend anymore. And he was a grown man, responsible for his own issues. But I couldn't help wondering if his almost obsessive practice with Sita—and his decreasing ability to keep her controlled and contained—was a sign that his self-imposed isolation wasn't good for him.

The new Indian art exhibit would be opening on Saturday, but I'd already determined that Jamaal would blow me off if I asked him to go see it with me. I needed a stronger temptation, something Jamaal couldn't get on his own. I glanced sidelong at Steph, who was quietly concentrating on driving. Through her extensive charity work, Steph knew practically everybody who was anybody in the D.C. area. Her virtual Rolodex contained a veritable cornucopia of the rich, famous, and powerful.

I didn't know how to bring up the subject gracefully, so I just blurted it out.

"Do you happen to know anyone who's a big muckety-muck at the Sackler Gallery?" I asked.

We conveniently came to a red light, so Steph could turn in her seat and give me a long, puzzled look. "The Sackler? Why? Have you developed a sudden interest in Asian art?"

There was something too knowing in her eyes as she stared at me. My sister's no dummy, and not only was she aware I had the hots for Jamaal—despite my repeated attempts to deny it—but she was also aware that he was the descendant of an Indian goddess. Even if I could have thought of a more innocuous-sounding reason for my interest, I didn't think Steph would buy it, not when the look in her eye said she'd already put two and two together.

The light turned green, and Steph returned her attention to the road. I let out a breath I hadn't realized I was holding. Steph disapproved of Jamaal almost as much as I disapproved of Blake, so asking for her help might not have been the smartest idea I'd ever had. However, I'd already committed to the course of action.

"There's a new Indian art exhibit opening up next weekend," I said. "I'd like to see if I can draw Jamaal out to go see it, but I know if I ask him, he'll say no. I was thinking maybe you had a contact who could get us in for a private tour, maybe before the exhibit is open to the public. I think he'd have a much harder time saying no to that."

Steph was silent for the next couple of blocks, and I forced myself to be quiet and let her think. If I tried too hard to persuade her, she might come to the conclusion that I was letting myself get too involved. Actually, she probably already thought that, but there was no reason to make it worse.

"Do you really think that's a good idea?" she finally asked me.

I shrugged, trying to look casual. "It wouldn't be that big a deal. Just a trip to a museum. But I think Jamaal needs to get out of his own head for a while."

"That's your professional opinion, eh?"

I bristled, but managed to refrain from making an angry retort. "It's my opinion as a fellow human being." I didn't think telling Steph about Sita's walkabout was going to incline her to see things my way, though it was that more than anything that convinced me Jamaal needed more human contact. "We're not meant to be solitary creatures. Or didn't they teach you that in psych class?" Steph had been a psych major in college, although she'd chosen not to pursue a career.

She raised an eyebrow at me. "No reason to get testy."

"I'm not!" I protested, though I knew I was.

Steph ignored me. "If I have to listen to you

telling me Blake isn't good for me, then you have to listen to me telling you that Jamaal is bad news for *any* woman."

I slumped in my seat. I thought I'd been getting better, refraining from editorializing about Blake, but maybe I hadn't. "You *don't* listen to me about Blake," I pointed out.

"That doesn't stop you from sharing your opinion."

"When was the last time I said anything to you about him?" I honestly couldn't remember. I'd bitten my tongue more times than I could count.

"You don't have to say anything to make your opinion clear. All I have to do is take one look at your face when I'm talking about him."

I glanced out the side window to orient myself, hoping we were almost at the mansion so I could escape this conversation. No such luck.

"I'm doing my best to keep my opinions to myself," I said. "That doesn't mean I don't *have* opinions, and I can't just turn them off like a light. Sorry."

Steph's hands had tightened on the wheel, and I hated the tension that radiated from her. She was a genuinely nice, good person, and she deserved to be happy. Ever since I'd become *Liberi,* I'd been dragging her down, and I wished I could make things better. But I *knew* Blake was bad for her. Eventually, they would both get tired of a relationship that didn't include sex, and then one of two things would happen: either Blake would sleep with her, thereby tying her to him for the rest of her life, or he'd dump her, breaking her heart. Neither of these alternatives was acceptable.

"I just want you to stop treating me like a child who's not capable of making her own decisions. I'm twenty-seven years old, and I don't need your guidance."

"What do you want me to do, Steph? Stop caring about you? Stop worrying about you? That isn't reasonable."

"Oh, but it's reasonable for you to ask me not to care that you're falling for Jamaal?"

"I'm not falling for him!" I snapped, which probably cemented her opinion that I was. I took a deep breath to calm my temper. Steph had seen me make a lot of bad relationship decisions over the years, and I couldn't blame her for trying to warn me away from what she saw as just one more. I took a second deep breath just for insurance, then continued in what I hoped was a calmer, more reasonable tone.

"Jamaal is a different story. I live in the same house with him, and unless the Olympians turn over a new leaf and decide to live and let live, I'll be stuck with him for the rest of my life. And in case you've forgotten, I'm immortal." Despite already having come back from the dead once, those words sounded almost laughably absurd. I supposed I'd get used to it someday, but that day sure hadn't come yet. "It's in my own best interests to try to help him, because I have to live with him either way, and he's not good to live with right now."

Everything I said was true, but it wasn't really the reason I wanted to help Jamaal, and we both knew it. Steph tapped her fingernails against the steering wheel, but the gesture seemed more restless than angry. Maybe we were making progress.

"Why does it have to be you who tries to help him?" she asked, and I decided we weren't making progress after all. "Why don't you let Anderson handle it? He's supposed to be in charge, right?"

It was a perfectly reasonable question. Anderson had certainly known Jamaal longer than I had, and Jamaal respected him a hell of a lot more. But I didn't think Anderson or any of his *Liberi* could connect to Jamaal the way I did. Our lives and backgrounds were completely different, and yet there were unmistakable similarities between our emotional landscapes. I knew what it was like to feel isolated, to hold everyone at arm's length and be completely self-sufficient. Anderson could see Jamaal's outward behavior, but he couldn't *understand* it like I could.

Of course, if I told Steph any of that, she'd read a whole lot more into it, and things felt rocky between us already.

"Anderson is too much of a guy to be much help," I said, and it was the truth, even if it wasn't the whole truth. "But he does have money up the wazoo, so maybe he'll have some contacts that can get me into the Sackler. I'll ask him about it tomorrow, and we can pretend we never had this conversation."

There was a long silence, and then Steph shook her head and sighed. "Don't bother. I know one of the trustees, and I can probably arrange something." I started to thank her, but she cut me off. "You can thank me by laying off me and Blake. What we do or don't do is our business, not yours. You've more than done your sisterly duty in trying to warn me, and you need to back the hell off."

I swallowed a protest. I *had* backed the hell off. Hadn't I? But maybe I needed to try harder.

"Okay, fine. It's a deal," I said.

Steph didn't respond.

The rest of the ride passed in silence.

NINE

It was still raining when I woke up on Monday, and a glance at the weather forecast showed me the rain was settling in for a lengthy visit. This did not increase my chances of hunting down Konstantin before he struck again, and I was tempted to drop-kick my computer for giving me the bad news.

I made another pot of coffee instead. Then I stretched out on the sofa in my sitting room with my laptop on my lap to make a show of keeping up to date with the news. I was brooding a little too much to read more than a couple of paragraphs here and there, and those only for the most interesting of stories.

My heart took a nosedive into my stomach when I saw the headline that read ARSON SUSPECTED IN CONDO FIRE THAT LEFT THREE DEAD.

There was no reason to think it had anything to do with me, but the words *arson* and *condo* jumped out at me like monsters at a horror movie.

My throat was tight, my every muscle taut, as I reluctantly clicked on the link to the full story. My breath whooshed out of my lungs when I saw the picture of a burned-out husk of a building. The roof had collapsed, and the brick facade was black as charcoal, but the shape of the building was familiar, as were the rows of granite planters that adorned the circular drive.

Without a doubt, it was *my* building.

Konstantin had struck again, and this time it wasn't an empty building he'd burned.

My eyes were clouded with tears as I took in the horrifying details the article revealed. The fire had occurred around ten last night, while Steph and I had been riding around the Beltway in our fruitless quest. The three dead were a ninety-two-year-old woman who was apparently overcome by the smoke before she'd even gotten out of bed, a twenty-five-year-old single mother whose broken leg had hampered her attempt to escape, and the three-month-old baby she'd been trying to carry to safety.

All dead because of me.

I shook my head violently. No, it was because of Konstantin. I had to remember that, had to keep it front and center in my mind, or I would go crazy. I'd done nothing wrong, nothing I'd had any reason to believe would endanger innocent civilians. Konstantin had always made it clear that he valued humans about as much as he valued insects. It was his contempt and malice that was behind the deaths, not me.

All sound, logical reasons why I shouldn't feel

guilty about what had happened. And not one of them did a thing to lessen the guilt that sat heavily on my shoulders.

I read the article about four or five times, under the guise of getting all the details down, but I think I was mostly just flogging myself with them. Maybe if I'd done a better job on one of my aborted hunts, I would have been able to stop Konstantin before he killed innocents. Maybe instead of giving Jamaal a hard time about his obsessive practicing with Sita, I should be practicing my own powers just as obsessively. I'd practiced throwing and shooting because I understood exactly how that worked, but I hadn't done a whole lot with the hunting because it was hard to figure out how to train for something I didn't understand. Maybe if I'd put some serious time and effort into it . . .

Frightening how easy it was for me to find reasons to blame myself, even when I knew that was exactly what Konstantin wanted and that I was playing into his hands.

For a while, I was too busy wallowing to notice the incongruity in last night's fire. But when my mind kept circling back to my failed hunts, something jumped out at me.

The article said the fire had started around ten last night. That was when I'd been dreaming about hedge mazes and directing Steph toward what was presumably Konstantin's location. My powers had cut out the moment the rain set in, but we'd been way across the city from my condo when that had happened.

I unfolded my D.C. metro area map. Steph said we'd been in Maryland when I'd directed her to get off the Beltway, and while I'd had her make quite a few turns as I homed in on the "signal," we'd been traveling in a northwesterly direction at the time my supernatural radar went silent. My condo was northeast of that location, and quite a distance away.

It didn't necessarily mean anything. I couldn't be certain my powers were actually leading me to Konstantin, and even if they were, he probably hired a third party to set the fire for him. He wasn't the type to do his own dirty work if he didn't have to. But that line of thought reminded me of my doubts about Konstantin being the culprit. He had always struck me as coldly calculating, cruel, and dangerous, but not *crazy*.

No, an attack that left three innocent civilians dead pointed more to a mind like Emma's, dangerously unhinged. Maybe Cyrus and I were both wrong about her. Maybe having Erin killed *hadn't* been the end all, be all of her revenge.

I'd been having a hard enough time tracking down Konstantin when I'd been sure he was behind the fires. Now I had another viable suspect, one who was just as much under the Olympians' protection. And yet, whoever the firebug was, I was going to have to catch them, and catch them soon. Before more innocents died.

I gave myself a few hours to get over the initial shock and horror of what had happened, locking myself in my suite and turning off my phone. If I didn't pull myself together before I talked to anyone, I was going to say something I would later regret. Either that, or I'd burst into tears, which was almost as bad. I didn't know what whoever it was had planned for the next attack, but I was sure the other shoe would drop soon, and it would be worse even than the condo fire. If I was going to stop it from happening, I had to keep my emotions as under control as humanly possible.

Hours of sitting alone in my room and brooding didn't do much to improve how I felt, and I eventually decided no Zen-like state of calm was going to descend on me out of the ether. I didn't have time to sit around anymore anyway.

I didn't like my chances of hunting down Konstantin in the next handful of days, especially not with the rain cutting off the moonlight. That meant my best chance of preventing another attack was through diplomacy. Whether the person behind the attack was Emma or Konstantin, they were both Olympians, and that meant they answered to Cyrus, at least in theory. I'd already seen evidence that Cyrus was not the nice guy he pretended to be, but I believed he genuinely wanted to avoid a war between the Olympians and Anderson's *Liberi*. Maybe he could be persuaded to put a leash on whoever was behind the fires.

It was a long shot, particularly if it really was Konstantin who was behind them. No matter what terms he and Cyrus had come to in order to effect their peaceful regime change, I didn't think there was a chance in hell Konstantin would take orders from his son. Maybe I would just have to hope that Emma was the guilty party and that she would be forced to obey Cyrus.

Of course, I was getting way ahead of myself. First, I had to find a way to convince Cyrus to call off the dogs.

My first inclination was to pick up the phone and call him, but even in my depleted mental state, I knew that wasn't a good idea. I didn't have enough clout to enter into a negotiation with Cyrus myself, and Anderson would *not* appreciate me going behind his back. I'd done it once before, and had the feeling I'd just barely escaped a date with his Hand of Doom.

I printed out the article about the fire, sticking it in a manila folder so I didn't have to see the headline and the photo anymore. Then I ducked into the bathroom to wash my face and put on some makeup, trying to make myself look more normal than I felt. The concealer lightened the dark circles under my eyes, but it didn't make them go away completely, and there wasn't any makeup in the world that could conceal the stark expression in my eyes. I wanted to look calm, strong, and completely reasonable when I pleaded my case to Anderson, but the reflection in the mirror told me I was falling short.

There was nothing to be done about it, so I grabbed the manila folder and marched down to the second floor, hoping Anderson would be in his study. The door was open, but when I stepped inside, Anderson wasn't at his desk. He didn't go out much, so chances were he was in the house, most likely somewhere else in his own private territory in the east wing. The rest of us weren't allowed to venture into the east wing except in case of emergency, and I wasn't sure this would qualify in his book, no matter how urgent it felt to me.

I stepped out into the hallway. "Anderson?" I called, hoping he was within earshot.

A door down the hall opened, and Anderson stuck his head out. His hair was slicked back from his face with water, and I caught a glimpse of bare shoulder, though he used the door to shield his body from view. If I weren't such an emotional wreck, I might have tried some wisecrack about our mutual propensity for interrupting showers, but I couldn't muster even a hint of humor.

I must have looked even worse than I thought, because Anderson didn't wait for me to speak.

"Just let me throw some clothes on," he said. "I'll be right back."

I nodded, my throat tightening up on me as my mind insisted on flashing me an image of the poor, injured mother trying desperately to get her baby to safety while the building burned around her and smoke stole her breath. I had always been a bit of a bleeding heart, and I had the unfortunate tendency to let other people's misery become my own. I would never have made it as a health-care worker of any kind, being completely unable to hold myself at the distance necessary to maintain sanity. I told myself not to think about the doomed woman, or to imagine what she must have felt in the final minutes of her life, how terrified and utterly devastated she must have been when she'd realized she wasn't getting her baby out.

I made a fist and banged it hard on my thigh, trying to force myself back from the brink. The last thing I wanted to do was start this conversation with tears already running down my cheeks, and my eyes were burning in that familiar, ominous way. At least I could hand the article to Anderson instead of having to tell him what had happened.

Taking as deep a breath as my tight throat would allow, I stepped into Anderson's office and took a seat in front of his desk. I swallowed convulsively, hoping that would loosen my throat—and hoping that Anderson would take his time getting dressed so I could regain my composure.

I was going to be asking Anderson to have a civilized conversation and even negotiate with the man who'd ordered Erin's death, and I was going to have to bring up the possibility that Emma was the one responsible for the fires. No matter how cold Anderson might have acted when Emma had come by to drop her bombshell, I knew he wasn't going to want to accept the possibility that the woman he'd loved and married had set a condo full of people on fire. I had to be in control of my emotions, because Anderson might well lose control of his, and that would be bad.

I no longer felt on the verge of tears when Anderson stepped into his office, but I still wasn't as put together as I'd have liked. Anderson had donned one of his endless collection of wrinkled shirts, and if he'd combed his wet hair at all, it had to have been with his fingers. He dropped into his desk chair looking even more safe and ordinary than usual, and though I knew it was an illusion, I grasped hold of it to help steady myself.

Wordlessly, I tossed the manila folder across the desk, still not trusting myself to talk. Anderson raised an eyebrow at me, but opened the folder and read the article while I averted my eyes to avoid the pictures. I heard the pages flipping as he read, but I didn't look up. An unfortunate, whiny voice in my head kept asking why everyone was so eager to blame me for everything that went wrong in their lives. I tried not to listen to it, because feeling sorry for myself wasn't going to help the situation one bit.

I heard the sound of the papers being tucked back into the folder, then the soft groan of Anderson's chair as he leaned back in it. Safe from the worry of catching another glimpse of the pictures, I raised my head and tried to interpret the look on his face.

The best word I can come up with to describe his expression was *neutral,* and I realized he was making a concerted effort to hide his feelings. He was doing a much better job of it than I was. I hadn't a clue what he was thinking or feeling behind that mask.

"In case you were wondering," I said, though I was sure he'd figured it out already, "that was *my* condo."

"So I gathered. Have you made any progress in your hunt?" he asked, his voice as neutral as his face.

"Depends how you define progress," I said. "I thought I was on his tail last night when the rain came in, but I have no way to be sure." I braced myself for trouble as I took a tentative step into dangerous territory. "I was on his tail right about the time the fire seems to have started, and he was nowhere near my condo."

Anderson kept his neutral mask firmly in place, though I was sure he knew what I was implying. "A man like Konstantin never does his own dirty work. He has people for that kind of thing."

I was certain that was the truth, but I still couldn't shake the uncomfortable suspicion that Emma was the true culprit. She had a much more obvious motive, at least in her own twisted version of reality, but Anderson wasn't going to believe that unless I came up with actual proof, and I didn't have it. At least not yet.

"It doesn't really matter who's behind it," I said, although it did matter, quite a lot. "Whoever it is, it's an Olympian, and Cyrus should be able to put a stop to it."

Anderson shook his head. "I don't care that Cyrus has supposedly taken Konstantin's place at the top. He doesn't have the kind of power that Konstantin does, and there's no way in hell he can control Konstantin's actions. Even if he wanted to."

I mentally cursed Anderson's stubbornness. If he'd only acknowledge the possibility that Emma was behind the fires, he'd probably have set up a meeting with Cyrus already. Cyrus might not be able to stop Konstantin from coming after me, but I'd bet good money he could stop Emma.

"So what you're telling me," I said through gritted teeth, "is that you're content to sit back and do nothing while whoever it is kills babies and old ladies." Anderson's narrowed eyes said he didn't appreciate my tone, but I was pissed enough not to care. "You're not even going to *try* to negotiate with Cyrus."

"I didn't say I wouldn't try." Despite the narrowed eyes, he sounded calm enough. "I was merely pointing out that it's not likely to work. We have no leverage."

No, we didn't have leverage. Not unless Anderson was willing to go to war with the Olympians for my sake, which he wasn't. And to tell you the truth, I was just as happy about that. The Olympians had too much of an advantage in numbers, and they would wipe us all out. Cyrus might not be eager to start that war, but not eager wasn't the same as not willing. Konstantin had laid off Anderson and his *Liberi* because he knew that Anderson was capable of killing him, and that was a risk he wasn't willing to take. Taking that thought to its logical conclusion . . .

"We'd have leverage if you'd let Cyrus know what you are, and what you can do."

I'd tried to broach this subject any number of times since I'd learned Anderson's secret, and he had always shut me down fast and hard. He'd even threatened to kill me—and whoever I told—if I revealed what I knew. I didn't think he was bluffing, but I couldn't for the life of me understand why he wasn't willing to reveal the deadly weapon that could act as a powerful deterrent and give us a leg up on the Olympians. It felt kind of like we had a nuclear bomb but didn't want anyone, not even our own people, to know it.

"I think I've made it perfectly clear that that is not an option," Anderson said in a low and menacing voice. "You'd be wise never to bring it up again."

I felt like grabbing him and shaking him. I couldn't think of a single reason why we shouldn't use his special power to our advantage. He obviously wasn't shy about using it, at least not when nobody but me could see. I'd already seen him kill three *Liberi*.

"I know you want me to shut up about it," I continued. "But letting Cyrus know you have the power to kill him might be the only way to motivate him to—"

"Enough!" Anderson pushed back his chair and practically jumped to his feet. His expression was dangerous enough that I stood, too, and took a couple of hasty steps back.

Anderson stepped around his desk, but instead of coming toward me, he stalked toward the study door and banged it shut, turning a dead-bolt lock I'd never noticed before. He swiveled toward me, and I made sure there was a chair between us. It wouldn't slow him down much, but it was better than nothing.

"What's it going to take to keep you quiet, Nikki?" He took a step toward me, and I took a corresponding step back as he raised his right hand. The Hand of Doom.

My heart was slamming in my chest, my every nerve on red alert, but frankly, I was getting sick to death of being bullied. I wanted to shout out my rage, but I shoved a muzzle and leash on my temper. If I wasn't careful, I could end up dead, or wishing I were dead, in no time flat.

"You could try explaining *why* you're so dead set against anyone knowing," I said.

Anderson blinked like he was startled. I guess he'd expected me to back down in the face of his threat. And why shouldn't he expect that? It's what I'd always done before.

"Innocent people's lives are at stake," I reminded him. "People are getting hurt, getting killed, losing everything they own, all because one of Cyrus's people has some psychotic vendetta against me. I couldn't live with myself if I didn't do everything in my power and explore every possible way to make it stop. Even if it means pissing you off yet again. I don't get why—"

"If I tell you why it's imperative that the truth doesn't get out, will you promise to stop asking questions?"

It was my turn to be startled. I don't know where I was expecting the conversation to go, except that it wasn't here. Anderson was actually backing down? It seemed impossible, and I was immediately wary.

"So after all the huffing and puffing, you're just going to give up and tell me?"

"I'll tell you what could happen if the truth got out. The answer won't satisfy your curiosity, and you'll want to ask me ten million questions in search of more details. You must swear to me that you won't ask even one, no matter how curious you are. Not now, not ever."

Scant seconds ago, I'd been in fight-or-flight mode, sure this conversation was going to end with something ugly. Now I felt like I was going to explode with curiosity. Nothing like telling me I'm not allowed to ask questions to make me desperate to ask questions.

"Or you *could* try taking my word for it," Anderson said. "Giving me the benefit of the doubt, believing that I'm not a shallow, selfish person acting on a whim."

Anderson wasn't human, and he never had been. At times, I was painfully aware that his thought processes weren't always the same as ours. How could a man who'd never been mortal, had never had to face the possibility of his own death, think like everyone else, or understand the specter we all have to live with? Even the *Liberi* could die, no matter how hard it was to kill them, but Anderson couldn't, and there was an inherent otherness that came with his true immortality. But despite that otherness, he *did* have feelings, and I realized for the first time that my insistence on knowing his reasoning had hurt them.

When you read mythology, you see examples aplenty of gods acting shallow and selfish. I mean for Pete's sake, the Trojan War started when a couple of goddesses got offended that a mortal said another goddess was prettier than they were. But I'd seen no sign that Anderson was like that, and I had yet to see him act on a whim. So the question became: did I believe Anderson had a good reason for keeping his secret?

I hadn't known Anderson all that long, admittedly, but I knew him well enough to feel certain the answer was yes. I was dying of curiosity, having been unable to form even a reasonable guess as to why keeping the secret was so important, but did I really want to draw this line in the sand over curiosity? Anderson was willing to tell me why he wouldn't reveal his identity, but I realized that if I pressed for it, it would change something between us. He would always feel that when it came right down to it, I didn't trust him. Once upon a time, that had been nothing but the truth. It still was, if you threw Emma into the mix. But this particular secret had nothing to do with her.

I swallowed hard, forcing my curiosity back down. I believed Anderson had a good reason, and it wasn't going to kill me not to know what it was.

Maybe Anderson was manipulating me. It was something he was very good at, though I liked to think I was aware whenever he tried to do it. Maybe his feelings weren't really hurt by my lack of faith, and he was just laying the guilt trip on me because he knew it was an effective tactic. But considering the things that had happened with Emma over the last few weeks, I figured Anderson was in enough pain already. No reason for me to add to it.

"All right," I said. "I'll trust you, even though I'm not very good at it. You've earned that."

He smiled at me, the tension easing out of his shoulders. "I appreciate it. More than you know."

If I didn't know better, I could swear he was a little choked up under that smile. I thought about giving him a hug, but decided it would feel awkward, for both of us.

"I'll call Cyrus and see if I can set up a meeting," he said. "I don't have high hopes we can reach a resolution, but we should at least try."

"Thank you." Going in there with such a defeatist attitude wasn't going to help our cause, and I worried that Anderson's refusal to suspect Emma would hamper any negotiations that occurred. But I'd gotten as much out of him as I was going to get.

Anderson stepped aside so I had a clear path to the door, the gesture something between a release and a dismissal.

"Um, sorry I got so pissy," I said, because I couldn't walk out without another word.

"Me, too," he replied, and the twinkle in his eye told me he'd deliberately left it up to interpretation as to whether he was apologizing to me or teasing me.

I shook my head as I reluctantly smiled back. I stepped up to the door and opened the dead bolt.

"If word of my existence reaches the wrong ears," Anderson said softly, "it could mean the death of every man, woman, and child on this earth."

I turned back to him, and I'm sure my expression was one of naked shock.

"When I say I have a good reason, I mean it."

What could I possibly say to that? My cheeks felt cold and bloodless, and my mouth gaped open. My mind could barely encompass what he'd just told me, and I desperately wanted to dismiss it as some kind of hyperbole. A shudder ran through me. When the first shock wore off, I was going to have a million questions—none of which Anderson would answer—but right now I couldn't think of a single thing to say. I opened my mouth a couple of times in hopes that I would magically say *something,* even if it wasn't something intelligent or meaningful, but nothing came out. So instead, I opened the door and hurried out of the room.

Ten

It was still raining later that afternoon when Anderson and I left for our meeting with Cyrus. Anderson had invited Cyrus to the mansion, but Cyrus insisted the meeting be held on neutral ground, so we were meeting him at a coffee bar downtown.

I whipped out my umbrella as Anderson and I walked from the main entrance of the mansion to the outbuilding that held the garage. Anderson didn't bother with an umbrella, stepping out into the steady rain without hesitation. He jogged ahead of me to the garage before I could offer to share my umbrella. I'd have suggested Anderson not make himself look any more disheveled than usual when going to meet Cyrus—I wasn't sure the frumpy look gave off quite the aura of power he would need to convince Cyrus he meant business—but he wouldn't have listened to me.

I followed at a more sedate pace. I was carrying

the manila folder with the article about the fire in it, and I'd also tucked in the email from Konstantin.

Anderson was waiting for me behind the wheel of his black Mercedes by the time I reached the garage, the engine already running. His car was more elegant than he was, but in this area of politicians and diplomats, black Mercedes were a dime a dozen, so his car didn't catch the eye any more than Anderson himself did. I took a deep breath as I slid into the passenger seat. I can't say I held out any great hope that we'd get Cyrus to see things our way, and I was more than a little worried about Anderson's temper.

"Are you sure you can have a civilized conversation with Cyrus after what happened to Erin?" I asked as Anderson drove out of the mansion's gates. I figured with his distorted view of Emma, he'd probably shifted a lot of the blame for Erin's death onto Cyrus.

"Yes," Anderson said in his familiar mild voice. "He's an Olympian. He did what Olympians do, and I know it was nothing personal on his part."

I was impressed with his stoicism, and wondered if that meant he was finally going to stop making excuses for Emma.

The rest of the drive passed in silence, except for the annoying squeak of the windshield wipers. The rain was just hard enough to make them necessary, but not enough to keep them silent. The noise grated on me, but that was just because of my generally crappy state of mind. It took a lot of effort to keep myself from dwelling on the deaths that had occurred because of me. I wasn't *responsible,* but I *was* part of the chain of events that had led to them. That was more than enough to have my conscience bothering me.

Cyrus was waiting for us at a corner table when we arrived at the coffee bar. Not surprisingly, he wasn't alone. No self-respecting Olympian would attend a meeting with Anderson and not have a pet Descendant in tow. It always seemed a bit rude to me—kind of like carrying a gun in your hand—but obviously they felt threatened by him, despite being under the impression that he couldn't kill them.

Not being a *Liberi,* Anderson couldn't be killed by the Descendant, so Cyrus's gun would be shooting blanks if it ever came to that. Of course, *I* could be killed by a Descendant, so I gave Cyrus's companion a careful once-over as Anderson and I approached the table.

He wasn't as goonish as most of the Descendants Olympians liked to use as bodyguards, though he wasn't a ninety-pound weakling, either. Blond, good-looking, and stylishly dressed, he reminded me more than a little of Blake. I darted a quick glance at Cyrus, wondering if the resemblance was coincidental.

Cyrus and his companion were standing when we reached the table. With his trademark friendly smile, he greeted us, shaking hands first with Anderson, then with me.

"This is my friend, Mark," he said, indicating the Descendant, who offered his hand. "I hope you don't mind him sitting in."

Anderson stared at Mark's extended hand, but made no move to shake it. There was a lightning bolt glyph on the back of Mark's hand, telling us he was a descendant of Zeus. I didn't like leaving him hanging there, but I took my cue from Anderson and didn't offer any pleasantries, either. I guess Anderson found the Descendant's presence as rude as I did.

Still smiling, Cyrus patted Mark's shoulder, and Mark lowered his hand.

"Just a precaution," Cyrus said, sitting back down. "I figured you probably weren't too happy with me right now. I also figured you probably wouldn't do anything stupid in a public place, but one can never be too careful." He reached over and stroked Mark's back like he was petting a dog. "I promise he won't interfere as long as we're just talking. You won't even know he's here."

Anderson was still standing, giving both Cyrus and Mark his best scowl. I'd never had much patience for posturing, so I pulled back my own chair and sat without waiting for Anderson.

"Were you hoping we'd bring Blake so you could make him jealous?" I asked Cyrus.

He grinned and looked over at Mark in a considering manner. "Yes, there is a certain resemblance, isn't there?" Mark looked more uncomfortable now than he had when we'd refused to shake his hand, and I felt momentarily bad for him. Then I reminded myself that he was an Olympian-wannabe, which meant he was not one of the good guys.

Anderson slowly took his seat.

"Would you like to order something before we begin?" Cyrus asked. Both he and Mark had cups of espresso in front of them, though it looked like Mark had barely touched his.

I'd have loved to have a cup of coffee to fidget with, if not to drink, but Anderson wasn't interested.

"This isn't a social call," he said coldly, "and there's no reason to pretend it is."

Cyrus stuck out his lower lip in a pout. "We can talk business without completely skipping the social niceties." He motioned to the barista, holding up two fingers. "Two more shots for my friends, please," he called.

"You know, the polite way to order at a coffee bar is to go up to the register and talk in a normal tone of voice," I said, not willing to be charmed by his genial manner.

Cyrus was hardly chastened by my rebuke. "I'm a regular, and I tip really, really well. Amazing the kind of service that buys me."

"You don't actually think we're buying your good-ole-boy act, do you?" Anderson asked.

"It's not an act. If you're expecting me to act all stodgy and self-important like my father, you can forget it. That's not my style."

The barista brought over two demitasse cups of steaming, fragrant espresso, putting them before me and Anderson. "Need anything else?" she asked Cyrus with a coquettish smile. She probably thought he would make a great catch with his good looks and his propensity for throwing money around.

"No thanks, Lacy," he said, and I wondered if he

actually remembered her name, or was just reading her name tag. "We're good for now."

She wandered away, disappointed.

"Now, since you're so anxious to get down to business," Cyrus said, "why don't you start talking."

Anderson turned to me, and I told Cyrus about the two fires that had devastated my life over the last week. He listened in silence, and I passed the folder with the news article and the printout of the email across the table to him.

I'm not a big fan of espresso, unless it has a lot of steamed milk in it, but I was too jittery to sit still while Cyrus read, so I took a sip. Anderson hadn't touched his.

Finally, Cyrus finished reading and tucked the papers back into the folder. He shook his head and gave me a look of genuine sympathy.

"I'm sorry you've had to deal with all this," he said. "I'm sure being tossed headfirst into our world is stressful enough without adding this crap to it." He slid the folder back to me with a sharp gesture that spoke of annoyance. "But I can assure you Konstantin isn't behind it."

Anderson snorted. "He claimed responsibility!"

Cyrus rolled his eyes. "As I told Nikki before, an anonymous email isn't proof of anything." He looked at me. "My father hates your guts, I won't lie. But not because he blames you for his troubles. He can be petty, but he's not stupid."

"Oh, so he readily accepts the blame for what happened with Justin Kerner?" Anderson asked with patent disbelief.

Cyrus smiled ruefully. "Of course not. It's the incompetents who didn't bury him deep enough, and Phoebe, whose visions weren't clear enough, and, hell, me because I met with you a couple of times and didn't stop his secret from getting out. There's plenty of blame to go around. And Nikki, he hates you, but you're nowhere near important enough to him to warrant this kind of attention."

I believed every word of what Cyrus was saying. For a while, I'd allowed myself to accept that Konstantin really was behind the fires, but the motive had never quite made sense. Hearing Cyrus shoot down the theory without even momentarily considering it just cemented my opinion.

Anderson, of course, saw things differently. "Did it ever occur to you that his misfortunes might have caused him to become a bit . . . unhinged?"

"No," Cyrus said. "It never did. I've been in regular contact with him, and I can assure you, he's acting like his usual, ornery, domineering self."

"And I'm supposed to take your word on it?"

"Why would I lie?" Cyrus picked up his cup and frowned at the contents. "Mine's gone cold. Are you going to drink that?" He gestured at Anderson's untouched espresso.

"You'd lie because that's what Olympians do."

"There's no reason to be such a dick," Cyrus said, reaching for the espresso without Anderson's go-ahead. "I'm telling you my father isn't behind these particular attacks. I'm not trying to tell you he's a nice person, and I'm not telling you he wouldn't take an opportunity to hurt Nikki if it fell into his lap. But he's not going to go through this elaborate bullshit in a quest for revenge."

"Of course, you also said Emma wouldn't do this," I pointed out, more to give Anderson a moment to cool down than because I thought the point needed to be raised, "and she's the only other person I can imagine wanting to hurt me. You're wrong about someone, either your father or Emma."

"I suppose it's possible," Cyrus conceded with a careless shrug. He took a sip of Anderson's espresso. "But I don't think it's likely, and you didn't ask for this meeting because you wanted to solve the mystery of who's behind the fires, now did you?"

I think Anderson wanted to snap something about there being no mystery, but he refrained. I suspected that somewhere down inside, he *had* to see where the evidence was pointing, even if he wasn't ready to admit it.

"No," he said, wiping the emotion from his face. "I asked for this meeting because I want you to put a stop to it."

Cyrus took another sip of espresso, as nonchalant as ever. "Can't help you there. Property damage isn't covered under our agreement."

"Property damage?" I cried in outrage, pushing my chair back so I could leap to my feet. "Three people were killed, including an *infant,* for Christ's sake. That's murder, not property damage!"

And here I'd been worried about Anderson losing his temper. Mark's hand had disappeared into his pocket, and he was watching me with studied intensity. I assumed his hand was on a weapon, and that he'd be on me in a heartbeat if I made anything that he could construe as a hostile motion toward Cyrus.

"Sit down, Nikki," Anderson said, still calm and unruffled.

"At ease, Mark," Cyrus said in a similar tone of voice.

I wondered if they were going to tell us to heel or fetch as a follow-up. Mark didn't seem to mind being given commands. He took his hand slowly out of his pocket, but he kept his eyes on me. I minded a lot more, but I knew emotional outbursts were counterproductive. I wished I hadn't just lost my temper in front of the enemy, but there was nothing I could do about it now except try not to make it worse. I sat down and tried to relax, though I was practically shaking with rage.

"Sorry," Cyrus said with a grimace. "I should have known you'd be more upset about the casualties than about your property. I'm sure the intent behind the attack was to destroy something that belonged to you, and that doesn't fall under the purview of our agreement. Nor do the incidental deaths that accompanied the damage."

This was exactly the response Anderson had warned me to expect, but that didn't make it go down any easier. Cyrus made such a good show of being a nice guy that no matter how much I reminded myself what he was, I couldn't ever seem to make the knowledge stick.

"So you're okay with your people burning down buildings filled with innocents, and it doesn't bother you in the least when those innocents die."

Cyrus shrugged. "*I* wouldn't do something like that, but I'm not going to get all worked up about it. If I got all worked up every time an Olympian killed somebody, I'd never have survived to adulthood." He leaned forward and gave me an earnest look. "Look, I'm sorry about what's happened. You seem like a good person, and I'd rather not see you get hurt. But unless the treaty is broken, my hands are tied."

"Spoken like a true Olympian," Anderson said sourly.

Cyrus raised an eyebrow. "You expected something different? I'd have thought Blake had told you all about my deficiencies of character."

"*I'm* not the one who expected something different."

"Ah." He gave me that earnest look again as his voice dropped until I could barely hear it over the roar of the espresso machine. "I've stopped the Olympian practice of disposing of Descendant children. You have no idea how far out on a limb I've already gone. I can't go forbidding my people to bother you just because Anderson asks me to."

If he thought I was going to sympathize with his delicate political situation, he was nuts. He was still looking at me, this time expectantly, though I didn't know what he was expecting.

Suddenly, Anderson gave a harsh bark of laughter. I didn't get the joke.

"What?" I asked, looking back and forth between the two of them.

"Let me translate what Cyrus just said," Anderson answered. "It comes down to: what's in it for me?"

I hadn't fully registered Cyrus's words until that moment. He hadn't said he wouldn't stop his people from tormenting me. He said he wouldn't stop them *just because Anderson asked him to.*

"You bastard," I said, scowling at Cyrus.

The insult rolled off him. "I'm not running a charitable organization, Nikki. I like you, but I'm not going to go sticking my neck out for you just because I'm a nice guy. You want my help, you have to make it worth my while."

"You're just a goddamn shakedown artist, aren't you?"

"Do you want to bargain with me or not?"

If it had been Konstantin offering me some kind of a deal, I'd have refused without even exploring the possibility. In fact, if it had been any other Olympian, I probably would have gotten up and walked away. But there was a part of me that still kept insisting there had to be some redeeming qualities to Cyrus. Naive? Maybe.

"All right, I'll play," I said. "What would it take to get you to order your people to leave me alone?"

I realized Cyrus had planned to take us into a negotiation all along, because he didn't even have to think a moment before he named his price.

"Give me an IOU for one hunt, to be cashed in at my convenience."

"No," I said instantly. I knew more innocents would likely die if I couldn't get Emma (or Konstantin, if I was wrong about him) off my back, but I wasn't willing to actively cause someone else's death. I'd just have to find some other way to fix things.

"I understand that you have severe moral qualms about hunting for us," Cyrus said. "How about if I promise that whomever you hunt will not be killed?"

I'd seen how creatively the Olympians could torture someone without killing them. "Not good enough. You'd have to take rape and torture off the menu, too."

Cyrus thought about that a moment, then nodded. "I could do that. We don't *always* have nefarious purposes when we're looking for people."

I glanced at Anderson, wondering if there was some big loophole I was overlooking. I was pretty sure that Cyrus would be getting the better of this deal, but as Anderson had told me, we had no leverage.

"I think Cyrus is about as close to honest as an Olympian can be," Anderson said in answer to my questioning look.

"Gee, thanks," Cyrus said with another of his grins.

"It's up to you whether you're willing to put yourself in his debt," Anderson finished.

It still wasn't exactly a rousing endorsement. The idea of owing Cyrus held no appeal, but if that was what it took to keep the other Olympians off my back, then I'd just have to suck it up. "Just to clarify,"

I said, "if I promise to hunt someone for you in the future, you will get whoever's been setting the fires to stop?"

Cyrus shook his head. "I can't promise it will stop. If I'm wrong and my father's behind this, he might not listen to me. But I will warn all of my people off, and if anyone acts against you after my warning, then they'll be disobeying my direct orders. I'm not as much of a hard ass as my father, but I will *not* tolerate disobedience." He leaned forward and looked back and forth between me and Anderson. No charming smiles this time, and the look in his eyes said that he was dead serious. "And let me make this perfectly clear: if you go after my father, all bets are off."

"What if he sets another fire after you warn him off?" I asked.

"Then I'll have to conclude I'm a gullible idiot and declare open season on him. But that's not going to happen, because he's not behind this in the first place."

Anderson leaned back in his chair and didn't say anything. I didn't for a moment think he was going to let Konstantin go for my sake, at least not in the long run. He would have his revenge, one way or another. But he would have to find a new way to convince me to find him if the agreement with Cyrus worked out. That was a problem for another day.

Both Cyrus and I were looking at Anderson expectantly.

"What?" he asked. "I've already agreed to let him be. Do you need me to agree again?"

"Yes, I think I do," Cyrus said, and I think he was as skeptical about Anderson's agreement as I was. After all, he'd already sort of caught me on the hunt after Anderson and I had both agreed to leave Konstantin alone.

"All right," Anderson said. "I'll say it again. Neither I nor any of my people will harm Konstantin as long as he is an Olympian, and as long as he commits no acts of aggression against us. Satisfied?"

"I guess I am." Cyrus didn't sound convinced, and I didn't blame him. "Shall we shake on it?"

A round of handshaking followed. This time, Mark didn't even try to participate.

I returned home from our meeting with Cyrus more than a little unsettled. I couldn't shake the feeling that although Anderson had raised no objection, I had made a tactical error in promising Cyrus a hunt. The fact that I'd specified no violence made me feel marginally better, but I imagined there were any number of ways Cyrus could twist my promise into something I'd later regret.

I was so worried about what I might have gotten myself into that I went looking for Blake, whom I usually preferred to avoid. The door to his suite was ajar when I arrived. I rapped on it as I pushed it open and stuck my head in, but apparently Blake didn't hear me, because he didn't look up. When I saw what he was doing, I wasn't sure whether to laugh or to gape in shock.

He hadn't heard me knock because he was

wearing earbuds, his head nodding along to whatever was playing on his iPod. He was sitting on his couch, one leg tucked under him, as he concentrated intensely on the pair of knitting needles he was holding. I couldn't tell what he was making—he only had about four or five inches of fabric so far—but the yarn was a thin, silky-looking crimson, and the little bit he had done was almost lacy. He executed some complex maneuver with the yarn and needles, his forehead creasing with the effort, then came to the end of his row and let out a sigh of what sounded like satisfaction.

If you had asked me what Blake did in his spare time, I'd have put knitting somewhere at about 1,001 on the list of possibilities. He wasn't as macho as guys like Jamaal and Logan, but despite his pretty-boy looks and his onetime romance with Cyrus, he'd never given me the impression that he might be the sort to engage in such a stereotypically feminine pursuit.

"What are you making?" I asked, loud enough that Blake could hear me over whatever was playing on his iPod.

He jumped and practically dropped his needles. He'd been concentrating so hard that I doubt there was any way I could have made my presence known without startling him, but I gave him a sheepish smile anyway.

"Sorry," I said, as Blake pulled out the earbuds and laid his knitting carefully on the coffee table. "I knocked, but you didn't hear me."

He eyed me suspiciously from his seat on the couch. I guess my sudden and unexpected appearance in his suite worried him. Maybe he thought I was going to try to warn him away from Steph for the millionth time.

"I'm making a scarf for Steph for Valentine's Day," he said, that wary look still on his face. "I haven't knitted for a long time, so I thought I'd get an early start."

The admission made me strangely uncomfortable. The idea that he was making something for Steph *by hand,* something he expected to take him nearly a month to complete, suggested a deeper attachment than I'd allowed myself to imagine. I'd known Blake was *fond* of Steph, and I'd even had to admit to myself that he genuinely cared about her, but I'd hoped it was something fun and casual. You don't spend a month knitting something for someone if the relationship is casual.

"I wouldn't have taken you for the knitting type," I said. My voice came out a bit tight. I'd promised not to *voice* my disapproval of his relationship with my sister, but that didn't mean I didn't *feel* it.

Blake shrugged. "I grew up with three sisters. I was a rebel, so when my parents told me boys don't knit, I immediately wanted to do it." He grinned. "I learned by unraveling a couple of my sisters' projects so I could figure out how it worked. Strangely enough, they weren't very happy with me when they found the piles of yarn I left behind."

I chuckled, reluctantly charmed. "How old were you?"

"Nine, the first time. Dad took his belt to me something fierce, so next time, I was more sneaky about it and buried the evidence. I'm pretty sure Dad knew it was me, but there was an outside chance the dog had made off with it, and he wasn't going to thrash me unless he was sure."

I imagined blue-eyed, blond-haired Blake had been a pro at looking angelically innocent as a child.

"But you didn't come here to talk about my hobbies," Blake said. "What's up?"

I hesitated, unsure if bringing up his relationship with Cyrus would come across as some kind of subtle rebuke under the circumstances. But it was why I'd come to Blake in the first place, so I straightened my spine and closed the door behind me. Blake hadn't invited me to sit, so I stood awkwardly and put my hands into my pockets so I wouldn't fidget.

"You know Anderson and I went to meet with Cyrus this afternoon, right?"

He nodded, and his suspicious look made a return appearance.

"Cyrus promised to tell all the Olympians to back off me if I promised to owe him a hunt someday." Blake's eyes widened in alarm and surprise, and I hastened to clarify the details of the deal we'd made. "My question is, is Cyrus like Konstantin? Will he try to find some way to make this deal hurt me despite the conditions I set?"

Blake thought about it a moment, and I decided to sit down despite the lack of invitation. I suspect it hadn't even occurred to him to issue one—he'd just assumed I'd make myself comfortable. He wasn't as formal as Anderson or as standoffish as Jamaal.

"Here's the thing to understand about Cyrus," Blake said slowly, thinking over his words carefully before he spoke. "Unlike Konstantin, there's no malice in him. He'd never go out of his way to hurt someone, and he's even capable of being a nice guy, when the spirit strikes him."

"Nice guys don't lead the Olympians!" I protested.

"I said he's *capable* of it. He's not in the least bit malicious, but what he *does* have in common with his daddy is a deep, abiding selfishness. He'll be nice and actually help someone, if it doesn't cost him anything and he's in the mood. But if you're standing between him and something that he wants, all bets are off. So in answer to your question, no, he won't look for a way to make the deal bite you in the ass. But he won't hesitate to exploit a loophole if he finds one and it's to his advantage."

I shook my head. "How the hell did you end up involved with someone like that?" I asked, not really expecting him to answer.

A hint of sadness crossed Blake's face. "I honestly thought I could change him. He was a good friend for a long time, and I've seen sides of him that no one else has seen. He could be a good person, if he wanted to be." Bitterness now colored Blake's voice, the sadness gone. "But I found out the hard way that he has no desire to change. And that's all I have to say on the subject."

From some of the things I'd heard Cyrus say to and about Blake, I got the feeling the desire to change each other had been mutual. Cyrus would have loved to convert Blake into a full-scale Olympian, and the fact that his current boy toy bore such a striking resemblance to Blake made me wonder if he'd ever fully abandoned that hope.

"Did this stuff make you feel better, or worse?" Blake inquired.

Honestly, I had no idea. "Knowledge is power, right?" I said with a shrug that was supposed to look careless, but probably didn't. "I'll just have to hope he finds some inoffensive use for me before anything potentially sticky comes up."

What I didn't say, but I suspect we both knew, was that if something sticky came up, I might balk at it despite it fitting the letter of our agreement. The consequences of balking might turn out to be disastrous—no way would Cyrus take it well if I failed to honor our agreement—but I would just have to cross that bridge when I came to it. And hope I never did.

ELEVEN

I'd turned my cell phone off during the meeting with Cyrus, and I didn't remember to turn it back on until I was in my suite after talking to Blake. I saw that I'd missed a call from Steph.

With the way my life had been going lately, I couldn't help bracing a bit in fear of bad news, but Steph's perky greeting instantly put me at ease.

"I got your message," I said. "What's up?"

"I called that trustee I know," she answered, and for a moment I didn't know what she was talking about. In all the stress and drama, I'd temporarily forgotten about my plan to draw Jamaal out of his shell.

"Wow. You work fast." I wouldn't have been surprised if she'd dragged her feet about it, considering how much she disapproved of my interest in Jamaal.

She breathed a delicate sigh. "Well, after what happened, I figured you'd be badly in need of an escape."

My heart swelled with love for my sister, who was way better to me than I had any right to expect. "You have enough balls in the air trying to get ready for the big homecoming. I don't want to add to your workload." I knew Steph had already talked to the insurance company multiple times, and that she had rented a furnished condo for the Glasses to stay in while the house was being rebuilt.

"It wasn't that much work. Just a few phone calls."

"Have I ever told you you're amazing?"

I could hear Steph's smile in her voice. "Will you still think I'm amazing if I tell you I've arranged for you to meet with the curator of the exhibit for a private showing at seven o'clock tonight?"

"Tonight?" I asked in a startled squeak.

"Yeah. Sorry for the short notice, but Dr. Prakash is going to be massively busy in the next few weeks, so the only time she could fit you in was today."

When I'd asked Steph if she could set something up, I'd imagined Jamaal and me being shown around during regular business hours by a docent. Not being given a special, after-hours showing with the curator, who was probably already overworked and underpaid.

"I don't want to put her out," I said, hedging.

"It's a done deal," Steph said firmly. "I've done a lot of favors for people who've donated a lot of money and art, and I was past due to call some of them in."

"Yeah, but the curator isn't—"

"She'll be excited to have a chance to show off the exhibit, especially if Jamaal is knowledgeable about art, which I gather he is."

The books in his room gave me the same impression, but I wasn't convinced Dr. Prakash was going to be as thrilled to show us around as Steph thought. If it were me, I'd resent being made to drop everything just because someone with connections wanted a special perk.

"She's already rearranged her schedule to fit you in," Steph said. "Don't you dare try to wriggle out of it. And instead of asking Jamaal if he wants to go, you'd better *tell* him he's going. It would be unspeakably rude to stand her up."

I glanced at my watch and saw that it was already three thirty. I didn't have a whole lot of time to track down Jamaal, convince him this was a good idea, and get to the museum. I wondered if putting me in such an awkward position was part of Steph's plan, if she was giving me extra fuel I could use to help me talk Jamaal into going. She can be a bit devious at times, though always for a good cause.

"I'll get Jamaal out there, one way or another," I promised. I wished I felt more certain that I could deliver, but I would at least do everything in my power. "Thanks so much. You're the best."

"I know. Now get off the phone and go give him the good news."

"Yes, Mom."

I could almost see Steph shaking her head and laughing as she hung up.

I'd have called Jamaal's cell in an effort to locate him, only I wasn't sure he'd answer if he saw my name on caller ID, and he might make himself scarce once he knew I was looking for him.

I headed down the stairs toward his suite, my pulse tripping along even as I rolled my eyes at myself for being nervous. I'm not a shy person, nor was I as intimidated by Jamaal as I probably should have been, but asking him out on what was essentially a date was well beyond my comfort zone. Especially when I felt sure it was going to turn into a battle of wills.

After a deep, calming breath, I knocked on his door. If he was out in the clearing working with Sita, then I was going to settle in and wait for him. Frankly, if I never saw another tiger for the rest of my life, that would be fine with me. I would never forget the feeling of her breath on my face.

Footsteps told me at once that Jamaal was in, and my pulse picked up even more speed. Damn, I was as nervous as a sixteen-year-old girl asking a boy to the junior prom. I wiped my palms on my pants legs in case they were sweaty, then tried my best to brace myself for the rejection that was sure to come. I might be able to talk him into coming with me, but I'd faint in shock if his first answer wasn't a resounding no.

The door opened, and I was suddenly face-to-face with Jamaal. Well, face to chest. Jamaal is about a foot taller than I am, so I always have to look up to meet his gaze.

His cheekbones looked a little sharper than usual, and I wondered if he had lost weight. But other than that, he looked good enough to eat, as always. He was still wearing the tiger-colored beads in his hair, and he had on torn jeans and a faded T-shirt. The outfit would have looked scruffy on, say, Anderson, but it somehow looked carelessly sexy on Jamaal.

He didn't scowl on seeing me on his doorstep, and I figured that was a good sign. He didn't smile, either, but then he didn't do a whole lot of smiling even at the best of times.

"If you're here to get on my case about what happened with Sita the other day, you can turn around and go back upstairs," he said. The scowl made its appearance after all.

"Really?" I said, crossing my arms over my chest and giving him an exasperated look. "You think I'd come down here and knock on your door to lecture you?" I didn't for a moment believe that was why he thought I was here. He was just trying to establish a sense of distance before we'd even started.

He leaned against the doorjamb. It would be nice if he'd invite me in, but I wasn't surprised he didn't. "I don't suppose we have much else to talk about."

It appeared I was lucky he hadn't slammed the door in my face. Whatever had caused the new friction between us, it wasn't getting better over time.

"Why don't you stop acting like a jerk and let me in?" I'd often found that tact was overrated when dealing with Jamaal.

His scowl darkened. "Like I said, we have nothing to talk about."

The fact that he still hadn't slammed the door in

my face made me think some hidden part of him was more interested in talking than he liked to admit.

"Yeah, actually, we do," I countered. "And I promise it won't involve any of that girlie-talking-about-feelings stuff you hate so much."

I thought I saw a flicker of amusement in his eyes before he shut it down. "In that case, we can talk about it right here."

"You hiding a girl in there or something?"

Jamaal gave a grunt of exasperation and stomped into his sitting room, leaving the door open. I guessed that was as much of an invitation as I was getting. I stepped inside and closed the door behind me. Jamaal watched me with suspicious eyes as I invited myself to take a seat on his futon sofa. I might have hoped he would join me, but he remained on his feet, giving off keep-away vibes.

"Did you hear about the new Indian exhibition opening at the Sackler later this week?" I asked, and was rewarded by a look of complete confusion on Jamaal's face. Bet he didn't see that one coming.

"Huh?"

"Sackler. Exhibition. Indian stuff." I nodded my head toward the small Indian painting that was the focal point of Jamaal's sitting room. "Did you hear about it?"

The look on his face told me he was still busily trying to figure out where I was going with this. "Yes," he admitted cautiously, as if he expected the answer to get him into some kind of trouble.

"Well, how would you like a chance to visit with

the curator and have her give you a personal guided tour of the exhibition before it even opens?"

Boy, did I ever have his attention now. I saw the spark of greed and excitement in his eye before he managed to hide it under his habitual grumpy face. "Are you claiming you have contacts at the museum?" He sounded skeptical, but I heard the undertone of hope.

"No, but Steph does."

Jamaal shook his head, rattling his beads in a way that had become familiar to me—and strangely endearing. "I don't know what you're trying to talk me into, but the answer is no."

"I'm trying to talk you into getting a sneak peek at the exhibit. That's all."

Another shake of his head. "No way. Offers like that come with strings attached."

Considering Jamaal's life experiences, his attitude and suspicion weren't surprising. "The only string is that I'm going with you." Of course, that might be the kind of string he considered a deal breaker.

His lip lifted in a faint sneer. "You've suddenly developed an interest in Indian art?"

"No, but I've developed an interest in fixing whatever's gone wrong between you and me. I thought maybe if we stopped avoiding each other and spent a little time together, we might figure out how to start acting normal again."

Jamaal rubbed his forehead like he had a headache, then reluctantly came to sit on the couch—as far away from me as he could get. I remembered our little make-out session on this couch with a pang of regret.

But asking Jamaal out wasn't about trying to get into his pants—though my libido thought that sounded like an excellent idea—it was about trying to keep him from withdrawing from everyone around him.

"I know you're the kind of woman who wants to fix everyone," Jamaal said. "But it's time for you to stop trying to fix *me*."

"Why? Because you'd prefer to be miserable so you can bitch and whine about it? Of course, you'd only bitch and whine to yourself, because you won't let anyone else near you."

Jamaal's temper would have normally risen to meet mine, but not today. "I've been broken in one way or another for more than a hundred years. What makes you think you can snap your fingers and make it all better?"

"I don't. I'm not completely naive, Jamaal. It took years for my adoptive parents to bring me back from the brink of becoming a juvenile delinquent, and I don't suppose I'll ever be as well adjusted as someone who spent their whole childhood in a good, loving home. But I'm in a lot better shape now than I was when the Glasses took me in.

"I'm not trying to *fix* you. I'm just trying to be a friend."

"You've been a much better friend than I had any right to expect," he said gruffly. "But now, you have to let me be."

"Why?" I demanded. "What's different now?"

"Didn't you promise we weren't going to talk about feelings?"

"I lied."

His lips lifted in the faintest of smiles. "At least you're honest about your dishonesty."

"And I'm not that easy to deflect. We have to live and work together for God only knows how long. We'll do a lot better job of it if you get whatever's bothering you out in the open."

"Haven't you interfered enough with my life already?" he snapped.

His attitude might have pissed me off if that weren't so clearly the reaction he was hoping for. "You think if you're a big enough asshole I'll flounce off in a huff and leave you alone? I'm way more stubborn than that."

He snorted, but the hostility faded and his shoulders slumped. "I've noticed."

Maybe what I needed to do was pull back a bit and stop trying to make him talk. Every emotional guard he had was up and running, and the chances of me slipping past them were low. I wished I could get him to spill whatever his problem was with me, but I didn't have to get him to do it *now*.

"All right," I said. "You don't have to tell me about your feelings. I wish you would, but I understand that it's hard for you." A little condescending, maybe, and I saw the spark of annoyance in Jamaal's eyes before I hurried on. "But please come with me to the museum. It would do you good to spend some time around people for a change, even if one of those people is me."

"Remember what I said about trying to fix me?"

What an exasperating man. But I hadn't expected any less. "My parents' house was burned down, and my condo was burned down with people inside, all because some nutcase has decided I'm responsible for all his or her problems. Did it ever occur to you that maybe *I'm* the one who could use some fixing right now? That maybe I want to go out to the museum as much for my sake as for yours?"

He flashed me a dry smile. "No, it never occurred to me. If you were just looking for a way to forget your troubles for a few hours, I doubt you'd do it by going to a museum."

He had a point. Maybe that argument had been a bit thin. "That's the opportunity that fell in my lap, thanks to Steph. Look, she's already arranged a meeting for us with Dr. Prakash, the curator. We're supposed to meet her at seven tonight."

Jamaal glared at me. "You didn't think it might be a good idea to ask me about it *before* setting something up?"

"If Steph had given me any warning, I'd have asked first. I only brought this up to her yesterday. I never dreamed she'd work this fast."

He looked at me suspiciously.

"She said Dr. Prakash had already rearranged her schedule to fit us in. Surely it won't kill you to spend a couple of hours in my presence, and I *know* you want to see the exhibit."

I could see from the look on his face that he was torn. He really, really didn't want to spend that much time with me. But he also really, really wanted that private look at the exhibit. I decided it was time to rest my case, so I clamped my lips shut and gave him some time to think. If this didn't work, I was going to have to have a talk with Anderson, see if there was something he or his other *Liberi* could do to persuade Jamaal to engage in some more human interaction. They were all glad not to have to tiptoe around his temper anymore, and they might not want to risk making him change back into the powder keg he'd been. His temper had been so volatile he'd almost been kicked out of the house, and he'd had to undergo a tribunal and a brutal punishment to prove how committed he was to trying to control himself.

Thankfully, Jamaal made such a drastic action unnecessary.

"All right," he said softly. "We'll go to the exhibit. But this isn't a date, and it isn't the start of a beautiful friendship. It's best for everybody involved if you and I stay at a safe distance."

"Why?" I asked.

But I wasn't surprised when he didn't answer.

Twelve

I had no idea what to wear for a private visit with a museum curator, so I decided to dress for comfort and warmth on this wet, gloomy winter night. I paired a teal cowl-neck sweater with soft black cords and water-resistant ankle boots, then examined myself in the mirror. I decided the outfit was dressy enough to be classy, but not so dressy as to look like I'd dressed up for a special occasion.

I met Jamaal in the foyer. He'd gone with what for him was a pretty dressed-up look, wearing black jeans with an orange polo shirt. Tiger colors again, I noted, though I kept the thought to myself. I didn't bother arguing with him about who would drive. He liked to refer to my Mini as "the clown car," and though he fit in it just fine, he liked his black Saab a hell of a lot better. He'd made a concession in agreeing to come with me tonight, so I made my own about transportation.

When we were in the car with the doors shut, I noticed the faint scent of clove cigarettes in the air. Before he'd learned to summon Sita, Jamaal had tried to keep his temper in check by chain-smoking clove cigarettes—or pot, when things got really bad.

"You still smoking?" I asked, though I don't know why I was surprised. People don't just quit without a concerted effort.

"Not as much," he said defensively. "Just because I don't *need* cigarettes anymore doesn't mean I don't like them anymore."

"I didn't mean anything by it. I was just curious." Had he smoked tonight because he needed the extra help to stay calm in my presence? His body language told me he was agitated in a way I hadn't seen for a long time.

We had to come to a brief stop while waiting for the gates at the head of the driveway to open, and Jamaal took that opportunity to roll his neck from side to side. The crackling sound made me wince.

Why was going out with me such an issue for him? If it wasn't about my attempt to leave, and it wasn't about our experiment with romance, I couldn't imagine what it *was* about. The curiosity was killing me, and his continued reticence just made it worse.

"How did you get into art, anyway?" I asked, just to make conversation. "You don't seem much like an art geek to me."

"By 'art geek,' do you mean rich white guy?"

I suspected he was trying to start a fight—maybe so he could use it as an excuse to turn the car around and go back—but I wasn't about to take the bait. "When I think of an art geek, I think of a sensitive beta male," I said calmly. "You don't fit the description."

The comment won me a reluctant laugh, and a little of the tension eased out of his shoulders. "You shouldn't put so much stock in stereotypes," he said, but there was no rancor in his voice.

"I'm sure you're not the only macho man who likes art. You're just the only macho man I *know* who likes art. Or at least who *admits* it."

"Macho man?" He sounded affronted, and there was no hint of a smile on his face, but I was 99 percent sure he was teasing.

"All right, you like 'alpha male' better. I'll keep that in mind for the future."

He made a little growling sound as he shifted gears, giving the Saab a little more gas. If he got pulled over and made us late, I was going to be seriously pissed.

"You going to answer my question, or just brood in silence?"

He shot me a quick look of annoyance. "You must be the most persistent female I've ever met."

I grinned. "Is that supposed to be an insult?"

He shook his head in resignation. "If you must know, I got into art because it's something I would never have dreamed could be a part of my life when I was a kid. I tried every highbrow cultural door that would open for me. I went to the opera and ballet. Learned to play golf. At least, tried to learn. I sucked at it, and it's not a good sport for someone with a temper problem. I went to fancy restaurants to eat foods I couldn't pronounce. And I visited art galleries. The art's the only thing that stuck."

"And you got into the Eastern stuff because you're descended from Kali, right?"

He nodded. "I thought I might collect paintings of her, because being an art collector was about as far from being a slave as it was possible to get. I went to an auction and bought the painting that's in my sitting room, but when I hung it, I decided I'd rather let the art go to museums. I should probably donate the one I have, but . . ."

"You're allowed to do something nice for yourself every once in a while."

He didn't say anything, but I saw the small smile on his lips. Maybe the walls he'd built around himself were starting to show cracks. Tiny ones, to be sure, but I was going to do my damnedest to widen them.

We were to meet Dr. Prakash at one of the side entrances to the museum. Jamaal and I arrived there a little before seven. Standing outside waiting in the rain wasn't my idea of a good time, especially not with the damp chill in the air.

Jamaal, of course, had no umbrella. If we'd just been walking straight from the parking lot and into the building, I'm sure he would have refused to share mine, but even *he* wasn't macho enough to stand around waiting in the rain as the temperature dipped toward its predicted nighttime low of thirty-five.

Sharing the umbrella meant Jamaal had to stand closer to me than he would have liked. I think he was trying not to show his discomfort, but I couldn't help noticing the stiffness of his posture, or the way the fingers on the hand that wasn't holding the umbrella were dancing nervously at his side.

"Do you need a cigarette while we wait?" I asked.

My question must have cued him in to his unconscious hand movements, and his fingers came to a stop. "I'm fine," he said.

I was debating whether to try to push him into telling me what was wrong when the door to the museum swung open.

I hadn't realized I'd built an image of a curator of Indian art in my head until I set eyes on a woman who looked absolutely nothing like that image. I'd pictured a petite Indian woman of mature years wearing a sari and sporting a red dot on her forehead. The woman who beckoned us into the museum was indeed of Indian descent, but that was about all I'd gotten right.

Dr. Kassandra Prakash was plump without being fat, and if she was over thirty, she was some kind of cosmetics genius. She wore a thoroughly Western wrap dress with ugly sensible shoes, and she had a smile that made her face look pretty despite an oversized nose and black eyebrows that were just short of being a unibrow.

I darted inside, leaving Jamaal to wrestle the umbrella into submission.

"I'm so sorry to leave you waiting in the rain!"

Dr. Prakash said earnestly. "I've been indoors all day and never realized it was raining."

"Don't worry about it," I said as Jamaal won his battle with the umbrella and joined me inside. "We just got here. And we can't thank you enough for taking the time—"

"Nonsense," Dr. Prakash interrupted with a cheery smile. "I'm like a proud mama showing off her baby." She held out her hand for me to shake. "I'm Kassandra Prakash, but you can just call me Kassie."

"Nikki Glass," I answered as I shook her hand. I could tell the moment she got her first good look at Jamaal, because her generically friendly smile turned into something with a hint of hubba-hubba behind it.

"And you must be Mr. Jones," she said.

I highly doubted Jamaal had been born with either his current first or last names, and I sometimes wondered why he'd chosen something as dull as "Jones" for his surname. It didn't fit his exotic good looks, but then I don't think Jamaal realizes just how attractive he is.

"Nice to meet you," Jamaal said dutifully as he shook Kassie's hand. There was a hint of strain behind his smile, and I wondered how long it had been since he'd had a normal, social interaction with someone other than Anderson's *Liberi*. He certainly wasn't used to smiling at people, and I was glad he'd made the effort, even if it did come off a little forced.

If Kassie noticed Jamaal's awkwardness, she didn't acknowledge it, instead leading us through the empty halls of the museum toward the exhibition. She chattered almost nonstop, and I decided Jamaal's lack of social graces probably wasn't going to be much of a handicap tonight. I didn't get the feeling that she was overly enamored of hearing herself talk, just that she was so excited about the exhibit that she couldn't contain herself. I wondered if she was always like this, or if she'd been overdosing on energy drinks to get her through her long and busy day.

I'd imagined this evening's outing as a chance for Jamaal and me to spend some time together and maybe try to ease ourselves back into something resembling a normal relationship. I thought maybe we'd bond a bit over this shared experience. I might even have thought Jamaal would be grateful to me for giving him this opportunity. Instead, I ended up feeling like a third wheel on someone else's date.

Kassie proceeded to give us a guided tour of the exhibit, which consisted mostly of paintings, with some bronzes and some stone carvings for variety. I knew absolutely nothing about Eastern art of any kind, and to tell you the truth, I didn't find the Indian paintings all that interesting to look at. A lot of them were pretty primitive, with stiff figures and wonky proportions. If I'd been on my own, I'd probably have been in and out of the exhibit in fifteen minutes, tops. Jamaal, on the other hand, was enthralled, and within minutes had forgotten all about being his normal surly self. His face was more animated than I'd ever seen it as he hung on Kassie's every word. He was even able to make intelligent conversation and ask intriguing questions whenever Kassie paused to take a breath.

I followed along beside them in silence, feeling inadequate and uncultured. Kassie tried to include me in the conversation a few times, and I appreciated the effort, but I didn't have much to contribute. Anything I said about the art would either make me look stupid or reveal that I wasn't that impressed with it, and with the two of them geeking out so much, I didn't think bringing in inane small talk would help.

Eventually, they kind of tuned me out. I told myself that tight feeling in my gut was just because of my inability to join the conversation, but I was pretty sure there was a hint of jealousy in there, too. Jamaal spoke more words to Kassie in those couple of hours than he'd spoken to me in the months I'd known him. And he smiled a lot more, too. I'd have loved to see him smiling at *me* like that.

Not that he was flirting, though. I'm not even sure Jamaal knows *how,* and though he was clearly enjoying his conversation with Kassie, his enthusiasm was directed at the paintings, not at her. That didn't stop me from feeling jealous, especially not when Kassie put her hand on his arm here and there. I didn't think *she* was flirting, either, at least not consciously, but it raised my hackles anyway.

I tried to hide my own discomfort, smiling and feigning interest whenever either of them glanced at me. Whether I was enjoying myself or not, I couldn't help feeling like this was good for Jamaal, and that was supposedly the reason I'd invited him out here. When we'd finally seen the last of the exhibit, I thought the ordeal was over, but then Kassie offered to show us the reserve collection—paintings the museum owned but that weren't currently on display. Jamaal's eyes lit up even more, and I had to suppress a groan. For Jamaal's sake, I faked my way again through the next hour or so, trying not to let myself glance at my watch every five minutes.

It was almost ten by the time we escape—I mean, by the time we regretfully said good-bye and thank you to Kassie. The rain had slowed to a desultory drizzle, but the temperature was close enough to freezing to make the damp night air feel thoroughly unpleasant. Despite the success of my plan to draw Jamaal out, I was in a crappy mood thanks to three hours of feeling like a moron while Jamaal and Kassie bonded over stuff that was over my head. Not to mention that I'd failed to eat dinner before we'd set out, and my stomach was howling in protest. I had planned to ask Jamaal if he wanted to grab a bite to eat when we left the museum, but now I just wanted to get back to the mansion and lick my wounds.

We didn't speak on the walk to the car, and I figured that meant Jamaal was back to his habitual brooding self already. Maybe I shouldn't have bothered trying to draw him out. Maybe it had done no good whatsoever and had just made me miserable instead. Maybe I really should butt out of his life as he'd repeatedly told me to do.

Okay, so maybe just this once, Jamaal wasn't the most broody person in the car.

"Thank you," he said softly as we pulled out of the parking lot.

A lump formed in my throat. I swallowed hard and tried to respond in a normal tone of voice. "You're welcome. I'm glad you had fun."

We drove for a couple more minutes in silence, then Jamaal pulled into an illegal parking spot against the curb. I looked around, trying to spot whatever had inspired Jamaal to pull over, but instead of parking the car, he left the engine running and turned toward me in his seat.

"That might be the nicest thing anyone's ever done for me," he said, meeting my eyes only briefly before looking away. "And I know it must have been painfully boring for you."

"It wasn't—" I started to protest automatically.

Jamaal met my eyes with a look of frank skepticism that killed my protest.

"You did a good job trying to hide it," he assured me. "And I'm an asshole for taking advantage of you and making you wait while I looked at the reserve collection."

"No, you're not. If I didn't want to do it, it was up to me to say no." And as badly as I'd wanted to escape, I couldn't have denied Jamaal the opportunity to see things the public might never see.

He straightened in his seat and leaned his head back into the headrest, closing his eyes. He was bracing himself for something, but I didn't know what. He opened his eyes and huffed out a breath.

"You remember you said once that Sita's attitude toward you might have something to do with how I feel about you?" he asked, looking out the windshield instead of at me.

"Yeah," I said, then held my breath, wondering if somehow, miraculously, he was going to talk about his feelings after all.

"You weren't wrong."

Even though I'd figured all along that Sita's dislike of me was a reflection of Jamaal's own feelings, I still felt a stab of pain. Things had been strained between us lately, but I'd allowed myself to hope that there was still a spark of friendship underneath it all. The ferocity of Sita's attitude toward me suggested maybe that had been wishful thinking.

"Okay," I said. My voice came out a tad raspy, and I cleared my throat.

To my shock, Jamaal reached out and brushed a strand of my hair back behind my ear. The touch sent a shiver through my whole body.

"You weren't wrong about Sita's attitude being related to my feelings," he said. "But you were wrong about what the feelings were. She's *jealous,* Nikki."

My eyes widened and my jaw dropped. "Your phantom tiger is jealous of me?" That might have been one of the most ridiculous things I'd ever heard. And it made me feel almost giddy with relief.

Jamaal graced me with one of his small, wry smiles. "Yeah. She's jealous of *anyone* who might steal any of my attention from her, and you're Public Enemy Number One."

"Oh." I wanted to say something more intelligent and useful, but my brain refused to feed me any words.

"I'm trying to learn to control her better. That's why I've been practicing so much. Right now, I can keep her focused on me and obeying me as long as I'm concentrating my full attention on her. But if I let my concentration waver . . ."

"Or if you practice so hard that you pass out?"

He grimaced. "Yeah. That, too."

"I don't get why you've made this into a state secret. Why wouldn't you just tell me what was going on?" He gave me a long, condescending look, until I answered my own question. "Because you didn't want to admit feeling anything that would make her jealous."

There was another long silence between us. I didn't know what to say to Jamaal's admission, and he didn't seem to have much idea what to say, either.

"I'm glad you told me," I finally said.

"It doesn't change anything. It's going to take everything I have to keep Sita under control the next time I summon her after tonight. It would be best if you weren't even in the house when I do it, just in case I can't stop her from going to look for you."

Trying to manifest his death magic in the form of an animal had been my idea in the first place, and I'd thought it had turned out to be a pretty good one. It was nice not having Jamaal ready to fly off the handle at any moment. Now I was beginning to wonder if an out-of-control phantom tiger was really any better than an out-of-control temper.

"It's an improvement," Jamaal said. Obviously, it was clear what I was thinking. "I *feel* a hell of a lot better. And Sita may be hard to control, but at least I can control when and where I let her out. When I was fighting the death magic instead of cooperating with it, everyone knew I could snap at any moment."

That was a bit of an exaggeration. Sure, his temper had been volatile, and he could be dangerous when his death magic got antsy, but he didn't go off without provocation. Of course, it hadn't taken much to provoke him . . .

"I'm glad you feel better," I said carefully. "But I hope you won't let Sita cut you off completely from the rest of us." Especially me. No matter how much my common sense told me I shouldn't let him get too close.

He shrugged. "I guess we'll see what happens. I've only been working with her a couple of weeks. Maybe my control will get better. And maybe she'll stop seeing everyone else as her competition. But until then, you have to give me my space. I had a great time tonight, but I never should have let you talk me into this. Sita is going to be one angry kitty next time I summon her."

He put the car back in gear and pulled out of the makeshift parking spot. I got the signal loud and clear: our heart-to-heart conversation was over.

I couldn't have told you how I felt about the night's revelations. There was good news and bad news, and I didn't know which was bigger. But at least I no longer thought Jamaal was avoiding me because he was pissed at me. That was a step in the right direction.

THIRTEEN

On Tuesday, I had to meet Steph so we could make the apartment she'd rented for the Glasses as welcoming as possible before they arrived the next day. The place was attractive enough, with good-quality, bland vanilla furniture, but the decoration was sparse, to say the least. Steph thought coming home to a bare-bones apartment was going to make the Glasses feel worse than they already did, so we spent the whole afternoon darting around from store to store buying things like throw pillows and wall hangings, and then spent the evening and well into the night installing our purchases.

The rain was finally starting to clear when I couldn't take decorating anymore and left Steph to finish up alone. The clouds were patchy, and at times I caught quick glimpses of the moon between them. I didn't think it was clear enough for a hunt yet, even if I weren't exhausted and I hadn't agreed to Cyrus's terms. Maybe by tomorrow night . . .

But no. I didn't believe Konstantin was the firebug, and if Cyrus thought for a moment that I'd continued the hunt despite my promise, there would be hell to pay.

Knowing Wednesday probably wasn't going to be any easier on me than Tuesday had been, I collapsed into bed the moment I got home.

The following day dawned bright and clear, not a cloud in the sky. The weather forecast said we'd be venturing up into the low fifties, and after the chilly rain of the last few days, it was going to feel like spring.

The cheerful weather did nothing to calm my rampaging nerves, however. Steph and I had agreed that she would pick up the Glasses at the airport when they arrived around noon. I'd have gone with her, except the Glasses had packed for a three-month trip and would need every spare inch in the car for their baggage. Steph would call when she was leaving the airport, and I'd meet them at the apartment.

I had missed my adoptive parents while they were away, and there was a part of me that was looking forward to seeing them again, whatever the circumstances. I *wasn't* looking forward to seeing their lingering grief over the loss of their house, nor was I looking forward to their worry when Steph told them about the fire at my condo. On paper, they were the owners of the apartment. There was no evidence that the police had linked the two fires—yet—but you could be certain the Glasses' insurance company would take a serious interest in the "coincidence." And, since I was supposedly living in the condo, the Glasses would probably worry I was in some kind of trouble, especially when they factored in the fire at my office building.

What I was dreading the most, however, was the distance I was going to be forced to put between us because of all the things I couldn't tell them.

I remembered what it had been like trying to tap-dance around the truth with Steph before she was dragged in so deeply that I had to tell her my secrets. I may be a good liar, but people who know me really well—like Steph and her parents—tend to see through me. Maybe they had enough crap on their plate that their parental Spidey senses wouldn't start nagging at them right away, but I knew it was only a matter of time before they came to the conclusion I was hiding something from them. I wasn't sure I could face their disappointment and hurt when that happened.

Jamaal was on the porch smoking a clove cigarette when I left the house to go meet the Glasses. I hadn't seen him at all the day before, but considering how little time I'd spent at home, that wasn't a surprise. He held a glass ashtray in one hand. There were three butts and a considerable heap of ashes in it already. I hoped they were old, because if Jamaal had started chain-smoking again, it was not a good sign. I tried to think of a tactful way to ask him about it, but it turned out I didn't have to.

"I didn't get to practice with Sita yesterday," he

told me, then took another drag off his cig. "You were out of the house, but I didn't know how long you would be gone."

I shook my head. "So you mean you were serious about not being willing to summon her when I'm nearby."

He nodded as he finished off his cigarette and stubbed it out in the ashtray. "Better safe than sorry. Any idea when you're coming back today?"

I had no clue, actually. However, I didn't think I'd have a hard time making myself scarce for hours on end if that was what Jamaal needed.

"How about I call you before I come home?" I asked. "If I don't get you, I'll figure you and Sita are still at it and I'll find some way to kill time. I'm sure it won't be hard."

He thought that over for a moment, then nodded his approval. "That'll work."

I started down the porch steps toward the garage, but paused midway down. "You know, you could have called me yesterday and asked me when I was coming back."

His only answer was a shrug. I understood now why he was so determined to keep distance between us, but it didn't really make me feel any better.

The Glasses had beaten me to the apartment. I closed my eyes and sucked in a deep breath as I pulled up next to Steph's car. I hated the anxious knot in my gut, and I hoped like hell I'd be able to cover my discomfort with a convincing veneer of normalcy.

By the time I'd reached the front door of the apartment, I'd put on my happy face. When Mrs. Glass opened the door, I let my cares and worries sink into the background and allowed myself to be swept into the warmth of her hug.

"I missed my girls so much," she said as she tried to hug the breath out of me.

"I missed you, too," I replied, hugging her back just as hard. I glanced over her shoulder at Steph, who was smiling fondly at us. Steph nodded slightly, confirming that she had told her parents about the fire at my condo on the ride from the airport. It was hard to see anything like a silver lining in a fire that had left three innocents dead, but at least it made it easier for me to explain why I was currently "staying with a friend."

"I'm so sorry about everything," I said, my voice suddenly hoarse. "Everything" encompassed a whole lot of things I couldn't talk about, as well as my condolences over the loss of property.

Mrs. Glass only hugged me tighter, holding on until Mr. Glass nudged her aside so he could take her place. He was a little more reserved than she, so my aching ribs survived his hug without greater damage.

"I just made a pot of coffee," Steph said. "Want some?"

"Is water wet?" I retorted.

Mr. Glass released me from his hug, but kept an arm around my shoulders as he guided me to the living room. I saw that Steph had already served her parents coffee and was steeping a cup of tea for herself. The tea was looking a little dark, so I removed the teabag while waiting for Steph to return from the kitchen with my coffee. I'd have told her she didn't have to serve me, except I didn't think the Glasses were going to let me out of their sight quite so soon.

They both had that weary, slumped-shouldered look of people who've been traveling way too long. They'd had to fly in from Hong Kong, and they had to be jet-lagged like nobody's business. Especially Mrs. Glass, who had never been able to sleep on an airplane, even in first class. I hoped that meant that we'd have a pleasant, stress-free visit today and that we'd leave any difficult conversations for a later date.

"So tell me about your trip," I prodded as Steph brought me my cup of coffee. Maybe if I started the ball rolling in the right direction, I could steer the conversation in the direction I wanted. In a perfect world, I'd be able to avoid talking about the fires and what they meant for my continued safety. But it had been a long time since I'd believed in a perfect world.

For a while, my strategy seemed to be working. Mrs. Glass came alive, apparently forgetting her jet lag completely, as she told Steph and me about all the exciting things they'd done and the exotic ports they'd visited. Mr. Glass provided visual aids in the form of photos, which the cruise ship had printed out for him—no doubt at an exorbitant fee. We were all aware of the elephant in the room, but at least we tried to pretend it wasn't there.

The stop-by-stop recounting of the cruise

eventually petered out, and that was when the Glasses invited the elephant in the room to join us for coffee. I spent a good fifteen minutes nonchalantly telling them the official version of the story, trying to pretend I genuinely didn't think the fires had anything to do with me. No one called me a liar, but I could see the skepticism on their faces.

"You'd tell us if you were in some kind of trouble, wouldn't you, Nikki?" Mr. Glass asked with fatherly concern.

"Of course," I lied.

"Because I can't help thinking that in your line of work, you might make the kind of enemies who would do something like this."

I had to look away, unable to lie convincingly when he was looking at me like that. The Glasses had never once criticized my choice of career, though I was sure they'd have preferred it if I'd taken a desk job of some sort—or lived off my trust fund and dedicated my life to charity, as Steph had. There had always been an element of danger to my job, and I imagined this wasn't the first time they'd worried about me.

"I'm not in any trouble, at least not that I know of," I said into my cup of coffee. I was acting squirrelly, and I knew it. I just couldn't get myself to stop, too uncomfortable with the direction of the conversation to act normal.

"And what about the rest of us?" he persisted, looking pointedly at his wife and his biological daughter. "Anything we should know about?"

Steph gave an exasperated huff, and I gathered

they'd already had this discussion in the car. "It's just a bizarre coincidence, Daddy," she said. "If Nikki thought someone might hurt us, I'm sure she'd tell us."

Steph isn't as good a liar as I am, and I could see her father mentally digging in his heels. I hated the very thought that they might be in danger because of me. I was doing everything I could to protect them, but it wasn't enough.

I received a reprieve from an unexpected source when Mrs. Glass patted her husband's leg. "Now, Ted," she said warningly, "I thought we'd agreed we weren't going to give Nikki the third degree."

My mouth dropped open, though I quickly snapped it shut. If anyone was going to press me for details, I'd have expected it to be my adoptive mother. That was what mothers did, wasn't it?

Mrs. Glass met my gaze with a sad smile. "I'm sure if there's something you're not telling us, it's for a good reason."

My throat squeezed tight, making it impossible for me to answer. There was no hint of reproach in her voice or her eyes. Just loving acceptance and trust. How I'd been lucky enough to be placed with this family when I'd been well on my way to being a lost cause, I'll never know. I swallowed hard, trying to scrape up my voice from wherever it was hiding, but I failed.

"This might be a good time for a change in subject," Steph said. She drained the last few drops of tea from her cup. "You said in the car you had something you wanted to tell us."

Mr. Glass was still looking at me as if he could read my every secret—and he wasn't happy with what he was reading. Mrs. Glass, however, looked suddenly uncomfortable and fidgeted with her empty coffee cup. I shared a quick, puzzled glance with Steph.

"Maybe now isn't a good time—" Mrs. Glass started.

"There never *will* be a good time, May," Mr. Glass said gently, which sent a bolt of adrenaline shooting through my veins.

"What's wrong?" I asked, my voice tight with alarm.

Mrs. Glass was still fidgety, and there was a sheen in her eyes that suggested she was fighting tears, which didn't make me any less alarmed.

"Nothing's wrong," Mr. Glass assured me and Steph, who looked as worried as I felt. "We just have something to tell you." He gave Mrs. Glass a pointed look, but her eyes were now swimming and she shook her head. He sighed. "We're not going to rebuild the house," he said. "Your grandma Rose is getting old, and she's all alone. Your mother and I have been talking for a long time about moving closer to her."

Grandma Rose was Mrs. Glass's mother, and she'd celebrated her seventy-fifth birthday last year, three years after being widowed.

"But Grandma Rose lives in San Francisco!" Steph said in a tone that suggested San Francisco was akin to Timbuktu.

Mrs. Glass rallied her mental forces and cleared

her throat. Her eyes were still shiny with tears, but her voice was firm and sure. "We've been talking about it ever since your grandpa passed," she said. "And it feels like the house burning down is almost like a sign from the universe that now is the time."

Mrs. Glass wasn't the only one with shiny eyes now. Steph looked completely stricken. Her whole life, she'd never lived more than a half hour away from her parents. She hadn't even left town to go to college, going to Georgetown because it was close to home. I couldn't imagine what she must be feeling at the moment.

Actually, I wasn't exactly sure what *I* was feeling at the moment. Despite the tears that shone in both Steph's and her mother's eyes, I wasn't feeling inclined to cry myself, nor did I feel the kind of sinking sensation in my stomach I might have expected. My adoptive parents were moving all the way across the country from me. Instead of being able to pop over and see them any day of the week, I would only be able to see them a handful of times a year. They had rescued me from a future that had looked unbearably bleak, and I loved them with all my heart.

And yet at that moment, I felt . . . nothing.

I'd experienced this kind of emotional numbness before. It meant my psyche wasn't ready to deal with my emotions just yet, so it had shut them down entirely.

Even numb as I was, I understood why my emotions had shut down. Despite all the many years I'd lived with the Glasses; despite the fact that they'd adopted me, and treated me in every way as though I were their biological daughter; despite the fact that even if they were living in San Francisco, I could see them as many times as I was willing to endure the long flight, I couldn't help flashing back to the many times in my childhood when I'd been abandoned. First, my biological mother had abandoned me in a church. Then foster family after foster family had given up on me and sent me away. The small child who lived in my core felt like she was being abandoned yet again, and it was more than I could deal with.

Steph was openly crying now and had moved to the sofa to hug her mother. I should have made a similar gesture, but I sat rooted in my chair, wondering when the dam within me would burst. Mr. Glass shot me a look of undiluted sympathy as he reached over to pat Steph's back, and I knew he understood. At least my less-than-normal reaction to the news wasn't hurting his feelings, and probably wasn't hurting Mrs. Glass's, either. They both knew me well enough to understand my abandonment issues. Maybe that was even part of the reason why they hadn't before now gotten past the stage of *talking* about moving.

My cell phone chirped. After the bombshell the Glasses had just dropped, I probably should have ignored it, but I dug my phone out of my purse anyway, acting more on reflex than considered thought. The caller ID announced the call was from Cyrus.

"I'm sorry," I said to no one in particular, "but I have to take this."

I didn't wait for anyone to acknowledge my words, bolting from my seat in search of privacy.

It wasn't until I was halfway to my rendezvous with Cyrus that I saw the similarity between my current situation and the series of bad choices that had landed me in my new and confusing life in the first place. That time, I'd been on the blind date from hell. I'd gotten a call from Emmitt, asking me to meet him under mysterious circumstances. My gut had been telling me something was wrong, and I'd ignored it, desperate for any excuse to get out of my date. This time, it wasn't a bad date I was running away from, it was the turmoil of my emotions. I had left Steph and her parents with a flurry of excuses, no doubt causing them to worry about me even more. But running away was easier than dealing with the announcement, and I was all for easy.

It could be argued that running off to meet Cyrus without Anderson or any of his other *Liberi* to back me up might be dangerous—and stupid. I didn't think there was any danger that he would hurt me, but he was a devious son of a bitch and could be setting me up for . . . something.

If I'd been able to put my finger on a specific suspicion, I probably would have turned around before I reached the rendezvous. However, I couldn't think of anything Cyrus could do to me in the middle of a public coffee bar, not when the truce between the Olympians and us was still intact. He wouldn't want to piss me off and have me start hunting for Konstantin again.

I drove past the coffee bar, trying to get a look inside before fully committing myself to the meeting, but the cheerfully sunny sky meant all I saw was a reflection of the street with a few shadowy figures moving behind it. I gave a mental shrug, then found myself a parking space. If I was walking into some kind of an ambush, then so be it.

To my surprise and relief, Cyrus was alone this time. At least, he appeared to be. I took a quick visual survey of the rest of the people milling around the coffee bar, and didn't spot anyone with any visible glyphs. Cyrus rose from his table and beckoned to me, like he thought I couldn't find him. I'm sure he knew exactly why I didn't immediately rush to join him. He then shouted an order to the barista—a different one this time, but she seemed just as unflustered by his manner as the previous one—for two espressos.

"I'm not a big espresso fan," I informed him as I approached.

"Make that a latte," he called to the barista, then smiled charmingly at me. "Better?"

Arguing with him over a beverage order seemed like more trouble than it was worth. "Whatever," I said, taking a seat. "I've had a long day already. Can we just cut to the chase without the whole dog and pony show?"

The espresso machine let out a shriek that set my teeth on edge, and Cyrus waited until it went silent before answering.

"No theatrics, I promise."

The barista brought our coffees over. I hadn't been planning to drink mine, but the scent was so enticing I couldn't resist.

"You don't think calling me for an urgent, private meeting is theatrical?" I asked.

He huffed. "Well, I wasn't trying to be, but I guess it was a bit at that. Sorry."

I sipped at my strong, rich coffee, being careful not to burn my tongue. "So what's the big emergency? And why did you need to talk to *me* particularly?"

"I said it was important, not that it was an emergency. But I don't think Anderson will like what I have to say, and I'm trying to spare everyone some drama."

This didn't sound good. I put down the coffee. "What is it?"

"We were speculating the other day about who might be behind the attacks against you. I promised I would warn all my people off, and I did. But I found I was curious myself, so I did a little investigating."

My heart gave a loud ka-thump in my chest. If Cyrus thought Anderson wasn't going to like what he was going to say, then that meant . . .

"It was Emma, wasn't it?"

Cyrus nodded. He pulled a folded sheet of paper from the inside pocket of his jacket. "I stopped by her place and poked around on her computer for a bit while she was out."

I must have looked shocked at his blatant invasion of Emma's privacy, because Cyrus gave me one of his wry grins. "I'm her boss, and she's living in a house that I pay for. I have every right to keep an eye on her, especially when her loyalty's been questionable from the start."

Add one more item to the long list of reasons I never wanted to be an Olympian.

Cyrus slid the paper across to me. "I didn't find anything interesting in her files or browser history. But I did find this in her recycle bin."

I unfolded the paper and saw a screen shot of a computer's recycle bin full of junk files. A number of them with nonsense names had been highlighted, and I could see a bunch of tiled windows that had opened up in WordPad.

"I found seven different versions in her recycle bin," Cyrus continued. "I don't remember exactly what the email you showed me said, but the one on top in that shot is the closest to what I remember."

I had memorized "Konstantin's" email claiming responsibility for the fire at the Glasses' house, and although the one on the screen shot wasn't *exactly* the same, it was close enough. Looked like I'd been right all along to suspect Emma as the author of all my woes. I reread the letter a couple of times as I tried to process what I'd learned. Obviously, Emma was the firebug and was responsible for the fires at the Glasses' house and my condo, but I had to conclude that the fire at my office was every bit as accidental as it had originally seemed. It predated my feud with Emma, and the circumstances were very different. Perhaps what had happened at my office had sparked the whole idea in Emma's head. No pun intended.

"I had a talk with her," Cyrus continued. "She claims she didn't write it and she has no idea how it showed up on her computer."

I gave a little snort of disbelief, and Cyrus's cynical smile said he was with me. The smile faded into a look of grave intensity.

"None of this changes anything in the long run," he told me. "Emma is still an Olympian and under my protection. I have made it abundantly clear that you are off-limits and that I won't tolerate disobedience. I don't expect you to have any more trouble with her. But I thought you should know. I'll leave it up to you whether you want to tell Anderson or not."

I stared at the incriminating paper, shaking my head once more at the irrational depths of Emma's hatred. Anderson wouldn't want to know how low she'd sunk. He had a hard enough time reconciling his image of Emma with the woman who had betrayed Erin to her death just to spite him, but this was even worse. However, this might be something he *needed* to know, whether he wanted to or not.

"Thanks," I said, putting a heavy dose of sarcasm in my voice.

Cyrus smiled. "You can see now why I didn't want him to hear it from me."

I rubbed my eyes, feeling tired and headachy. I didn't exactly want Anderson to hear it from *me,* either.

I wondered if Cyrus thought I was rubbing my

eyes to stave off tears, because his voice suddenly went all soft and sympathetic. "I wouldn't take it personally if I were you. Emma's . . . not well."

"No kidding?"

"Her maid tells me she has nightmares every night," Cyrus continued after giving me a reproachful look. "I can see with my own two eyes that she's losing weight. She shouldn't have left Anderson when she did. In retrospect, I can see she was being self-destructive, and I probably served as an enabler."

I'd been so furious at Emma and the things she'd done that I'd never put a moment's thought into what her life might be like now. She was jealous, vindictive, and spiteful as all hell. More than once, I'd thought of her as crazy, but I'd never quite made the jump from "crazy" to "clinically insane." Until now.

"I'm trying to help her," Cyrus said, "but I don't think she's too interested in being helped. I made it very, very clear to her what the consequences of disobeying me would be, but I'm not sure she doesn't have a death wish. I'll try to keep an eye on her, but watch your back, just in case."

My stomach felt sour. I'd be the first to admit I'd disliked Emma from the moment she'd recovered from the catatonic state she'd been in when we first dragged her from the pond. She'd started out being merely annoying with her self-centeredness and bitchy comments, then graduated to being downright mean, consumed by unfounded jealousy and her understandable desire for revenge. She'd stopped having any redeeming features in my mind when she'd threatened Steph. And yet . . .

And yet, I had saved her life. Saved her from an eternity of repeatedly drowning to death. Finding her and rescuing her had been the single greatest victory of my life. I didn't want her to die after all that, didn't want to undo the good I had done.

Of course, I also didn't want her setting another fire.

"You'd better keep more than an eye on her, Cyrus," I said, though I had no ammunition with which to back up my ultimatum.

"I'll do my best."

His assurance didn't exactly fill me with confidence, but then nothing he said would. I picked up the incriminating screen shot. "Can I keep this?"

Cyrus nodded. "Be my guest. And if you tell Anderson and he takes the news as badly as I fear he might, let me remind you that you will always be welcome among the Olympians."

I paused with the paper halfway to my purse as a disturbing thought hit me. "How do I know this isn't all some kind of twisted setup so I'll have a falling-out with Anderson?" I asked. That would certainly explain his reluctance to break the news to Anderson himself. Hell, if I was going to be paranoid, I could even imagine he'd created the screen shots just so he could give me bad news to deliver.

He laughed. "An interesting idea. My father is capable of scheming and manipulation on that level, but I'm not as complicated as he is."

"Yeah, you're just a plain old everyman."

"Well, I didn't say *that*. But I wouldn't make trouble for you with Anderson unless I was sure it would make you join the Olympians. I'm not much of a gambler. Give me the sure thing any day."

Is it weird that Cyrus admitting his own potential for dishonesty made me more inclined to believe him?

What tipped the scales in the end was my absolute conviction that Cyrus wasn't an idiot. He knew that if Anderson kicked me out, I'd make a run for it rather than join the Olympians.

"I'm *never* going to become an Olympian," I told him, just to hammer home the point.

There was a glint in his eye when he smiled at me, and I wondered if making myself into a challenge to be conquered had been a tactical error. "Never is a long time, Nikki. A long, long time."

FOURTEEN

I wasn't in any hurry to deliver Cyrus's news to Anderson, so I decided to go for a run as soon as I got back to the mansion. As luck would have it, Maggie had the same idea, so I had company. I wasn't exactly feeling sociable, but running with Maggie isn't much of a social occasion for me anyway. She's five eleven to my five two, and she can cover a daunting amount of ground in a single stride. I have to run like my life depends on it to keep up, and I don't usually last all that long or have the breath to do a lot of talking.

On a day like today, running like my life depended on it was just what I needed. The effort of keeping up the aggressive pace left no room in my mind for inconvenient thoughts and worries. For just a little while, I left my problems behind me and didn't think about anything at all. My muscles burned and protested, my chest heaved with effort, I was sweating buckets despite the chilly temperature, and I adored every painful, oblivious moment of it. I pushed well past my usual limits and didn't even notice I was doing it.

By the time we started our cool-down walk, my legs were shaking with fatigue, and I was really glad I wasn't just an ordinary human being anymore or I'd never have been able to get out of bed the next day. Much of my hair had slipped free of the ponytail I'd tied it in, damp tendrils clinging to my face and neck. Maggie was panting delicately, and her face was glowing a bit with the exertion and a touch of sweat, but her curly auburn hair was pristine in its French braid. She looked like she was just about to *start* a run, while I looked more like someone staggering over the finish line of a marathon. She gave me almost as much of an inferiority complex as Steph did, but she was a good friend anyway.

"So, are you going to tell me what's wrong?" Maggie prompted when I was no longer breathing so hard I couldn't answer.

"Wrong?" I asked, giving her innocent wide eyes. "What makes you think something's wrong?"

"You don't love running enough to push yourself that hard. Not unless you're trying to run away from something that's on your mind."

I grimaced, realizing she was right. There were times when I enjoyed running, but mostly I did it because it was good for me, not because I loved it. And usually I'd quit long before I'd worked myself into such a lather.

I was sick to death of lying and trying to hide my

feelings. Or maybe I was just too exhausted, both mentally and physically, to hold it all inside. Instead of pretending nothing was wrong, I told Maggie about my disturbing conversation with Cyrus. My lips were chapped with the cold, but that didn't stop me from chewing on them, making them worse.

"What do you think I should do?" I asked. "Should I tell Anderson?"

I realized I knew her answer before she even spoke. Unlike me, Maggie's first instinct is always to follow the rules. Hiding the truth from Anderson might not be technically breaking any rules, but I suspected it would feel that way to her.

"Of course you should tell him," she said, as if it were the most obvious thing in the world. "He has a right to know. And he would *want* to know."

"But—"

"Besides," she interrupted, "he's likely to find out eventually, and he'll be pissed off that you didn't tell him."

She had a point. I kicked out at a pinecone in frustration, sending it straight into a tree so that it almost ricocheted back at us.

"I just don't get it," I said, restraining the urge to give the pinecone another kick. "Where is Emma getting all this crazy shit from? What have I ever done to give her the slightest hint that I might be after Anderson?"

I'd meant them as rhetorical questions, and wasn't expecting Maggie to answer. And yet there was a kind of waiting quality to her silence. Something that told me she had something to say but was thinking her words over carefully. I came to a stop, shivering in the cold now that I was finally cooling down.

"What is it? What are you thinking?"

Maggie gave me an almost apologetic smile. "I don't think it has anything to do with you or what you've done. I think it's more about Anderson."

I frowned in confusion. "Anderson's never done anything that would give her reason to be jealous, either. Not if she were sane, that is."

Maggie shrugged and turned as if to start heading back toward the house, but I grabbed her arm to stop her. Obviously, she had more to say, even if she was reluctant to say it.

"Come on, Maggie. Help me out here. Is there something going on I don't know about?"

She looked distinctly uncomfortable, but like a true friend, she answered me anyway. "I've known Anderson a long time. I even knew him back when he and Erin were together." She gave me the apologetic smile again. "I can see the way he looks at you when you're not looking, Nikki. It's just like how he used to look at Emma when his relationship with Erin was going south. Emma's a crazy bitch, but she's not making it all up."

I opened and closed my mouth a few times, but I couldn't come up with anything to say. Never once had I picked up that kind of a vibe from Anderson, but now I had to wonder . . . was it because there'd been nothing to pick up, or had I been completely blind to the signals?

I shook my head. "You're wrong," I said. "You *have* to be. I can be clueless sometimes, but not *that* clueless." My voice went up at the end, making my words sound more like a question than a statement of fact.

"Maybe," Maggie said with an unconvincing shrug. "But I bet you anything that Emma's seen the same thing I have, and that's what set her off."

"Guess that means you're *both* nuts," I grumbled. So much for the peaceful oblivion I'd been looking for when I decided to go running.

I was in even less of a mood to deliver bad news to Anderson now than I had been before. How could I look him in the eye after what Maggie had just said? I wouldn't be able to stop myself from overanalyzing every nuance of his behavior, looking for any hint that Maggie was right. If Anderson had the hots for me, I didn't want to know it. I had more than enough complications in my life as it was.

I took a long, hot shower, and by the time I got out, I'd convinced myself I *had* to tell Anderson that Emma was behind the fires, no matter how much I didn't want to. It could turn out to be dangerous for him to underestimate her level of malice, and the sooner he accepted what she had turned into, the safer we would all be.

Dread making my stomach feel twisted and cold, I descended the stairs to the second floor and forced myself toward Anderson's study. The door was open, but when I stepped inside, I found the room empty.

I could have gone looking for him, or I could have tried again later. Instead, I decided to take the coward's way out. Maybe the "right" thing to do would have been to wait until I had a chance to sit down with Anderson and deliver the news in person, but I'd had more than enough confrontation for one day, and I just couldn't face more.

Hoping Anderson wouldn't come back and catch me in the act, I rummaged through his desk for a pen. Then I took the screen shot that Cyrus had given me and scrawled a brief note on it. *I saw Cyrus today, and he gave me this. He says he got it off of Emma's computer. Remember not to shoot the messenger.* I left the paper on the seat of his chair, and then hustled out of there, glad to have escaped without having to face him.

FIFTEEN

Thursday and Friday passed without me once catching a glimpse of Anderson in the house. I kept expecting him to show up on my doorstep, or call me and demand I come to his study, but he didn't. I might have thought he'd gone off somewhere for a vacation, except when I casually asked Maggie at lunch one day if she'd seen him lately, she told me he was home. I wondered if he had just chosen to ignore the message I'd left him, or whether he was pissed at me for being the bearer of bad tidings and was simply avoiding me.

Another storm was due to roll into town sometime Saturday morning, with a slight chance of snowfall. As usual, it was still dark out when I woke up in the morning, but I could almost *feel* the threat of the approaching storm. I needed to make a grocery run, and it looked like I'd better do it soon if I didn't want to risk having to drive in the snow. The only grocery store I knew of that was open at six in the morning was a good twenty minutes away, but it would be worth it if the snow came.

It started raining as soon as I pulled into the grocery store's parking lot, but it was nothing more than a chill drizzle. No snow yet, but the temperature had dropped ominously. Predictably, the parking lot was almost deserted at this time in the morning, and I hoped that meant the hoarders hadn't hit the shelves yet and bought out all the milk, bread, and eggs as sometimes happens before a snowfall.

It was raining a little harder when I exited the store, and if I hadn't had two paper grocery bags in my arms, I would have put up my umbrella. Instead, I merely hurried a little more, ducking my head to keep the droplets out of my eyes.

The parking lot was still mostly deserted, and though it was somewhere around dawn, the clouds were heavy enough to keep the rising sun from showing through yet. I noticed that even with about a hundred open spaces available throughout the parking lot, some jackass had parked his car so close to mine I'd have to perform contortions to get into the driver's seat.

I'd planned ahead and had put my keys in one hand before scooping a grocery bag into each arm. I popped the trunk, then used my knee to nudge it open enough so I could put the bags in. I heard the sound of a car door closing, and out of the corner of my eye, I saw someone walking around the car beside me. I shoved my bags into the trunk, planning to ask the driver nicely if he would pull up so I could get into my driver's seat.

I slammed the trunk closed, then turned to the driver beside me. He had opened his own trunk, although I was sure he hadn't gone into the grocery store yet. He turned his head toward me and grinned. I frowned, not knowing what he was so happy about. Until his hand emerged from the trunk and I saw the tire iron in it.

It had taken me way too long to recognize the threat, and though I tried to ward off the blow with my shoulder, the tire iron still connected solidly with my skull, sending a stab of pain through my head. It felt like the parking lot pitched below me, and though I desperately tried to stay on my feet so I could take evasive action, I couldn't do it. The ground rushed up to meet me, and my attacker took another step toward me, raising the tire iron.

My head throbbed, and my brain felt all woozy. I tried screaming for help, though I doubted there was anyone nearby who could hear me.

The lunatic swung at me again, and I rolled violently to the side to avoid the blow. I heard the metallic clank of the weapon striking the pavement, and my attacker's curse at having missed. My stomach didn't like the sudden movement, threatening to toss my breakfast. I wondered if that meant I had a concussion from that first blow.

I didn't have time to bemoan my miseries, not unless I wanted to add more to the list. Swallowing my gorge, I tried to push to my feet. If the world would stop spinning enough for me to stand up, maybe I could run into the store, where there were at least a handful of people who might help me.

The tire iron connected with my back at shoulder blade level, knocking me flat on my face and forcing the air out of my lungs. My reeling mind ordered me to pull myself together and get up, but my body was having none of it. Pain and nausea roiled through me, along with a good dose of fear. No, my attacker couldn't kill me, at least not permanently. However, he could do a whole lot of very unpleasant things to me if I didn't find some way to muster my strength for an escape.

I was still struggling to get up when I heard the scrape of a footstep on the pavement right by my head. I looked around just in time to see my attacker's foot coming for my face.

I blacked out for a while, but either I wasn't as badly hurt as it seemed, or my supernatural healing was working overtime, because I woke up what had to be no more than a few seconds later. Pain screamed through my head, and I wanted to shrivel up and hide in some dark corner until it went away.

I was draped over a hard, bony shoulder, a pair of arms clamped around my legs. I struggled feebly, but the only effect was to let my attacker know I was conscious again. He slung me off his shoulder, and I tried once again to scream for help. I don't think a whole lot of sound made it out of my mouth.

I thumped down on the ground much sooner than I was expecting to, and in my weakened state even that relatively mild impact was almost enough to knock me out again. Like I said, my mind was pretty fuzzy, and it took me an agonizing minute to realize I'd been dumped into the trunk of my attacker's car.

This couldn't be good.

My attacker leaned into the trunk, and I got a good look at his face for the first time. He was no one I knew, and I didn't see any sign of a glyph anywhere on him. I hoped that meant he was just some random human thug who'd seen a delicate-looking woman alone in a darkened parking lot and decided to take advantage of the situation. If that was the case, I might be able to surprise him with my supernatural healing ability and make my escape.

The possibility that he might *not* be some random human, that he might have been after *me* specifically, was not something I cared to contemplate.

I was in no shape to make a flashy getaway from the car in my current condition, and I decided my best chance of escape—at least while my head was still reeling from what I was now sure was a concussion—was to attract attention and get help. I drew in breath to scream, but even that turned out to be more than my body could handle, as the ribs in my back sent a breath-stealing blast of pain through me. Maybe I had some broken ribs to go with the concussion.

My midsection hurt so much I barely even felt it when my attacker punched me and I blacked out again.

When next I woke up, my situation had not improved. My head felt even more woozy, and the car felt like it was pitching and bucking beneath me. I was lying on my stomach, my hands bound behind my back. I heard the distinctive ripping sound of duct tape, and felt something being wound around my ankles. I tried to voice a protest, but there was duct tape over my mouth, too. I swallowed a few times in rapid succession. This would be a really bad time to throw up, no matter how bad the nausea was.

Once again, my struggles served only to let my captor know I was awake.

"Damn, you are one tough bitch," I heard him mutter.

He grabbed me by the hair and slammed my head down against the floor of the trunk. If I hadn't already been hurt, I don't know if the impact of my head against the carpet would have done much, but as it was, it stunned me into semiconsciousness.

In the last few moments of light before the trunk slammed shut, I caught sight of something that struck terror into my heart: lying next to me, on the floor of the trunk beside the roll of duct tape my attacker had thrown in when he was finished with it, was a shovel.

Sixteen

I closed my eyes in the darkness of the trunk and tried not to panic. Panic would steal my ability to think rationally even better than the aftereffects of the concussion would.

It could be just a coincidence that there was a shovel in the trunk with me. Maybe my captor was a gardener, or a handyman or something. It didn't mean he was planning to bury me alive.

Or bury me after killing me, which was just as bad.

My attempts to comfort myself didn't do a whole lot of good, and fear stole my breath. Ever since I'd first heard about what Konstantin had done to Emma, chaining her at the bottom of a lake so that she would revive and die over and over again for all eternity, facing a similar fate had become my worst nightmare. Immortality might have its perks, but making a fate like that possible was one hell of an awful drawback.

Until I had joined the fold, Anderson had been searching for Emma for ten years, unable to locate and rescue her without a descendant of Artemis to help in the hunt. And if my attacker buried me, Anderson wouldn't have a descendant of Artemis to help him find me.

Which meant that no matter what it took, I had to make sure I didn't find myself planted in the ground.

I felt the vibration through my body as my captor started the car, then the lurch as he pulled out of the parking space and a bump when he pulled out of the lot. I didn't know where he was taking me, but I hoped it was a long way away. The more time I had to recover and plan, the better the chances I would be able to get myself out of this nightmare.

At least, that's what I tried to tell myself to keep the panic under control.

I tried wriggling my arms around, seeing if there was any leeway in my bindings, but there wasn't. I tried to fit my body through the circle of my bound arms so at least I could get my hands in front of me, but there wasn't a whole lot of room to maneuver, and my injuries seriously hampered my efforts. I forced myself to lie still for a moment, sucking in deep breaths, reminding myself my life might depend on me staying as calm and rational as possible under the circumstances.

If I wanted to survive this encounter—or at least survive this encounter in a manner that didn't make me wish I hadn't—I *had* to get free. I could try to position myself so I could give my attacker a kick to the face with my bound legs when he opened the trunk, but if I wasn't able to run for it, that would only delay the inevitable. I'd heard that escaping duct tape wasn't all that hard, but I wasn't sure I believed it, and I didn't know any tricky methods to accomplish it. The best I could do was try to wriggle my hands and wrists until the tape either broke or stretched, or until I somehow had enough space to get my hands through.

There wasn't a whole lot of wiggle room at first, that was for sure. I was painfully aware of the passage of time, painfully aware that every second I spent struggling, we were closer to wherever my attacker planned to take me to finish things. Panic kept trying to take over my brain, and though it was cold in the trunk, I was sweating from a combination of exertion and terror.

The sweat worked to my advantage, giving my wrists a little lubrication as I twisted and pulled and writhed, trying to find a way out. I definitely had a little more freedom of movement now than I'd had when I first started, and I seized on to that tiny hint of success to fuel my efforts to keep trying.

Those efforts were complicated by the fact that my attacker was a terrible driver. The car lurched whenever he hit the brakes, and he took every corner just a little too fast. Having no way to brace myself, I was thrown around the trunk like a sack of groceries, and the repeated, jarring impacts weren't doing my head a whole lot of good. It didn't help that the damn shovel was getting tossed around, too. I landed on it—or it landed on me—more than once. I tried to push it out of the way, trying to make sure the metal blade wouldn't come into contact with my head, but there wasn't anywhere to move it to.

I didn't know how much time had passed—it seemed like some weird combination of forever and not long enough—before I started to feel like I had a chance of getting out of the duct tape after all. The car had stopped doing so much starting, stopping, and turning, and I figured that meant we were on a highway somewhere. The steadiness meant that I didn't keep losing my progress every time I was tossed around, and I had slipped one hand up and one hand down so that only the ball of my thumb was holding me in. If I could just get that big part of my thumb out, I would be free, and the shovel would become my best friend. I almost grinned thinking about the look on my attacker's face when he opened the trunk, expecting to see a helpless, bound female, and instead found a heavy metal shovel coming at his face.

My thumb was coming free millimeter by millimeter, and I knew that at any moment now it would slip all the way through the tape, and I would be out.

Suddenly, a car horn blared from way too close.

Even from the trunk, I could hear my attacker's shouted curse as he stomped the brake pedal. Tires shrieked in protest, and I could tell the idiot at the wheel didn't know to pump the brakes, because we were skidding wildly.

I slammed into the side of the trunk, hitting it

with my forehead while the shovel thunked into me from behind.

More shrieking tires, more frantic blaring of horns. And then, impact.

I can only guess at exactly what happened next, because the sound of the impact is the last thing I remember of the accident. I think I took another blow or two to the head, either from the shovel or from the side of the car. It's also possible my head was thrown against the side of the trunk so hard that my neck snapped.

Whatever exactly happened, it killed me.

One moment, I was hurtling around in the trunk of the car, the next, I was nothing but a consciousness in the dark.

Having been dead once before, I knew exactly what was happening this time. I could feel my body, but I think I felt it in the way that an amputee sometimes feels a lost limb. I was aware of its existence, and I felt physical sensations, but I was utterly paralyzed, unable even to breathe, though my nonexistent lungs screamed for oxygen. My similarly nonexistent eyes felt like they were open, but I could see nothing but impenetrable darkness.

As far as I could tell, there was nothing above me, and nothing below me. I felt physical sensations, but only within myself, nothing from outside my body. No sensation of my weight resting on something, no heat or cold or breeze or movement.

Phantom adrenaline flooded my system as my

phantom lungs continued their desperate screaming for air. I knew I didn't really need to breathe, knew that my body was right now dead and had no needs whatsoever, but that primal need to flee, to fight, to *survive* was louder and more urgent than any logic. I honestly don't know which is worse: the feeling of suffocation, or the soul-tearing, uncontrollable panic that feeling engenders. There was a very good reason that even the immortal *Liberi* feared death, even when they knew they would come back from it.

The last time I'd died, my body had been completely destroyed, burned to ashes. The seed of immortality meant that I eventually grew a new body, but it had taken days for that to happen, and the time I'd spent in the dark, airless confines of death had felt more like years. I was fairly certain I wouldn't stay dead as long this time. I might have thought that knowledge would make death easier to bear, but it didn't.

I suffered, and it felt like it would go on forever.

I came to to the feeling of someone's fingers sliding off the skin of my neck.

"She's dead," a voice said, sounding like it came from far away.

I sucked in a frantic breath and opened my eyes, but whoever had been feeling for a pulse had already pulled away, and there was enough background noise that no one seemed to hear. Which was probably just as well, because it gave me a little time to gather my wits about me.

I took a moment to appreciate the luxury of breathing, practically hyperventilating in my effort to get as much air as possible into my lungs. The duct tape over my mouth hampered my efforts to fill my lungs, and I lost a few seconds to incoherent panic before I finally calmed down enough to assess my situation.

I was still in the trunk of the car, but I was crumpled awkwardly against one side of it, my head pressed against it, bending my neck at a painful angle. The trunk had been so badly mangled by the crash that I didn't at first realize the car had come to rest on its side. There was no way anyone could have pried the trunk open, but one side of it had buckled enough to create a sizable opening, which was letting in a steady patter of cold rain. I guess whoever had been checking my pulse must have crawled through that opening to get to me. Or perhaps been dangled through by someone holding his legs.

I was probably lucky I'd ended up wedged in like I was; otherwise, I might already be at the morgue. I imagined coming back to life there might have caused some serious issues for everyone involved. I was probably going to startle the hell out of some people even now, and I bet the guy who'd declared me dead was never going to hear the end of it.

The thought might have been amusing, except I had some clue how weird things were going to get when I made it known I was alive. I twisted around so that my neck was no longer in such an awkward position, and twisting like that was enough to show me that any injuries I might have sustained in the accident had already healed. I was utterly exhausted, which I knew was a side effect of the supernatural healing, but otherwise, I doubted I had more than a bruise or two on me. That was going to have a lot of people scratching their heads after I'd been tossed about so violently I'd been declared dead.

But there was no help for it. They knew I was in here, so it wasn't like I had any hope of sneaking away undetected. Even if I weren't still trussed up in duct tape. I was just going to have to feign ignorance and rely on the EMTs to believe they'd witnessed a miracle.

It took a while of kicking at the side of the trunk with my bound legs before someone heard me and came to check it out. There was quite a flurry of activity after that. They pried the trunk open to get me out. I wished they'd just grab me and drag me out through the small opening the EMT had crawled through, but I guess they were too worried about my injuries to manhandle me like that. Not surprisingly, I soon found myself on a gurney being rushed toward a waiting ambulance. I decided not to protest the treatment, because I knew no one would believe me if I said I was fine. I *did* try to protest having my head immobilized, but I couldn't blame them for thinking I had a head injury considering the position I'd been in when they'd first found me.

I had a couple of minutes to take in the scene around me while the EMTs were fussing around, trying to get me strapped onto the gurney and immobilized. The car I'd been in had done its best impression of an accordion, its trunk and hood crumpled to show there'd been solid impact from both ends before it had skidded into a ditch and ended up on its side. Through the shattered windshield, I saw the deflated airbag drooping from the steering wheel, its white fabric spotted with dark blood. Despite the extent of the damage, it was a pretty good-sized car, and I thought it possible my abductor had survived the crash. More's the pity.

There was another, smaller car a little farther up the road, and it looked like it was in even worse shape. I didn't think there was much chance its driver had made it. He or she had probably saved me from a fate worse than death, and I hoped I was wrong about their survival chances.

The ambulance doors closed, cutting off all sight of the wreckage and the flashing lights of an impressive array of emergency vehicles. One of the EMTs gunned the engine of the ambulance, hitting the siren, while the other climbed into the back with me, continuing to try to assess my injuries. I tried to tell the guy I wasn't that badly hurt, but I wasn't surprised he didn't take my word for it. He probably thought I was in shock or delirious or something.

The ride to the hospital didn't take long, but by the time we got there, there was already a lot of head scratching going on in the back of the ambulance as the EMT failed to find anything wrong with me. I kept repeating that I was okay, except for a little soreness here and there, but he was still sure I had to have some kind of dire injury he had so far missed. I tried to remain calm and patient, knowing he was just doing his job and that there was no reasonable explanation for my condition. I didn't blame him for being confused. I guess toward the end I was getting a little bit testy despite my best efforts, because he gave me a ferocious glare.

"You are *not* all right!" he snapped. "You had no pulse when I first checked you."

I could see why he might find that a cause for concern. "Well, I have one now. And I really want out of this head contraption."

The siren stopped wailing, and the ambulance came to a stop. The EMT took our arrival at the hospital as an excuse to ignore my request, and I knew I was about to go through the whole rigmarole again, because the doctors and nurses of the ER weren't going to believe their eyes, either.

SEVENTEEN

I was right about my reception at the emergency room. I once again had the delightful experience of being ignored when I claimed I was all right, and though I understood why, I couldn't help getting crankier as time went on. I wanted to get the hell out of there. I wanted a little quiet time in which I could try to process everything I'd just gone through. And I was so bone tired, I wanted a little time to sleep it off, too. None of which I was getting.

I put my foot down when they started talking about skull X-rays and an MRI. If they started ordering tests where I'd have to wait my turn to get in and then wait for the results, I was going to be in there all day. I had a right to refuse medical treatment, and I asserted it with a vengeance.

I swear every person in the entire ER tried to talk me out of checking myself out. It felt like I had to repeat myself to about twenty people, everyone from the attending physician to the freaking janitor, before I was finally given some papers to fill out that basically said it wasn't their fault if I died a horrible death due to leaving the hospital against medical advice. If I'd been merely human, they might have scared me so much with their warnings and predictions that I'd have caved.

I was mere moments from escape when the police caught up with me.

For a little while there, I'd almost forgotten that I'd been found bound in duct tape in the trunk of a car. Naturally, the police wanted to know how I'd gotten there. The authorities had caught on to the fact that I was a common denominator between three separate fires—thanks to the Glasses' insurance company, no doubt. I'd never been a direct target, and the first fire had been declared an accident, but it didn't exactly lead them to believe my abduction was a random act by some wandering psycho.

I saw no reason not to tell them the truth about the abduction, with a few errors and omissions. Like how I never mentioned being hit in the head with a tire iron, which would be completely unbelievable when I didn't have any obvious wounds on my head. I knew there was some blood in my hair, because everyone had been looking for its source, but the wound itself was gone. I didn't know how anyone was going to explain away the blood, and frankly, I didn't care.

The policemen shared a couple of significant looks as I told them about my abduction. Maybe they thought I was too shaken up to notice. I knew those looks meant something about my story was striking a false note, but I didn't know what—unless my abductor was still alive and had told all, including the stuff I was leaving out.

"Did the guy who tried to kidnap me survive the crash?" I asked, surprised that I hadn't thought to ask before. Though maybe I'd been too preoccupied trying to get myself out of the hospital to think about anything else.

The cops looked at each other again. Then one of them, a Detective Taylor, answered me.

"A few broken bones, a lot of stitches, and even more bruises, but yeah, the lucky son of a bitch survived. He's got a list of priors longer than my arm, and he was real eager to talk."

Shit. That probably wasn't good for me. The more stuff didn't add up, the more suspicious the cops were going to be, and the more determined they were going to be to get to the truth.

"Are you sure you don't know someone who might have a serious beef with you?" Taylor continued.

I gave him my best baffled face. "I have no idea. I've made enemies because of my job, but I don't know of anyone who would hate me enough to do all this to get back at me."

Taylor gave me a piercing look, no doubt trying to convey the message that he could see right through me. "Think hard."

I made a show of thinking about it, furrowing

my brow as if I were racking my brain. Then I shook my head. "I'm sorry, Detective, but I can't think of anyone."

"A woman, maybe?" he prompted, still not satisfied with my answer.

"I assume you have a reason for asking that," I said, hoping my face had shown no reaction. If they had reason to suspect a woman was gunning for me, there was only one logical suspect on my list.

"I told you the guy was eager to talk. Said he was hired over the phone by some woman. Never met her in person, though, and of course never got a name."

I nodded sagely and pretended to think it over some more. Then I raised my hands in a gesture of defeat and shook my head some more. "I still don't have a clue. Sorry."

Taylor gave me his card and asked me to call him if anything came to mind. Neither he nor his partner made much effort to hide the fact that they didn't believe me. I was real glad I was the victim rather than the suspect, or I don't think they would have let me off quite so easily. Even so, I felt their eyes on me as I retreated to the emergency room entrance, where I was able to borrow a cell phone and make a call.

There were lots of people I could have called to come pick me up at the hospital. I could have called Steph, although I wouldn't have wanted to worry her. I could have called Anderson, who, once he heard that an unknown woman had hired some thug to kill me and presumably bury me, would have to finally see Emma for what she really was. Or I could have called any of my friends at the mansion who would have driven me home without any hints of drama or complication.

So who did I end up calling? Jamaal, of course.

As far as I knew, he was the only one of Anderson's *Liberi* who knew what it was like to die, having gone through the experience at least three times already. So far, I had held myself together through sheer force of will, but once I had a moment of anything resembling privacy, I was going to fall apart, and Jamaal was the only one who would truly understand why.

"Sita's not going to like it," he reminded me when I called.

"I died, Jamaal. I *died*." There was a tremor in my voice, and for a moment I feared I was going to fall apart in front of an audience after all. Not that people in an emergency room waiting area are all that concerned with other peoples' distress, but it would have been embarrassing to break down in tears in front of them anyway. Especially when I wasn't sure I'd be able to get myself under control any time this century.

"I'll be there as soon as I can," Jamaal said after a brief hesitation.

He hung up before I could thank him. I closed my eyes and tried to breathe slowly and deeply to calm myself. After my last experience with death, I should have known better.

It wasn't truly dark when I closed my eyes. The

fluorescent lighting created a golden red glow behind my closed lids that was nothing like the darkness of death. My adrenal glands didn't appreciate the difference, however, and terror shot through me from head to toe. I gasped and opened my eyes, my heart hammering, my skin clammy with sweat.

"Are you all right, dear?" asked the nice old lady who'd loaned me her phone.

I plastered on what I was sure was a patently false smile. "I'm fine," I told her. "Thanks for letting me use your phone."

Her brow furrowed with concern, and I could see I had one more name I could add to the list of people who hadn't believed me when I'd said I was fine today. Of course, I didn't know her name, so it would be hard to add to the list.

The thought struck me as funny, and I knew that my body was trying to find another outlet for all the turmoil I was holding inside. I had successfully blocked the hysterical tears that wanted to rise up, but the inappropriate laughter almost had its way with me. A sound reminiscent of a bark escaped my lips before I changed it into a fake cough and clamped down even harder on my emotions.

"I'm going to wait for my ride outside," I said, then turned on my heel and practically sprinted for the exit. I knew I was being rude to the little old lady, but if I hadn't gotten myself away from her, I was sure all my walls were going to crack and I would make a fool of myself in front of everyone.

I had kind of forgotten I'd gotten such an early

start to my day because of the predicted weather front coming through. One step out of the emergency room doors was all it took to remind me. My kidnapper had removed my coat so he could bind my wrists more easily, and I had no idea where that coat had ended up. My clothes were still slightly damp from the time I'd spent crumpled in the trunk with the rain beating down through the gap the crash had created, and that first blast of cold air practically took my breath away.

The temperature had dropped since I'd last been out, and the rain had changed into a light snow that so far was only sticking in patches here and there. My breath steamed, and I wrapped my arms around myself for warmth. It didn't help, and within seconds, I was shivering.

The smart thing to do would be to go inside and wait where it was warm. However, the biting cold served two purposes: it kept me awake despite the exhaustion that dragged at me, and it made me so uncomfortable there wasn't room in my brain to handle thoughts of death.

I stood shivering in the cold and watched as the snowfall grew heavier, until there was a dusting of white over every exposed surface. So much for the "slight chance" of snow. Exhaustion had made my knees weak, and I was leaning against the side of the building to keep myself upright when I finally saw Jamaal's black Saab turning into the entrance. I pushed away from the wall as he pulled up to the curb, and my legs were so shaky I almost fell. I was in rough shape, and I hoped I wouldn't need Jamaal to help me into the car.

The passenger door sprang open, and I saw that Jamaal had leaned across the seat to open it for me. He was watching me intently as I approached, I think trying to gauge whether I could make it on my own or not. If he hadn't opened the door for me, I don't know if I could have. I collapsed into the passenger seat in a boneless heap, shivering even more violently when the blast of heated air hit me.

Jamaal reached over me to pull the door closed. I'd kind of forgotten that little detail in the blissful glory of sitting down and feeling the warmth of the heater. Despite my fear of the darkness, my eyelids weighed about a ton each, and sleep was pressing in on me from all sides. I was so out of it I'd forgotten about the seat belt, too. I thought about trying to take over as Jamaal buckled me in, but that simple task loomed like a Herculean labor, and I couldn't find the energy to even start.

I was asleep before the car started moving again.

There's no sleep quite so deep and dreamless as that which occurs after a lot of supernatural healing. I didn't wake up when we arrived at the mansion, nor when Jamaal picked me up and carried me through the snow from the garage to the main house, nor when he carried me up to my room on the third floor. When I *did* wake up, it was dark outside. Someone—Jamaal, presumably—had considerately turned my bedside lamp on so that I wouldn't wake up to a dark room. I smiled at that small act of kindness, even as my fuzzy brain realized I didn't remember a thing since collapsing into the seat of Jamaal's car.

My body still felt strangely heavy, and I knew that if I curled up and tried to sleep some more, I'd probably drift off again. But that effort would require me to lie there with my eyes closed for a while, and I knew from experience I'd have to face panicky memories of being dead.

Deciding I'd rather wait until the exhaustion had a mind of its own again before facing that ordeal, I pushed myself into a sitting position, and that's when I noticed a number of things.

For one, I wasn't wearing my clothes. I glanced down at myself and saw the straps of my bra peeking out from beneath the covers, so at least I wasn't completely naked, but *someone* had undressed me.

Second, I noticed the heavenly scent of coffee. I breathed in deep, wondering if I had the strength to wander into the sitting room and fetch myself a cup.

Then, and only then, did I realize I wasn't alone in the room.

I gave a startled little squeak when I caught sight of the shadowed form sitting quietly in an armchair in the corner. Jamaal leaned forward so that the light from my bedside lamp illuminated his face better. Not that I'd had any doubt who was there once I'd noticed him.

"Coffee?" he asked in a gruff voice, not meeting my eyes.

I wondered if he was the one who'd undressed

me, and the thought made my cheeks heat with a blush. "Yes, please," I answered, taking a page from his book and looking away. I felt almost like I was waking up on the dreaded morning after.

Jamaal walked to the sitting room without another word. I wondered if I should scurry out of bed and grab a robe or something, but that seemed both prudish and pointless. I had sheets to cover myself with, after all, and Jamaal was likely the one who'd removed my clothes in the first place.

I had the guilty thought that I wished I'd been awake for that, but I shoved it aside. Now was not the time to indulge in fantasy and wishful thinking.

Jamaal returned with coffee moments later. He handed me the steaming mug, and I wrapped my hands around it, even though I was no longer chilled to the bone. Then he stood awkwardly by the side of the bed, and I wondered if he was having trouble deciding whether to go back to his chair or sit down beside me.

"How long was I asleep?" I asked, hoping a little normal conversation would help dispel the awkwardness.

"A couple of hours," he answered, then came to a decision and sat hesitantly on the side of my bed.

"Have you been here the whole time?"

He shook his head, making his beads rattle and click, a sound I would forever associate with him. "Maggie and I went to pick up your car before the snow got too bad. You didn't exactly tell me the whole story when you called for a ride, did you?"

There was a hint of reproach in his voice, which suggested he'd filled in some of the blanks already one way or another.

I tried to think back to what exactly I'd told him. I'd been nearly out of my mind with exhaustion and stress and leftover fear, and it would have taken more strength than I had to tell him everything that had happened. My memory felt a little hazy, but I'm pretty sure all I'd said was that I was in a car accident and that I'd been temporarily dead.

"I wasn't in any shape for a long explanation at the time," I told him, taking a sip of my coffee. It tasted warm and soothing, and in a little while, I'd be enjoying a caffeine kick that might help me feel less like the walking dead.

"No, I suppose not," Jamaal said drily.

Clearly, he knew something about what had happened. "What have you heard? And where did you hear it?"

He shrugged and pulled at a loose string hanging off the edge of an artful tear in the knee of his jeans. "I figured the police would be called to the scene of an accident as bad as the one you must have been in, so I asked Leo to look up the police reports."

"I don't know that I'm ever going to get used to him being able to do that." I guess that explained how Jamaal had known where my car was to go pick it up.

"They said you were found in the trunk of a car, bound in duct tape. They also said that the first responders had reported you dead."

"Did the reports also say the guy who'd tried to kidnap me confessed he was hired by some unknown woman?"

He nodded. "Yeah. Thanks to Leo, we actually got a look at his full confession. The guy's orders were to kill you and then get you buried within an hour of your death."

I shuddered and hugged the covers closer to me. I had come so very, very close to facing my worst nightmare. If it hadn't been for the accident . . .

All day long, I'd been fighting to keep control of my emotions, to keep them contained inside me where they wouldn't threaten my ability to think rationally. And all at once, I couldn't hold them back another instant. Lord knows I tried, but after the first tears escaped, everything crumbled. I covered my face with my hands and sobbed, letting the aftermath of the terror have its way with me.

I've never been a big fan of crying in front of people, and if I had to name the top-ten people I didn't want to cry in front of, Jamaal would head the list. But there are some things in life you can't control, and this particular burst of emotion was one of them.

Covering my face with my hands didn't seem like enough, so I bent over double, pulling my knees up and burying my face against them as I hugged them. I felt the sheets sliding away from my skin, but I was too distraught to care. I imagined a manly stoic like Jamaal was appalled enough by my outburst not to notice the expanses of skin I inadvertently revealed.

These were not delicate, ladylike tears. These were wrenching, noisy, messy sobs.

I expected Jamaal to sit there and look befuddled, or maybe even to beat a hasty retreat so he didn't have to witness my meltdown. When I felt the tentative touch of his hand on the bare skin of my back, it was almost enough to startle me into silence. However, this meltdown wasn't about to let a sympathetic touch derail it.

Surely *now* Jamaal would retreat, I thought, but he remained beside me, his hand stroking gently up and down my back, more confident now that I hadn't rebuffed him. For his sake—and yeah, okay, for the sake of my own dignity—I tried to get a handle on myself, but it seemed like the harder I fought to suppress the tears, the more determined they were to escape.

Jamaal slid closer to me on the bed. He slipped his arm around me and pulled me against his chest, one hand on my back, one on the back of my head. I resisted for all of about one and a half seconds, then melted against him, clinging to him as if he were a life raft in a stormy sea. He rocked me back and forth like a child, and he made no obvious attempt to get me to stop crying.

His acceptance of my tears, and his strong, silent support, warmed me from the inside out. And that was *before* he started singing to me.

I'd only heard him sing once before, but it was one of those rare moments in my life that I'd have loved to bottle up so I could experience it again. His voice was a lovely unpolished baritone, and the tune had the soothing lilt of a lullaby, though I didn't recognize the language.

There was a part of me that felt faintly ridiculous about cuddling up in a man's arms, being rocked like a baby while he sang me a lullaby. That part of me was drowned out by the part that was touched and moved beyond words. Jamaal was not a man from whom I expected tenderness, and that was hardly surprising in light of the horrors of his life. But it was moments like this when I knew for sure that all the years of abuse he'd endured, and all the torments of trying to control his death magic, had not destroyed the decent human being he was destined to be, no matter how hard they had tried. There was a *reason* I felt such a strong connection to him, a reason I felt the need to reach out to him even when he tried to hold himself aloof.

My tears ran their course, slowing to sniffles and hiccups, but Jamaal didn't let go of me, nor did he stop singing. I took as many deep breaths as I could manage. My head felt swollen and achy, my nose was completely stuffed up, and my chest hurt from the violence of my sobs. And yet for all that, I felt almost . . . peaceful.

Finally, the song ended, and I reluctantly extricated myself from Jamaal's arms, wiping at my eyes with the backs of my hands, unable to look into his face when I felt so raw.

"That was beautiful," I said in a scratchy whisper I could barely recognize as my own voice.

"Matilda used to sing it to me when I was very little," he said. "I should hate it and want to burn it out of my memory, but it's stayed with me all these years."

Matilda had been his owner's wife. She'd been unable to have children of her own, and had treated Jamaal like a surrogate child—right up until the time she found out her husband was Jamaal's father. Then she'd insisted that her husband sell both Jamaal and his mother, and both their lives had gone to hell.

"What language is it?"

Jamaal chuckled, and even brief laughter from him was so rare that I had to look up at his face after all.

"I'm not sure," he admitted. "I think it's Swedish or Finnish or something like that. Matilda's family was from Scandinavia somewhere. I'm sure I'm butchering the pronunciation."

"Whatever language it was, it was beautiful," I told him again, still wiping at my tears.

He shrugged, uncomfortable with the praise. And possibly with the tenderness he'd just shown me. He started plucking at the string on his jeans again. I had a feeling that the discomfort was going to get to be too much for him soon, and he would retreat, leaving me alone to recover. Maybe that would have been the best thing for me, but the last thing I wanted was to be alone.

I reached out and touched the place on his chest where my head had rested. Not surprisingly, his shirt was damp.

"I'm sorry I got your shirt wet," I murmured as I continued to skim my fingers over the wet spot.

"Nikki . . ." There was an unmistakable warning in his voice, but I didn't feel inclined to listen, and despite the warning, he wasn't pulling away.

"It must feel kind of clammy against your skin. Maybe you should take it off."

He shook his head and pulled my hand away from his chest, but he couldn't hide the flare of heat in his eyes. I'm not a ravishing beauty under the best of circumstances, and I didn't want to know how awful I looked after a crying jag like I'd just been through. But I knew Jamaal found me attractive anyway, and I *was* sitting there in front of him wearing nothing but a bra and panties. Mismatched, and not exactly pretty, but I've found men rarely care about such things.

"We've given Sita enough fuel to feed her jealousy already," he said, fingers still wrapped around my hand even as he verbally pushed me away.

I snorted. "Sita can bite me! And probably will, if she gets a chance."

The dirty look Jamaal gave me suggested he didn't find my attempt at a joke all that funny. I guess I didn't, either, because I really didn't look forward to having his psycho tiger even more mad at me than she already was.

"You can't let her run your life, Jamaal."

He tried to stand up, but I anticipated it and grabbed a handful of his shirt. He could have torn away from me easily, but he settled for a halfhearted glare instead.

"The death magic has run my life ever since I first became *Liberi,*" he growled at me. "Whether it's contained inside me, or in the form of a tiger, it doesn't matter. It always wins."

He was trying to look and sound fierce and angry, but I could hear the wealth of pain under the facade. Still holding on to my handful of shirt, I got to my knees beside him so my head could be level with his as I looked into his eyes. It would have been more effective if he hadn't turned his face away from me.

"You've always been fighting it solo," I reminded him, then cupped my hand around his face so I could turn him toward me. There was fear in his eyes when he met my gaze, but there was desire, also. "You're not in this fight alone anymore."

"I have to be," he said. I caressed his face, feeling the racing of his pulse beneath my fingertips. "It's too dangerous . . ."

"After what I faced today, I'm not intimidated by a jealous cat." We both knew that wasn't true, of course. Only an idiot wouldn't be afraid of a magical tiger with a grudge. "And besides, I think you're worth fighting for."

Jamaal closed his eyes as if those words hurt, but he leaned forward and rested his forehead against mine, so I guess they didn't.

"I don't want you to get hurt because of me," he whispered, his breath tickling against my skin.

I kissed his temple and felt the shudder of desire that ripped through him. Encouraged, I started kissing my way down the side of his face. One of his hands came to rest on my back, and one on my hip, just above the waistband of my panties. I took that as another positive sign and propped his chin on my palm so that his mouth was at the perfect angle.

His hands clamped down tighter when our lips first touched, and he held himself rigidly still, fighting his desire. But when I ran my tongue along the seam of his lips, he lost all that hard-fought control. A little moan escaped him as his mouth opened for me.

I kissed him hard and thoroughly, and he loved every minute of it. He shifted his grip so that both hands were under my butt, then effortlessly dragged me forward until I was straddling his lap, still on my knees. I pressed myself tightly against him, savoring the scent, the feel, the taste of him. When we'd kissed before, his tongue had been highly flavored by the smoke of his clove cigarettes, and I'd found it surprisingly erotic, perhaps just because clove cigarettes and Jamaal were so closely associated in my mind. I tasted them now, though the flavor was faint because he was smoking so much less.

I played with his braids while I kissed him, enjoying the coarseness of his hair contrasted with the smoothness of the beads. And all the while, I was aware of him hardening beneath me.

My hands slid out of his hair to caress the broad expanse of his back over the thin T-shirt he wore. I desperately wanted to get my hands on bare skin, but the last time we'd tried giving in to our attraction, it had all come to a screeching halt when I'd touched his scars. I didn't want that to happen again, so I forced myself to let Jamaal set the pace.

His hands explored my every curve while staying maddeningly clear of my erogenous zones. I wasn't sure if he was doing it to torture me, or if even now he was fighting what was happening between us, trying to keep the distance I so badly wanted to remove.

I was determined to let Jamaal take the lead, but it was a powerful test of my self-control. Without even meaning to, I was grinding myself against him, and I had to clench my hands into fists to resist the urge to tug at his shirt. His mouth left mine as he trailed kisses down my throat. I arched into them and moaned, wanting him more than I could ever remember wanting anyone in my life.

Jamaal put his hand under my butt again, and I thought we were finally getting somewhere when he lifted me and laid me down on the bed. His body came to rest on top of mine, a warm, solid weight that might have crushed me if he weren't partially supporting himself with his arms.

I thought I might spontaneously combust when he nudged the cup of my bra downward and sucked my nipple into the delicious heat of his mouth. My mind short-circuited with pleasure as my back arched off the bed. I forgot all about letting him set the pace, and about keeping my hands away from his scars. In that pleasure-fogged moment of carelessness, I slid my hands under Jamaal's shirt.

If I'd been thinking rationally—or thinking at all, more like it—I might have expected Jamaal to be so overcome by pleasure that he forgot whatever it was that made him so touchy about the scars. But either he wasn't as lost in the pleasure as I was, or whatever emotional wound those scars triggered was far too deep to be defeated by sensual pleasure.

Whatever the reason, Jamaal's body jerked as though I'd given him an electric shock, and every muscle in his body went tense and rigid. I desperately wanted to hold on to him, but my instincts told me that was a terrible idea, so I kept my hands to myself as he rolled off of me. He came to rest beside me on the bed, lifting his forearm to cover his eyes. His chest rose and fell with panted breaths, but the bulge in his jeans was fading before my eyes.

I had enough sexual frustration coursing through my body to set off an explosion or three, but I swallowed it down as best I could. Whatever Jamaal was going through right now was far more important than my carnal needs. I turned to face him, propping my head on my hand, but I didn't say anything at first, giving him time to gather himself.

"I'm sorry," he said, arm still over his eyes.

"Hey, I blubbered all over you a little while ago and you wouldn't let me apologize for *that*."

He moved his arm so he could give me a look that was both skeptical and strangely tentative. "Not exactly in the same league."

It was hard to shrug in the position I was in, but I gave it a shot. "It's all emotional crap neither one of us is all that comfortable letting others see."

"Still not the same," he said stubbornly.

My heart ached for him, for whatever trauma had happened to him to make him so sensitive about his scars. I wanted to know what was behind it, but I knew I had to tread very delicately or risk scaring him off for good. I reached out and put my hand on his chest—over his shirt, of course—and felt the continued racing of his heart. The one thing I knew I couldn't afford to do was ask him why having me touch the scars freaked him out so much, no matter how badly I wanted to know. He would tell me when and if he was ready, and he didn't need me pushing at him.

"I'm sorry I let myself get carried away," I told him. "I knew better than to touch you like that, and I had every intention of keeping my hands to myself." I smiled at him, trying to convey the message that whatever was wrong, it was no big deal to me. "Maybe next time you should put some handcuffs on me."

He growled and sat up. "There won't *be* a next time," he said, predictably. "I'm too fucked-up, Nikki. I can't do . . . this." He made a vague gesture with his hand, and I didn't know whether his *this* referred to a relationship, or just sex.

"Maybe you can't do it right now," I said as gently as possible, "but I'm more than willing to wait."

"You can't fix me!"

"So you've said. And you're right, I can't. But I can be here for you whenever you decide you want to fix yourself."

"Ain't gonna happen." He had closed down

entirely, the expression on his face distant and almost forbidding. If I didn't understand so thoroughly his need to protect himself from the fear and the pain that welled inside him, I might have been hurt at being shut out like that. He slid off the other side of the bed, no longer able to look me in the eye.

I wished there were magic words I could say to make all his pain go away, or at least get him to open up enough to me to let me help him. But for now, he was out of my reach once more, and I blinked away the burning sensation of another bout of tears as he walked out of my room without another word.

EIGHTEEN

After Jamaal left, I felt drained and melancholy. I dragged myself into the shower and stood under the hot spray for way longer than was environmentally correct, washing away the lingering traces of blood, sweat, dirt, and tears that clung to me. I didn't have any plans to go out, having checked out the window and seen the pristine blanket of snow that covered everything in sight. It was still coming down, and only in the direst emergency would I consider trying to drive through it. I wasn't sure why I felt the need to blow-dry my hair and put on makeup, but I did it anyway. Maybe just because it made me feel more normal, though my concealer wasn't up to the challenge of hiding the dark circles under my eyes.

I probably should have left my room in search of Anderson as soon as I was dressed. No doubt Jamaal and Leo had told him what they'd found in the police report and he would expect me to fill in any missing details for him. But I wasn't up to facing him after what I'd been through. Maybe he'd had enough time to absorb the blow, especially after I'd left him that screen shot the other day, but I didn't think it was likely. He had loved Emma so much, and though I suspected she had always been self-absorbed and bitchy, the years she'd spent as Konstantin's prisoner had made Anderson forget her true nature. She had become a paragon in his memory, and I didn't want to see his pain at having that paragon irrevocably destroyed.

I guess that meant my plan was to hole up in my room for the rest of the evening so I could avoid any chance of running into Anderson. Or anyone else, for that matter. My stomach grumbled its disapproval of my plan, reminding me I hadn't eaten all day and my body had burned up tons of energy bringing itself back from the dead. I contemplated a run to the kitchen, but decided I'd dip into the box of granola bars I kept in the filing cabinet in my sitting room instead. Buying myself a filing cabinet had been silly, since most of my paper files had been destroyed by the sprinkler system in my old office, and I rarely kept much in the way of paper files anymore. But it made for a handy pantry, and I grabbed a chocolate bar for dessert while I was at it. It wasn't exactly the healthiest meal I'd ever eaten, but it was damn convenient.

Crunching on my granola bar, I opened up my laptop and went in search of something, *anything,* to keep my mind occupied so I wouldn't keep thinking about what had almost happened to me this afternoon. It was worth a try anyway.

I was just finishing my chocolate bar and trying to resist the urge to go foraging in my filing cabinet again when there was a knock on my door. I had the cowardly urge not to answer. I didn't want to talk to anyone right now, wanted to lose myself in something completely mindless—not that I'd had a whole lot of success with that so far.

"Come in," I finally said with weary acceptance.

The door opened, and Anderson stepped inside. No doubt he would have let himself in whether I'd invited him or not. I closed my laptop and laid it on the coffee table, then stood up, scattering a bunch of granola crumbs all over the place. I brushed at my clothes to dislodge any remaining crumbs, giving the task way more attention than it deserved. It looked like I was going to have to talk about all the things I didn't want to talk about after all, and if I could put it off for a few seconds, I was all for it.

Finally, I was as crumb-free as I was going to be, and I raised my head to look at Anderson. I expected to see pain, anger, and even sorrow, but what I saw on his face was none of the above. Instead, I saw a frozen, almost lifeless calm. I'd seen him run both hot and cold with anger, but I'd never seen anything quite like this before, and there was something so forbidding about it I had to fight the urge to take a step back.

"I came to offer my apologies," he said, and his voice was off-the-charts weird, too. Completely flat and noninflected. Inhuman, almost, though not exactly godlike, either.

"Umm . . ." I couldn't think of what to say. The man who stood in front of me wasn't Anderson, at least not the Anderson I knew.

"I was blind to Emma's faults, and you almost paid an unspeakable price for it."

He was saying the right words, but without any emotion behind them it was hard to tell if he actually meant them or not.

"A-are you all right?" Stupid question, of course, because he was obviously anything but all right. I realized his face was so immobile he wasn't even blinking, like his body was some kind of automaton. Was the Anderson I knew even in there?

His head moved slightly in a sad imitation of a head shake. "No. I am far from 'all right.' I am dangerous in my current condition." There was still no emotion in his voice, like he was reading off cue cards. "I cannot afford to feel anything just yet. I will try to act more like myself when we meet with Cyrus tomorrow."

I shivered, more freaked out than I wanted to admit by the talking husk Anderson had left behind. "We're meeting with Cyrus?"

"One of his Olympians has broken the treaty. We will meet to discuss the consequences."

Not a conversation I particularly wanted to participate in. "Do you really need me—"

"You are the injured party. You are coming."

Not much chance he was going to be flexible

about that. "You're not going to kill her, are you?" I didn't know *what* this faux-Anderson was capable of. Maybe in his current state he wouldn't mind letting the world know just who and what he was.

"No."

He turned to leave, and I should have just let him go. But of course I had to open my big mouth again.

"So what exactly are you hoping to accomplish at this meeting?"

After what Emma had tried to do to me, I should have been screaming for her blood. I should have been begging Anderson to kill her. But despite the horrors I'd seen in the last few months, becoming *Liberi* hadn't stopped me from being a bleeding heart. I wanted Emma to pay for what she'd done— and tried to do—and I wanted her not to be able to hurt me again, but I didn't want her to pay with her life. If she were tried in a court of law, she might well get a verdict of not guilty by reason of insanity. Confinement in a mental institution might be the most appropriate sentence, but I was under no illusion that it was an option.

For the first time since he'd set foot in my sitting room, something stirred behind Anderson's eyes. I couldn't have said what it was—the expression was gone almost before I had a chance to notice the change—but it made my heart skip a beat in primal terror. I dropped my gaze to the floor, an instinctive gesture of submission, and held my breath. I didn't like this lifeless talking shell of his, but even that one tiny glimpse of what lay beneath had told me in no uncertain terms that the shell was the lesser of two evils. If and when Anderson unleashed everything he was suppressing, I didn't want to be anywhere near him.

I felt his eyes boring through me for what felt like forever. I kept my own gaze pinned to the floor, and my lungs started to burn with the pressure of holding my breath.

I didn't give in to the need to breathe until Anderson had left the room and closed the door behind him.

I didn't get a whole lot of sleep on Saturday night, despite my exhaustion. When I lay down to try to relax, I kept obsessing about what had almost happened to me. Just thinking about it flooded my system with adrenaline. And to make matters worse, when I closed my eyes I was immediately transported into the memory of the darkness of death.

I knew from previous experience—and from talking with Jamaal about his own experiences— that my fear of the darkness would fade over time. Every night, it would be just a little bit easier. But that didn't help me much on this first night. I wished Jamaal would come up to my room and sing me asleep as he had the first time I'd died, but it wasn't going to happen.

Eventually, exhaustion won out over terror, though it did so not when I was lying comfortably in my bed, but when I was on the couch in the sitting room playing solitaire on my laptop. I remember waking up briefly hours later, when there was a roll of thunder so violent it made the whole house shake. My laptop slid off my lap and onto the floor, but I wasn't awake enough to bother picking it up.

I'd fallen asleep sitting up, and during that brief period of wakefulness, I stretched myself out on the couch, clutching a throw pillow under my head. I had the brief, hazy thought that it was unusual to have violent thunder in the midst of a snowstorm, but the phenomenon wasn't interesting enough to keep me awake. I drifted back into sleep and didn't wake up until the sun had risen.

I was stiff from spending the night on the couch, and I didn't exactly feel well rested. I checked my laptop and found, to my relief, that it had survived the fall. I'd have followed my morning ritual of making coffee in my room while perusing the news, except my stomach was growling at me that my granola-and-candy meal last night had been woefully inadequate.

Though the mansion felt more and more like my home every day, I didn't feel at home enough to go downstairs in my bathrobe, so I showered and dressed before heading down to the kitchen. I'd slept in enough that for once I wasn't the first person up and about, which meant there was already a pot of coffee brewed. I poured myself a cup, then frowned when I noticed someone had left dirty dishes in the sink. There were drawbacks to living in a house with so many other people in it. I put the dirty dishes into the dishwasher, then made myself some scrambled eggs and toast. And cleaned up my own damn mess when I was finished.

I sat down at the kitchen table with my food and coffee, taking a moment to admire the view through the windows. It looked like it had snowed about four inches all told, and the back lawn was a pristine white carpet that glittered in the light of the sun. A dark blot was moving across the snow, and the glare was bright enough I had to squint to make out Jamaal's form as he tromped toward the house. At a guess, I'd say he was coming from the clearing.

I'd have thought after our make-out session yesterday he'd have waited until I was out of the house before summoning Sita again, but apparently not. Maybe he thought the fact that he'd ultimately rebuffed my advances was enough to calm Sita's jealousy. Or maybe I'd ruffled his composure so much he felt he *needed* to vent the death magic immediately, whether he wanted to or not.

I had wolfed down half my eggs and all of my toast by the time Jamaal made it back to the house and into the kitchen. The first bite had proved to me that I was starving, and I'd started shoveling it in as fast as I could chew and swallow. Jamaal nodded at me in greeting before turning his back on me to pour himself a cup of coffee.

Even in that one brief glance, I'd been able to see his turmoil, so when he turned as if to leave with his coffee, I paused between bites to ask, "Did Sita give you a hard time this morning?"

He reluctantly turned back toward me. "No."

If he thought he was going to put me off with one-syllable responses, he had another think coming. There was a haunted, troubled look in his eyes that worried me.

"Then what's wrong?" I asked.

He took a couple of steps closer to me, though he leaned against the end of the kitchen counter instead of coming all the way into the breakfast nook. "I went to the clearing to practice this morning."

"Yeah, I gathered that." My remaining eggs were getting cold, and my stomach was far from satisfied with what I'd eaten already, so I went ahead and shoved another forkful into my mouth while Jamaal paused to give me a dirty look. "Sorry," I said with my mouth full. Dying had not had a good influence on my table manners. "What happened?"

He shook his head. "Finish your breakfast. I'll show you."

The words sounded ominous, and the expression on his face made them even more so. I wanted to ask him to explain, but he was obviously not in a talking mood, and I didn't want him to get annoyed with me and wander off. I finished my eggs in two big bites, then loaded my dishes into the dishwasher.

"Okay," I said, closing the dishwasher, "time for show-and-tell."

I snatched my parka from the coat closet. Jamaal waited for me impatiently, his edginess making me nervous. What the hell had he seen out in the clearing that had rattled him so much? And was I going to regret going to get a look for myself?

The snow was a little deeper than I'd thought, and I wished I'd run up to my room for boots as my feet sank into it. Of course, I doubt Jamaal would have waited for me. He was agitated enough that he lit a cigarette and puffed on it steadily as we made our way out to the clearing, following the narrow path his shoes had already left in the snow. The air bit into my cheeks, and snow trickled in around the edges of my shoes. I buried my hands in my pockets and shivered.

The first thing I noticed as we approached the clearing was that there were a bunch of trees down. I certainly hadn't thought the storm was violent enough to take down trees, especially not as many as I saw. I glanced at Jamaal, wondering if this was what he wanted to show me, thinking that he could just as easily have *told* me a bunch of trees had fallen.

Jamaal looked grim and kept walking. I followed, and the closer we got to the clearing, the more fallen trees I saw, lying like discarded children's toys among the ones left standing. We had to weave our way around the trees to get to the clearing. Most of the trees were pines, and they were all green and healthy looking.

When we stepped around the last set of branches that were obscuring our view, I finally got a good look at the clearing, and I gasped.

There wasn't a flake of snow anywhere in the clearing, as if someone had come out here and gone to work with a snow blower, doing such a thorough job of it that all you could see was grass. That was weird as hell, but it wasn't what took my breath away.

Mouth gaping open, I continued forward until my feet left the snow, blinking a couple of times as if that might make what I saw go away.

I said there were "a bunch" of trees down. Now that I was in the clearing proper, I could see that there were *dozens* down. Some had been torn up by the roots, and some had snapped in two. Not a single tree that had fronted the clearing was left upright. And the weirdest thing of all? They had all fallen *away* from the clearing. Almost like a bomb had gone off in the center.

Jamaal stood beside me, his arms crossed over his chest as he surveyed the sight. He must have smoked that cigarette in record time, but I had to admit, if I were a smoker, I'd have been diving for the cigs myself.

"What the hell happened here?" I whispered, my words steaming in the brisk air.

Jamaal swallowed hard. "There was a loud noise in the middle of the night. Woke me up and shook the bed under me."

I remembered. "I thought it was thunder," I murmured.

"I did, too, at the time."

I was pretty sure I had at least a clue of what had happened. Or at least *who* had happened. Anderson had made himself into a walking, talking automaton in his effort to contain his fury over what Emma had done. He had promised me he would be more like himself when we met with Cyrus today, and the only way that was possible was if he let out some of that repressed fury. I had the distinct feeling we were looking at the results right now.

Jamaal didn't know what I did about Anderson's origins, but his mind was obviously traveling similar paths.

"No one knows who Anderson is descended from," he said. "I don't know why he's so mysterious about it, but he is. I've never seen him do anything other than that trick with his hand. I have no idea what he's capable of. What I *do* know is that none of the rest of us are capable of this." He indicated the clearing with a sweep of his hand.

I didn't know what Anderson was capable of, either, although I knew more than Jamaal. "If he has a power that lets him do this, I'm just as happy he keep it and any other powers he might have under wraps."

Jamaal grunted something that might have been an agreement.

"You think we should ask him about this?" I asked.

Jamaal gave me a look of disbelief. "You go right ahead. Just tell me when you're going to do it so I can arrange to be in the next county over."

Okay, it had been a dumb question. It didn't take a rocket scientist to know that Anderson would not be open to discussion about whatever had happened out here. And even if he had vented some of his fury last night, he wasn't exactly going to be in a good mood in the foreseeable future. Asking him questions he didn't want to answer would be a poor survival tactic.

"I don't want to be there when he confronts Cyrus," I said. "Not that I have a choice."

I wished he'd at least given himself a couple of days to absorb everything and calm down as much as he could before squaring off with someone who could start a war that could kill every one of Anderson's *Liberi* if he wanted to.

"He'll keep a lid on it," Jamaal assured me, not very convincingly.

"Uh-huh."

I sure as hell hoped he did, despite my skepticism. Because if Anderson let loose whatever it was he'd let loose in this clearing, I didn't think anyone near him, even immortal *Liberi,* would survive.

Nineteen

As a general rule, Olympians seem to have a taste for palatial homes set on acres of land in the most upscale of neighborhoods. Cyrus, however, lived in an impressive brownstone in Georgetown, perhaps too much of a city boy to enjoy the comforts of a country estate. I had driven by the place before when I'd been investigating Olympian properties, but now I was going to have an up-close-and-personal look at the interior. I wasn't what you'd call thrilled at the prospect.

Because of the sensitive subject matter we'd be discussing, a neutral site with witnesses was deemed unacceptable. Anderson was apparently through with letting Olympians set foot within the borders of his own personal territory, and so we were meeting at Cyrus's house instead. Walking into the lion's den and making accusations didn't seem like the best idea to me, but Anderson hadn't asked my opinion. He seemed closer to normal than he had the day before, able to speak in a natural tone of voice, but I still felt like I was in the presence of a bomb that could go off at the slightest provocation. All I had to do was think of what I'd seen in that clearing, and my desire to question Anderson's decisions melted away.

Anderson didn't have any pet Descendants he could take with him to keep the Olympians honest, but he was wary enough of them not to walk into Cyrus's house completely "unarmed," so Blake had the pleasure of coming with us. He couldn't kill anybody, but he could make it so that all the bad guys were so overcome with lust for each other there wasn't room in their brains for thoughts of attack. I didn't get the feeling Blake was any happier to be going than I was, but he wasn't stupid enough to argue with Anderson's decisions, either.

Thanks to the snow, which showed no sign of melting anytime soon, we had to leave extra early if we hoped to make it to Cyrus's house by our scheduled three o'clock appointment time. Anderson knew that as well as anybody, but he wasn't ready to leave until almost two thirty. There was no question in my mind the delay had been deliberate and that he was making some kind of power play by making Cyrus wait.

I didn't trust Anderson's mood, but when he announced he was driving, I once again didn't feel up to arguing with him. Blake and I shared a doubtful look as we followed him out to the garage; then we both shrugged our acceptance. It wasn't like a car accident would kill us anyway.

The drive was excruciating. All but the main roads were a mess, and there was the usual collection of idiots out who mistakenly thought they knew how to drive in the snow. We did a lot of stopping and starting and threading our way around stranded motorists, then had the always-enjoyable situation of being stuck behind a salt truck.

The ride was made just that much more unpleasant by the tense silence in the car. Anderson was in no mood to make conversation, and his presence was like an oppressive blanket, weighing us down. Blake dealt with the tension by incessantly cracking his knuckles until I turned around and gave him a pointed look. I don't think Anderson even noticed the effect he was having on us.

Parking on the street in Georgetown is a pain in the butt on any day, but it was well-nigh impossible with the snow. The streets in the heart of the city had been cleared, but that meant there were mountains of dirty snow lining the curbs, blocking off a large percentage of what would ordinarily be parking spaces. Anderson didn't even bother cruising in search of one, instead pulling into a garage.

Blake was out of the car almost before it had come to a full stop. I took my life into my hands and touched Anderson's arm as he was turning the car off.

"Are you going to be all right?" I asked him softly.

He looked at me and blinked a couple of times, as if he didn't quite know what I was talking about.

Then he frowned. "I'm in control of myself, if that's what you're asking. I'm still angry, but I'm not going to do anything rash. Come on. I think we've kept Cyrus waiting long enough."

We were back to uncomfortable silence as the three of us walked from the garage to Cyrus's house, now more than a half hour late. Anderson rang the bell, and moments later, the door was opened by a middle-aged man in a stuffy suit. I should have known better than to expect Cyrus to answer his own door. Even having grown up with the ultrarich Glasses, I'd never visited a house that had a butler before, but I guess there's a first time for everything.

"Mr. Galanos has been expecting you," the butler said with just a touch of reproof in his voice. "May I take your coats?"

Anderson hadn't bothered with a coat, making do with a weathered-looking sport jacket. Blake handed over his stylish wool coat, and I handed over my not-so-stylish, but probably much warmer, parka. When the butler laid the coats over his arm, I caught a glimpse of a trident-shaped glyph on the inside of his wrist. I made an educated guess that he was a mortal Descendant whose divine ancestor was Poseidon. I also guessed that since he was middle aged and working as a butler, he was never going to be given the honor of becoming a *Liberi*.

Coats still draped over his arm, the butler led us to a two-story library that would make any reader drool. I don't know how many books, both modern and antique, were on those floor-to-ceiling bookshelves, but it was a lot. I breathed in deep to take in the comforting scent of ink and paper, even as I mentally rolled my eyes at the rest of the decor. The room would have fit right in as the set of some period drama taking place in one of those British men's clubs the aristocracy was so fond of, all dark colors and manly leather-and-wood furniture. It seemed awfully formal and stodgy for someone like Cyrus.

Cyrus was reclining in a forest-green leather armchair, holding a highball glass filled with something amber colored on the rocks. His pet goon, Mark, had been sitting on the arm of the chair when I first caught sight of him, but he rose to his feet and stood at full bodyguard attention when Anderson, Blake, and I entered the room. He had an enormous, angry-red hickey on his neck, and I had the immediate suspicion that Anderson wasn't the only one who was already playing mind games. Either Anderson had told Cyrus he was bringing Blake, or Cyrus had guessed his old flame would be joining the party.

I stole a quick glance at Blake out of the corner of my eye, but he gave no indication that he'd noticed Mark one way or the other. He and I hung back just a little as Anderson stepped forward.

Smiling, Cyrus put down his drink and rose from his chair. "So nice of you to join us," he said, holding out his hand for Anderson to shake. "I was beginning to worry you'd had an accident. I hear the roads are terrible."

Cyrus had to know that our late arrival was deliberate, but he didn't let it show in either his voice or his face. If I didn't know better, I would have sworn that he actually meant it and had been worried. Anderson paused just long enough for it to be noticeable before he shook Cyrus's hand.

"Sorry to keep you waiting," Anderson said, making no attempt to sound like he meant it. "The weather delayed us."

Cyrus's smile broadened. "No worries. Mark and I managed to keep ourselves entertained while we waited." He reached out to pat Mark's shoulder, and I doubted it was an accident that his hand landed right near the hickey. "You remember Mark, don't you?"

Anderson nodded, but Blake shook his head.

"I don't believe we've met," he said. He sounded ruefully amused. Either he was a good actor, or he wasn't even a smidge jealous. I wondered if he'd noticed that he and Mark resembled one another. He didn't try to shake Mark's hand, and Mark didn't offer.

"Can I get anyone a drink?" Cyrus asked, playing the gracious host.

"Don't be more of an ass about this than you have to be," Blake said. "We're not here to make friendly."

Cyrus sighed dramatically. "When did you become so serious all the time?"

Blake stiffened, and his eyes narrowed. "When you—"

"Blake," Anderson said mildly, but that one word was enough to shut Blake up.

Score one for Team Evil. They'd managed to

provoke us, and they hadn't even had to work at it very hard. Blake shut up as ordered.

"Will you sit down, at least?" Cyrus asked. "Or would that be too civilized?"

"We're here because one of your Olympians attacked one of my people," Anderson countered. "I'm not feeling terribly civilized."

Interesting how Emma had suddenly been transformed from Anderson's ex-wife into "one of your Olympians." I wondered if this meant Anderson was officially over her.

Cyrus sighed again. "Understandable, I suppose. Why don't you tell me what happened."

"I already told you on the phone," Anderson snapped. He'd been willing to put up with Cyrus's feigned friendliness the last time we'd talked, but apparently that was not the case today.

"So you did, but I wasn't asking you, I was asking Nikki." He turned an unusually grave look toward me. "I'd like to hear it in your own words."

Anderson raised no objection. I didn't particularly want to talk about my abduction to anyone, much less Cyrus and his pet. I didn't want to relive the memory, and I was also afraid I'd let too much emotion show. Showing Olympians signs of weakness was a recipe for disaster. Not to mention that I didn't like the feeling that I was tattling, and that I was afraid the consequences would be dire. However, it wasn't like I had a whole lot of choice.

I tried to remain as impassive as possible as I recounted the events of the day before. It's hard to keep the emotion out of your voice when you're talking about your own death, and especially about a deranged woman's plan to bury you alive and leave you to suffer eternal torment. I could hear the occasional quaver in my voice, and there was nothing I could do to control it.

Cyrus made sympathetic faces while I spoke, but I couldn't help noticing that Mark seemed to be enjoying the story. There was an eager glint in his eye, and he even licked his lips like a dog looking forward to its meal. I decided Cyrus had creepy taste in men.

There was a long silence after I finished my story. I took a moment to glare at Mark while Cyrus frowned thoughtfully.

"I knew she was unstable when I invited her to join us," Cyrus finally said. "I could hardly blame her after what my father did to her. I thought that perhaps her moods would even out over time."

"That's what I thought, too," Anderson agreed grimly. "But her actions yesterday tell me she has been irrevocably altered. The Emma I knew died years ago when your father raped her and drowned her in that pond."

Anderson was keeping control of himself, but there was no missing the fury behind his words, and something about the look in his eyes raised the hairs on the back of my neck. Whatever it was, Cyrus saw it, too, and his face lost just a little of its color. If he knew what Anderson really was, he'd be curled up in the fetal position.

"I am not my father," Cyrus reminded Anderson. "And you won't have to go medieval on my ass to get me to honor the treaty, if that's what you're thinking." He looked over his shoulder at Mark. "Go fetch our other guest, will you?"

There was a visible flare of excitement in Mark's eyes as he nodded and then hurried from the room. It occurred to me that he might have been present for reasons other than to try to make Blake jealous. Like maybe Cyrus planned to give him Emma's immortality. The fact that Emma was already a "guest" in Cyrus's house did not bode well for her.

Anderson and Cyrus stared at each other, and the tension in the room was so thick it was hard to breathe. I wanted to say something in protest of what I feared would happen, but the atmosphere was so oppressive I couldn't find the courage to speak.

Moments later, we all heard Emma's voice raised in annoyance. "I'm getting really tired of being jerked around!" she complained, presumably at Mark. "I could have—"

Both her voice and her footsteps faltered when she stepped through the library door and saw our little gathering. Her eyes darted from me, to Anderson, to Cyrus, and she seemed to shrink in on herself. There was something naturally fragile looking about her, though perhaps that was just because I knew how badly she had suffered when she'd been Konstantin's prisoner. No matter what she'd done—or tried to do—it was hard for me to forget that she'd been a victim.

And maybe, in a way, she still was. I didn't like it when Anderson made excuses for her, and I didn't think she'd ever been a truly nice person. But today, when she hadn't been expecting to see Anderson and me and therefore had obviously not bothered to dress to impress, or even put on makeup, I could see more plainly than ever that she was still suffering. Even if she brought some of that suffering on herself. Her face was gaunt, and her clothes hung loosely on her thin frame. Her eyes were red around the edges, as if she'd been crying when Mark had come to get her. I remembered Cyrus telling me she had nightmares every night. Yesterday, I had almost suffered a fate similar to hers, and I wondered if I'd have all my marbles if someone had dug me up ten years from now.

Emma drew herself up and raised her chin in a semblance of dignity, but it wasn't very convincing. She looked tired and scared, and I wished like hell she'd come out of that pond with her mind intact. I suspect her marriage to Anderson would have ended anyway, and it probably wouldn't have been a nice breakup—if there is such a thing—but she might have had a chance at a decent life. But as it was, there was no room in her heart for anything but bitterness, jealousy, resentment, and fear.

"What's going on?" she asked.

"Please do come in, my dear," Cyrus said, gesturing her forward. "We have something very important to discuss." He was smiling his usual pleasant smile, but his voice came out uncharacteristically flat.

I glanced at Anderson, wondering how he was taking all this. He wasn't looking at Emma like the rest of us were, was instead staring straight ahead. His face was a stony mask, and I didn't know what emotions that mask hid.

Emma obviously sensed the dangerous undercurrents in the room. She stood rooted in the doorway and turned a beseeching look on Anderson. When she saw him facing forward, refusing to look at her, she recoiled as if he'd slapped her.

Apparently, she was taking too long to follow Cyrus's orders, because Mark suddenly gave her a shove from behind, propelling her into the room. The shove was so violent that she tripped over the edge of the rug and landed on her hands and knees with a cry of surprise and pain. Neither Anderson nor Cyrus objected to the rough handling.

Emma scrambled to her feet and whirled on Mark. "How *dare* you," she snarled. I suppose she was trying to go on the offensive, but the shrill edge in her voice detracted from the attempt. She had to know the jig was up.

"I'd ask the same question of you," Cyrus said, and Emma reluctantly turned to face him. The little darting glances she sent over her shoulder said that after what had just happened, she didn't like having Mark behind her.

"What are you talking about?"

"Did we not have a discussion the other day in which I *specifically* forbade you from taking any hostile action toward Anderson or any of his *Liberi*?"

Emma blinked as if in surprise. "Yes. And I *specifically* told you I hadn't done anything." Her lip curled in distaste as she looked me up and down. "Whatever that bitch might have told you."

I'd have been more outraged, both by her attitude and her denial, if I didn't fear she was a hair's breadth away from a death sentence.

Cyrus grunted in exasperation. "And I believed you. Right up until I found those drafts of the letter you wrote in my father's name on your computer."

"Those weren't mine!" There were twin spots of angry color on her pale cheeks now. She certainly could put on a convincing righteous indignation act. "Someone used my computer to write them, but it wasn't me. Maybe you should have a word with your daddy about it."

Cyrus rolled his eyes. "Yes, that makes perfect sense. He broke into your house to use your computer to compose a letter that he then took to a FedEx to email. All because he's batshit crazy enough to blame Nikki for his misfortunes. Strangely, that sounds rather more like you than like him."

"I don't know who wrote it or why. All I know is it wasn't me."

"You hired a hit man to kill Nikki and bury her in the woods where no one would ever find her," Anderson interrupted, the rage in his voice enough to make Emma flinch from it.

"What?" she shrieked, looking back and forth frantically between Anderson and Cyrus.

"You gave Erin to your new friends just to spite

me," Anderson continued, taking a step closer to her. He looked intimidating enough that she took a step back. "But that wasn't enough for you, was it? You had to drive the dagger in deeper, so you had to destroy Nikki, too. Just because in your sick, twisted mind you decided she was the reason our marriage fell apart. But it was *you,* Emma. You're the only reason, the only one to blame."

Tears glistened in Emma's eyes. "I loved you," she said in a scratchy whisper. "And you loved me, too. Until *she* came into our lives." She reached out toward him briefly, then snatched her hand back as if to deny the gesture. "I could see from the moment I went back home that she'd already taken you from me. You were perfectly happy to let the monster who . . . who *defiled* me run free because you were too wrapped up in your new love to care."

Sometimes I wondered if Emma inhabited the same reality the rest of us did. Until I came into her life, she'd been chained at the bottom of a pond, continually drowning and coming back to life. How she managed to twist that into her vendetta against me I'll never understand.

"I loved you," Emma repeated. "And you abandoned me."

If Emma's tears affected Anderson in the slightest, he didn't show it. His face was stony and ice cold. "You're the one who did the leaving."

She shook her head. "What good would staying have done?" She was still sniffling, but there was a hard glint in her eye, a reminder of the ugliness that had settled into her soul. She was genuinely hurt by Anderson's perceived desertion, but she was also really, really angry. At him, at me, at Konstantin, at the world in general. "I had no desire to watch another woman parade around my home like she owned the place. Like she owned my *husband*."

I almost interjected a denial, but countering paranoia with logic was a pointless endeavor.

"I'll admit I loved you once," Anderson said. "But I don't love you anymore. You are nothing to me."

Emma gasped in a sob, covering her mouth with her hand as if that could somehow keep the sound contained. She was more than capable of crocodile tears, but that's not what these were. For all the efforts she'd taken to hurt Anderson, both through Erin and through myself, I think there was always a part of her that clung to the hope that she would one day win him back. Maybe she thought that after she eliminated the "competition," he would somehow fall in love with her all over again. She was already living in a dream world anyway, so what did one more delusion matter?

Anderson turned away from Emma and faced Cyrus. "I demand satisfaction."

Those words sent a slash of cold dread through my chest. I'd really been hoping it wouldn't come to this, no matter how obviously the signs had pointed to it. Emma had apparently been hoping the same, hoping his cold rejection of her love would be the only price she had to pay for her attempt to murder me.

"No!" she cried, her face going white. "Anderson, you can't mean that!"

Anderson ignored her. I didn't believe that all his love for her had disappeared so suddenly that no trace remained. What she'd tried to do to me was terrible, but though I knew he cared about me in an abstract sort of way, I wasn't *important* to him. Considering how long he'd been alive—not that I actually knew how old he was, except that he was ancient—the time he'd known me was nothing more than a blink of the eye. *Emma* was important to him, and there was no way her attack against me had changed that. But whatever feelings for her lingered in his heart, he wasn't allowing a hint of them to show.

"Are you sure that's what you want?" Cyrus asked softly. There was what might have been genuine sympathy in his eyes, as if he, too, must be certain that Anderson was in dire pain despite the mask of coldness he hid behind.

"Anderson, please!" Emma begged. Tears were streaming freely down her cheeks now. "I admit I betrayed Erin, but the rest of it wasn't me, I swear it."

"Oh, so you'll only admit to the one crime that Cyrus won't condemn you for?" There was a hint of amusement in Anderson's voice, but that had to be an act. Jesus, I *hoped* it was an act. "How very convenient."

Suddenly, the room went black.

I don't mean the lights went out. I mean it went *black,* as in a total absence of light. I'd seen Emma pull this stunt before, so I knew immediately what it was. She was a descendant of Nyx, the Greek goddess of night, and she had called this darkness to her, no doubt in a desperate attempt to escape. Adrenaline flooded my system as I remembered the darkness of death. I tried to focus on the sensation of breath going in and out of my lungs, proving to myself that I wasn't dead.

I didn't really think about what I did next, just acted out of pure instinct. I knew Anderson was going to lunge at Emma, or at least at Emma's last known position. Now that he'd condemned her, he wasn't going to risk letting her get away.

I stepped into what I calculated would be Anderson's path, and sure enough, he plowed into me. We both went down in a tangle of limbs. I hoped he would think my interference was nothing more than an accident. Having him mad at me in his current state would be a bad, bad thing.

Emma's most immediate threat was no doubt Mark, who'd been between her and the door, but I thought her chances of escape would be slightly higher if I delayed Anderson some more. He tried to get up, and I "accidentally" swept his legs out from under him as I rolled to my feet.

"Sorry!" I said as he went down again, knowing I'd given Emma as much time as I could afford to. If I tripped Anderson up a third time, there was zero chance he would think it was an accident.

Emma gave a high-pitched shriek that practically shattered my eardrums. There was a thud, and then the light reappeared, blinding after the total darkness. I blinked a couple of times to clear my vision.

Emma had made it about two steps into the hall before Mark had caught her in a tackle. She was flailing wildly and screaming as Mark hauled her to her feet and dragged her back into the library.

A very sane and sensible side of my brain told me there was nothing I could do and that I should stay out of it. Emma was a danger, to me, to Anderson, to the rest of his *Liberi,* and even to my loved ones. Because of her madness, I couldn't say I felt she *deserved* to die, but I could say her death would not be unjust. I could even say I wouldn't be unhappy if she were dead. But I'd drawn my line in the sand when I'd refused to hunt Konstantin for Anderson. I could not condone killing someone for revenge, and that was all that this would be.

Knowing I would be fighting one hell of an uphill battle, I held my chin high and got between Anderson and Emma yet again.

TWENTY

"Can we talk about this a bit?" I asked. I hated how tentative I sounded, but Anderson was really freaking me out. I almost liked the emotionless machine he'd been last night better, though I supposed it was a good thing he'd let some of that out considering the destruction in the clearing.

"There's nothing to talk about," Anderson said, fixing me with his laserlike stare. "She broke the treaty. And she's proven she can't be trusted."

"Anderson, please," she begged, sobbing. "Please believe me! I didn't do it!"

Anderson might as well have been struck deaf for all the attention he paid her.

"But *I'm* the injured party here," I argued. "And I don't think she needs to die."

"Your opinion is duly noted."

And ignored, obviously. I tried to think up some

argument that Anderson might listen to, but Cyrus spoke up before I could.

"Actually, Nikki, you're not the injured party here. *I* am. I gave her a direct order to leave you alone, and she disobeyed me. I can't allow that."

For the first time since I'd met him, there was cold steel in Cyrus's voice. He'd dropped the friendly smile, and there was a predatory sharpness in his eyes. Usually, the only resemblance I saw between him and his father was in their coloring, but the look on his face now suggested they might be more alike than I'd guessed.

Emma seemed to realize there was no reaching Anderson, so she switched her focus to Cyrus.

"I didn't disobey you! I swear to you, I'm being framed. That bitch probably set the whole thing up to try to get me out of the way."

My jaw dropped open. Even now, when I was the only one in the room trying to save her life, Emma was trying to stick it to me. If I'd had any sense, I would have washed my hands of her right there and then. Surely there was a straw that broke the camel's back somewhere in her ravings.

And yet they really *were* ravings. I'd always thought of her irrational behavior like it was some kind of character flaw, but maybe instead of hating her and being angry with her for her behavior, I should have been trying to get her to seek professional help. Maybe if she'd been put on meds shortly after she'd emerged from the pond, she wouldn't be what she was today.

"It's not fair to blame her for being crazy when

it was your own father's decade of torture that made her that way," I told Cyrus, deciding it was best to ignore Emma's wild accusation. "You always said you were sorry for what he did to her. Prove it!"

"What caused her to do it is irrelevant. I told her what would happen if she disobeyed me, and she did it anyway. I might have spared her if Anderson were willing to claim her as his own again, but that seems not to be the case." He raised an inquiring eyebrow at Anderson, who shook his head.

I was still scrambling for an argument that might work. I supposed I could try throwing something at Mark and giving Emma another chance to run for it, but I couldn't risk breaking the treaty. If my choices were to let Emma die or to trigger a war we couldn't win between us and the Olympians, I had to let Emma die.

I practically jumped out of my shoes when Blake put his arm around my shoulders, giving them a firm squeeze while whispering in my ear. "There's nothing you can do, Nikki."

"Proceed," Cyrus said to Mark.

Emma started making gasping, gurgling sounds, and I saw that Mark's forearm was across her throat, muscles bulging as he choked her. Emma kicked and flailed, but she was no match against Mark's brute strength.

"*You* could stop it," I hissed at Blake. He could use his power to distract both Cyrus and Mark with uncontrollable lust. That might interfere with their plans, but it wasn't technically breaking the treaty.

"I suspect it would annoy Anderson almost as much as it annoyed me if you tried it," Cyrus said to Blake. I guess my whisper hadn't been as quiet as I'd thought.

"Don't even think about it," Anderson said. He was looking at Emma now, and his face wasn't quite so impassive anymore. His Adam's apple bobbed a couple of times in quick succession. Emma's lips were turning blue, and her struggles became even more frantic.

"You don't have to do this," I said lamely, my eyes blurring with tears. Yes, I was crying over the impending death of a woman who'd tried to have me buried alive.

"Yes, I do," Cyrus answered, showing no signs that he felt any regret over ordering Emma's death. "You'd better grow a thicker skin if you're going to hang around with *Liberi* for the rest of your life."

If Blake hadn't clamped his arm around my shoulders harder, I might not have been able to resist the temptation to go slug Cyrus. I'd reminded myself time and again that he was one of the bad guys.

After today, I knew I would never forget it again.

Cyrus didn't chortle or rub his hands together with glee as someone like Konstantin might have done, enjoying the suffering of others. But his callous indifference was almost worse. At least if he'd reveled in it, it would have told me the death of a fellow human being actually *meant* something to him.

Emma went limp in Mark's arms. Unlike Cyrus, *he* looked like he was having a great time, but then he was in the process of becoming *Liberi*, stealing Emma's immortality so that he could live forever himself. I guess that could be quite a rush for someone who was raised believing in the Olympian ideal.

Mark didn't let Emma's body fall to the floor until long after she stopped moving.

Before that awful day when my car crashed into Emmitt and changed my life forever, I'd never once seen anyone die. On the way back to our car, I tried to figure out how many people had died in front of me since I'd become *Liberi*. The fact that I had to think about it before I could be sure freaked me out.

There was Emmitt, of course. Then there was Alexis and his two cronies, who had died when Anderson and I rescued Emma from the pond. There was Justin Kerner, and one of his victims, whom I'd tried unsuccessfully to save. And now there was Emma. That brought the death toll up to seven, if you didn't count the two times I'd seen Jamaal executed. Seven permanent deaths witnessed over the course of two months.

But today's was the worst of all. I'd seen Anderson be ruthless before. I knew he had it in him. He was the son of a Fury, for God's sake. But Emma was his *wife*. Okay, ex-wife, though they hadn't exactly filed for divorce in a court of law. The principle was the same. He had stood there and watched her die when he could have saved her.

I kept having to dab at my eyes as we made the silent walk from Cyrus's house to the garage where we had parked. Anderson was stone-faced, staring straight ahead as he walked. When we reached the car, Anderson pulled the keys out of his jacket pocket and handed them to Blake.

"I'm not fit to drive," he said. His voice was gravelly, and for the first time I noticed the rim of red around his eyes.

It made me feel a little better to know that Anderson was hurting after what he'd done. I don't know if I could have borne it if he'd been as indifferent as he'd pretended to be while we were at Cyrus's. Maybe he'd just been trying to hide his true emotions in front of the enemy.

"It had to be done, boss," Blake said as he took the keys.

A glint of anger flashed in Anderson's eyes. He'd called for Emma's death himself, had stood idly by while Mark killed her, but apparently he didn't like the implication that she'd needed to die. "You never did like her, did you?"

"There are a lot of people I don't like, and only a couple of them I'd like to see die. Emma wasn't one of them. But she wasn't right in the head, and she was getting worse over time instead of better. I just wanted you to know I thought you did the right thing."

Blake gave me a look that held both warning and reproach, probably worried I was going to argue, but what would be the point? I'd made my position clear already. Anderson was obviously suffering—as he had been almost from the moment we'd pulled

Emma from the pond and he'd seen what she'd become. I wasn't going to give him an "atta boy" like Blake had, but I wasn't going to kick him while he was down, either.

Anderson nodded a thank-you at Blake, then climbed into the back of the car. The ride home was even longer and more miserable than the ride out had been.

TWENTY-ONE

I felt far from social when we returned to the mansion, so I made a beeline for my suite and locked the door behind me. A long, scalding-hot shower failed to erase my memories, and my mind was stuck on a continuous loop, replaying Emma's death over and over again.

Was there something I could have said or done to save her? Some way to convince Anderson or Cyrus that it wasn't fair to hold an insane woman responsible for her actions?

In some traditions, when you save a person's life, you then become responsible for that person. It was a cruel, capricious universe that made my rescue the first step on Emma's path to destruction. In a fair world, Emma would have come out of that pond sane and healthy. Maybe her marriage to Anderson would have dissolved anyway—from what I'd heard, their marriage had already been on shaky footing when Emma was kidnapped—but she would not have fixated on me, nor would she have run off to join the Olympians to spite Anderson.

It burned me somewhere deep inside that I had rescued Emma only to have her die while Anderson looked on.

Because I wasn't feeling wretched enough already, my mind insisted on dangling my conversation with Maggie in front of me, the conversation during which Maggie had suggested that Emma's jealousy wasn't entirely misplaced. No matter how I looked at it, I still saw no sign that Anderson was interested in me that way, but then maybe I didn't know where to look. Maybe I just didn't know Anderson well enough yet to pick up the cues. And maybe if I *had* picked them up, I'd have been able to find some way to discourage him, and then—

My thoughts were spiraling out of control, and I knew it. Logic told me in no uncertain terms that Emma's death was not my fault. I'd done everything I could to prevent it, and I had absolutely nothing to feel guilty about. But logic was a cold comfort, and despite my attempts to distract myself and stop thinking about it, I was brooding myself into a deep, dark funk.

I tried everything I could think of to occupy my mind with something else, but Emma's death loomed over me like a massive shadow blocking out the light of the sun.

And then, as I sat on my couch with my computer on my lap and clicked from one website to another, looking for my magic potion of forgetfulness, I clicked by the page where I'd seen the ad for the Indian art exhibit at the Sackler, and I remembered the mixture of comfort and passion I'd experienced in Jamaal's arms last night, before he'd pulled away from me yet again.

Jamaal had a way of occupying my mind like nothing else in the world did, and as I closed my eyes and tried to remember every touch and caress, every word, every scent, every sound, the rest of the world seemed to fade away. He was such a hard, angry man, and yet his lips were deliciously soft, his hands gentle. I shivered in remembered pleasure, wishing I had kept my wits about me and not touched his scars.

How would things have worked out if I hadn't made that crucial mistake? If Jamaal were an ordinary man, I knew exactly where things would have led, but Jamaal was anything but ordinary, and there was more than just his scars holding him back.

I was very aware that I was reaching for a distraction, looking for an excuse to end my self-imposed isolation, but it occurred to me that Jamaal had probably gone back out to the clearing to practice with Sita this afternoon once I was safely out of the house. There was good reason to think she might be a bit cranky today after our aborted attempt at romance. I wondered if there was any chance she would take her anger out on Jamaal if I wasn't around. The thought sent a chill of alarm through me.

Was my sudden concern nothing but a big, fat rationalization, an excuse to fling myself at Jamaal when he'd made it clear he thought we should maintain our distance? Yes. But I didn't care. I needed a distraction, and Jamaal was the biggest, best distraction I could imagine.

It was a little after eleven at night when I rapped on Jamaal's door. It didn't occur to me until after I'd knocked that some people like to get a full night's sleep and go to bed at a reasonable hour. I had the vague impression that Jamaal was a night owl, but I didn't have much evidence to support it.

If he didn't answer the door, should I assume he was asleep? Or should I worry that my fears were more than a flimsy rationalization and Sita had hurt him?

Luckily, I didn't have to make that decision, because the door opened, and Jamaal stood there in all his manly glory, looking good enough to eat.

He hadn't been in bed yet, or he wouldn't have gotten to the door so fast, but he had changed into a pair of plaid pajama bottoms topped with a wife-beater. Instinct told me he wore the top to cover his scars, even in his sleep, and the thought made me hurt somewhere deep inside.

"What do you want?" he asked curtly when I just stood there in his doorway staring at him.

If I'd come down just because I was worried Sita might have hurt him, I could turn around and go back to my room now. He was obviously fine. Besides, he was blasting out keep-away vibes so hard I couldn't possibly miss them.

"Did you practice with Sita while I was gone

today?" I asked, instead of acting on the unsubtle message.

Jamaal sighed and rubbed his eyes like he was tired. I didn't think he was. I didn't feel like standing in the hall, so I pushed past him into his sitting room. The door to his bedroom was open, and I could see that the covers on his bed had been neatly pulled back. Jamaal was the kind of neat freak who makes his bed every day, so I knew this meant he'd been about to turn in for the night.

"Go to bed, Nikki," Jamaal said, a hint of pleading in his voice.

"Tell me what happened with Sita. Was she pissed off because of last night?"

Jamaal looked like he wanted to strangle me. Once upon a time, I'd have been intimidated by that look, but not anymore. As long as he was in control of himself, he would never hurt me, and he was firmly in control. I crossed my arms and gave him my best stubborn, implacable look.

He closed his sitting room door. It wasn't quite a slam, but it was close.

"Yes, she was pissed off," he said.

"Did she hurt you?" If she had, he was okay now, but that didn't stop my blood pressure from rising at the thought.

He rolled his eyes. "Of course not. But she tried to go looking for you even though I told her you weren't in the house."

That didn't sound good. "Maybe she didn't understand you." I still had trouble wrapping my brain around the idea that Sita understood *anything* people said to her. How the hell did a tiger learn English?

I shook my head at myself. I had to stop thinking of Sita as a tiger. That was the form she took, but that wasn't what she actually was. She was magic, and who knew what her limits were?

"She understood," Jamaal said grimly. "I wasn't sure she wasn't going to pick on someone else to punish me, so I put her away. You have to keep your distance, Nikki. It's not safe to be around me."

I heard the hint of bitterness in my own laugh. "I think *safe* is a thing of my past. In the last couple of months, I've been beaten, bitten, kidnapped, murdered—twice!—and threatened with fates worse than death. I doubt I'll ever feel safe again." I shivered, suddenly chilled by my own recap of what I'd been through. I was lucky I wasn't as insane as Emma by this point.

Jamaal took a step toward me, and I think he was planning to give me a hug, but he stopped himself and clenched his fists at his sides.

"The closest I've come to feeling safe," I continued, and this time I took the step forward, "was last night when I was in your arms. When you kissed me, I forgot the rest of the world existed." I reached out to touch his chest. The fabric of his shirt was thin enough that I could feel the ridges of his scars beneath it. I looked up into his eyes. "I need to forget for a while. Please."

"It's too dangerous," Jamaal said, but he didn't

move away from me, and his eyes were dark with desire. "Sita—"

"Is going to have to learn to live with it. And if she can't, then you'll just have to go back to coping with your death magic the old-fashioned way. You managed to do it for a century before her."

His face hardened. "If you can call what I did 'managing.' You remember that long list of bad things that have happened to you? Who was it who *beat* you?"

I'd thought Jamaal had forgiven himself for that. Apparently, I was wrong. "Even when your temper flared, you wouldn't have done that to one of your friends," I said. "You thought I was the enemy. Look, I don't like it when you go off like a powder keg, and I know fighting the death magic made you miserable, but if using Sita to vent it means you have to live your life in complete isolation from the rest of us, then it isn't worth it. I'd rather deal with your temper."

Jamaal shook his head. He opened his mouth to argue, but I reached up and put my fingers on his lips to stop him.

"You deserve to have a life," I told him, caressing the fullness of his lower lip with my thumb as I closed the last remaining distance between us. Almost against his will, he put his arms around me. There was a look very like fear in his eyes, and I was determined to extinguish it. I raised up on my tiptoes and kissed him, and a small sound of need escaped me.

"This is a bad idea, Nikki," he said against my lips, but the sexy rasp in his voice and the way his hands gripped me tighter said he was in as much of a mood to be bad as I was.

I breathed deep, taking in his scent of smoke and cloves and something else I suspected was hair product. And underneath was the scent of *him,* of the man who could chase all other thoughts from my mind with the lightest brush of skin against skin, or even with the faintest hint of a smile. I slid my hands up his chest and looped them around his neck, pulling his head down toward me.

For all his protests, he didn't resist. His lips came down on mine, and there was no longer room in my brain for anything but the taste of him, the feel of him against me. He was rapidly hardening beneath those soft flannel PJs of his, and I wished I were taller so I could grind something other than my belly against him.

Jamaal apparently had a similar thought, because his hands slid down my back to my butt and he boosted me up with casual strength. I groaned into his mouth and wrapped my legs around him, reveling in the feel of him. His tongue stroked mine rhythmically, and I grabbed hold of a double handful of his hair to remind myself not to let my hands wander. It was hard to remember *anything* at the moment, hard to think of anything but how glorious his lips felt as he kissed me.

My heart was already tripping along happily in my chest, but when Jamaal carried me through the sitting room and into his bedroom, I thought it might burst. I wanted him more than I wanted my next breath, wanted to lose myself in the sensations he sparked in my body, but I knew from past experience that I needed to keep some small section of my brain on-line and functional if I didn't want to scare him off again.

Jamaal laid me down on the crisp white sheets of his bed, pushing the covers further aside without breaking the kiss. He came to rest on top of me, his lower body held in the cradle of my legs, which I kept wrapped around him. My hands yearned to explore, to tear away the clothing that separated us. I wanted to feel his skin, hot and slick against mine, but I didn't dare make any overtures.

I let go of Jamaal's hair and groped for the headboard. I hadn't paused to examine it when Jamaal had carried me in, but I had a vague impression it was carved of dark wood and had some posts I could hold on to. Maybe if I kept my hands out of the fray entirely, I could keep them from wandering when they shouldn't. I found a couple of handholds and latched on, still kissing him for all I was worth and holding him close with my legs.

I almost howled in protest when he broke the kiss, but he didn't withdraw from me, merely cupped the side of my face in his hand and stared down into my eyes. With his erection pressed up tight against me, there was no missing his desire. Unfortunately, there was no missing the hint of fear in his eyes, either.

"I want you," he whispered, then rolled his hips against me to emphasize his point. I gasped in pleasure and arched my back. "But you know I have . . . issues."

I let go of the headboard long enough to run my fingers down the side of his face in a caress that I hoped was equal parts sensual and comforting. "I know. I don't care about your issues. Tie my hands so I don't get careless, and then have your way with me."

A tremor ran through him, and he closed his eyes. Shit. I was losing him.

"Don't you dare stop now!" I said, clamping my legs even more firmly around him.

"You deserve better than me."

"*I'll* decide what I deserve." I was somewhat heartened by the fact that despite his words, he was still rock hard against me. There was a part of him trying to withdraw, but it wasn't all of him. "I want you inside me."

He shook his head. "You don't understand. I had an owner once . . . The scars turned her on. She—"

I shut him up with a kiss, gently taking hold of his lip between my teeth when he would have pulled away. Apparently, he found that sexy, because he momentarily forgot his objections and returned my kiss with an intensity that took my breath away.

He was panting heavily when he ended the kiss. "Have to keep my shirt on," he said between breaths.

"Don't care," I said, and realized I was panting with need, too. Actually, I *did* care, but the time to talk to Jamaal about whatever had been done to him to make him so skittish about the scars was not now. I didn't want him thinking about anything that might make him back off yet again, so I channeled my inner porn star. I'm not usually into talking dirty, but for Jamaal I was more than willing to make an exception. "Fuck me. Now!"

It's amazing the effect those two little words can have on a guy. Jamaal forgot all about his excuses and apologies and explanations. He pushed up to his knees so he could get to the fly of my jeans, and he had them open and down before I could even offer to help. I'd have liked to have taken them off entirely, but he seemed in too much of a hurry and I wasn't about to complain.

I groaned when he dropped his pajamas and I got a good look at his erection. I'd known from the feel of him against me that he was, shall we say, well endowed, but naked and ready for action, he was nothing short of magnificent. My fingers itched to reach out and touch him, to stroke the smooth hardness of him, but since I hadn't let him pour out his whole tale of woe, I didn't dare, not knowing what might trigger traumatic memories.

A shiver of need passed through me, along with a tiny twinge of anxiety. I'm no virgin, but my spectacular ability to fall for inappropriate or unavailable men meant I wasn't the most sexually experienced twenty-five-year-old in the world, and Jamaal's size promised an uncomfortable beginning. I hoped it wouldn't hurt so much that I couldn't hide it. The last thing I wanted was for Jamaal to feel even a twinge of guilt.

"Condom," I reminded him as he stretched out above me, having barely remembered in time.

"Not necessary," he assured me. "The lines don't mix."

I took that to mean that descendants of different divinities couldn't have children together, which I stored away as something to ask questions about some other time. Right now, I was more than prepared to take Jamaal's word for it. I spread my legs as wide as I could with my damn jeans and panties restricting the motion. Jamaal didn't take me up on my offer to let him tie my hands, but he did pin my wrists to the pillow above my head. I had no objections.

I arched toward him in anticipation . . .

And felt like I'd been plummeted into a pool of ice-cold water when I heard a feline growl, way too close to me.

Jamaal cursed and shoved me aside, putting himself between me and the five-hundred-pound tiger that had suddenly appeared on the bed beside us. I rolled off the side of the bed, frantically pulling up my pants as I did. Sita growled again, the sound just short of a roar.

"I did *not* summon you!" Jamaal shouted at her.

Staying out of sight might have been my wisest choice, but I couldn't help peeking up over the side of the bed. Jamaal was on his knees, his arms spread wide as if that would block Sita from getting to me. We both knew she could jump right over him if she wanted to. He hadn't bothered to pull his pajamas back up, and I saw that his backside was as scarred as the rest of his torso. He reached out as if to touch

Sita—which he seemed to need to do to put her away—but she danced out of reach, baring a very intimidating set of teeth. Her eyes seemed to glow in the darkness of the room, and they locked on me like laser beams.

Jamaal moved to put himself between us again, trying to cut off her line of sight, but I didn't want him getting hurt because of me, and I worried Sita wasn't above taking out her temper on him. The idea that she'd just appeared out of nowhere without being summoned wasn't what you'd call a comfortable one. I wasn't about to cower while Jamaal took the heat for me, so I rose to my feet and glared at the tiger.

"Jamaal has a right to a life, Sita," I said. "You can't keep him entirely to yourself."

"Shut up, Nikki!" Jamaal snapped at me as Sita growled her disapproval. "Just get out of here while you can."

There wasn't much I could do to help, but leaving Jamaal to face an angry tiger by himself didn't seem like such a hot idea. Of course, staying and getting mauled didn't sound so great, either.

I shook my finger at Sita like I was scolding a small child. "If you hurt him, I swear to God I'm—"

Sita interrupted me with a roar that rattled my teeth.

"She won't hurt me," Jamaal said with conviction. "Now get the fuck out of my room."

There were a lot of things I wanted to say just then, but I swallowed them all. Jamaal said he hadn't summoned her, but could I be sure that was entirely true? We'd taken some slapdash steps to avoid triggering his issues, but maybe it hadn't been enough. Maybe we'd avoided the conscious issues, but the unconscious ones were deeper and more insidious. So insidious his subconscious had called for Sita to intervene. Maybe he would have to talk through whatever had happened to him in his slave days before he would be able to let someone get so close again.

Or maybe Sita was as out of control as his temper had been, before he'd learned to summon her.

I knew I couldn't help him. Not right now, anyway. I didn't want to leave him to face Sita's wrath alone, but I suspected my continued presence would just make her more angry.

Mentally promising myself that this was not over, that I was not going to give up on Jamaal no matter how difficult the situation, I slowly backed out of the room.

I was awakened in the night by another blast of thunder. I was surprised to discover that I'd fallen asleep at all, considering how long I had tossed and turned, searching for a solution to the Sita problem—one that didn't involve Jamaal having to shut one or the other of us out of his life. And wondering if he was just one more on the list of unavailable men I was destined to fall for.

I rose from my bed and went to the window, hoping to see that it was pouring down rain, but the sky was clear enough that I could have counted the stars if I'd wanted to. I wondered how big the clearing was going to be when Anderson had finished venting his pain and rage. Hopefully, we'd still have *some* woods left.

I slept only fitfully after that, waking up every forty minutes or so, brooding about Emma, and Jamaal, and my most recent brush with death. By 4 A.M., I was lying in bed debating whether I should try to get some more sleep or just give up and get out of bed. The decision was taken out of my hands when the phone beside my bed rang.

Phones ringing at four in the morning are rarely a good thing. The only person I'd given my land line number to was Steph. The last time she'd called so early, it was because the Glasses' house burned down.

Dread pooled in my stomach as I sat up and turned on the light. I blinked in the glare, trying to see the caller ID before picking up the phone.

My hand was halfway to the phone when my vision cleared enough for me to read the caller ID: Cyrus Galanos.

TWENTY-TWO

I was an emotional wreck when I got off the phone with Cyrus. I spent a few minutes indulging in a crying jag, a little piece of my heart breaking. When the worst of it was over, I went into the bathroom and splashed some cold water on my face. My eyes were red and puffy, and I had shopping bags under them from not sleeping. The hair around my face was wet from the splashes of water, and the hair that wasn't wet was tangled and frizzy. I wanted to get into the shower and put myself back together, but there wasn't time.

I threw on the first pair of jeans I could get my hands on and grabbed a warm, comfortable flannel shirt. Then I dug out my one pair of waterproof boots, nice and fleecy to keep my feet warm in the snow. I braided my hair sloppily as I made my way down the stairs to the second floor. The house was dark and quiet. I glanced at my watch and saw that it was now twenty after four. I'd wasted too much time having my pity party. The moon would set in less than two hours, and I would need every spare second of that time.

Of course, it was possible I wouldn't survive relaying to Anderson what Cyrus had told me when he called. I wished Cyrus had had the guts to tell Anderson himself without using me as his messenger service. After all, Anderson couldn't kill the messenger over the phone.

I hesitated when I reached the hallway leading to Anderson's wing. We were forbidden from going into the east wing past his study, except in case of emergency. This was an emergency, but that didn't exactly make me eager to trespass. Not with the message I bore.

I gave myself a swift kick in the pants and reminded myself once again that I didn't have time for hesitation. I needed to be at my hunting best, and that meant I needed the moon.

Heart throbbing in my chest, I hurried down the hall. I wasn't sure which room was his bedroom, but I made an educated guess that it would be next to the bathroom he'd stuck his head out of the other day. I didn't know how I was going to break the news, and I didn't have time to come up with a carefully worded plan.

I knocked on the door, rapping hard because I assumed Anderson would be fast asleep. "Anderson!" I called, hoping I wasn't shouting so loud I'd wake the entire house. "Wake up! I need to talk to you."

"I'm not asleep," he answered, startling me, and moments later there was a glow of light around the edges of the door and the sound of approaching footsteps.

The door swung open. Anderson was still wearing yesterday's clothes, and a quick glance over his shoulder showed me that his bed was neatly made. I didn't know what he'd been doing sitting around in his room in the dark, but I didn't wonder enough to ask. He looked even more rumpled than usual, his beard bristling with scraggly whiskers he hadn't bothered to shave, his shaggy hair standing up straight in places and lying flat in others. His eyes were bloodshot, and there was a faint scent of stale alcohol clinging to him. That answered my question about what he'd been doing alone and awake in the dark.

"What is it?" he asked, and he didn't sound as alarmed as a knock on the door at this hour of the morning should make him. He just sounded resigned and very, very tired.

I wished like hell I could turn around and leave him to his grieving. I wished I didn't have to make him feel worse than he already did. Yesterday, I had wanted him to feel bad for what I saw as his cold-bloodedness, but now I wished I could spare him.

I decided to ease my way into the conversation by telling him the easy part first.

"I just got a phone call from Cyrus."

A crease of worry appeared between Anderson's brows. "That was . . . unexpected."

No kidding. "Someone tried to murder him in his sleep."

Anderson no longer looked so weary and apathetic. I didn't know if that would turn out to be a good thing or a bad thing for me, though I supposed even if he'd remained flat and dull-eyed, he would be fully roused and ready to embrace his Fury heritage by the time I was finished.

"Come in," he said, turning his back abruptly and heading toward an armchair in the corner. I reluctantly followed as he sat and grabbed the pair of battered sneakers lying beside the chair. "Cyrus wouldn't call you just to report an attempt on his life," he said, shoving one foot into a sneaker. "Tell me what's going on."

I wanted to sit down. My knees were a little weak and trembly. But Anderson was sitting in the only chair, and sitting on the edge of his bed seemed too familiar and informal. I settled for grabbing one of the bedposts to steady myself, gripping it harder than was strictly necessary. Why the hell was *I* the one who had to have this conversation with Anderson? I swallowed hard.

"The guy who tried to kill Cyrus was a Descendant. One of Konstantin's cronies."

Anderson looked up from tying his sneakers. "You say that like it's some kind of surprise. I told you Konstantin has never trusted his children. I'm frankly surprised Cyrus has lived as long as he has. It might have seemed natural to him to step into his father's shoes, but it was probably the worst possible thing he could have done if he wanted Konstantin to keep him alive. Having his child usurp his 'throne' is one of his biggest fears, which is why he's killed all the others before Cyrus."

"But Cyrus took over in name only," I protested. I'd warned Cyrus myself that Konstantin would turn on him one day, but I still had a hard time understanding how someone could kill their own child. I don't think there's a more heinous crime in the universe.

"Doesn't matter," Anderson said. He finished tying his shoes, but remained in his chair, his body language fraught with tension. "Maybe Konstantin thought he'd be okay with it at first, but when he saw Cyrus taking over his role—and making some decisions he didn't agree with—he realized he couldn't stomach it. He might even think killing Cyrus would make the rest of the Olympians forgive his past mistakes and let him lead them again." He raked his hand through his hair. I don't know if that was a stress reaction, or if he actually thought he was finger-combing it. If the latter, he failed spectacularly.

"You still haven't told me why Cyrus called *you* of all people. And why you're at my doorstep at this hour of the morning."

No, I hadn't. And I didn't want to. My throat tightened up on me, and I couldn't think of what to say. I didn't like the idea of sitting on Anderson's bed, but my shaky knees wouldn't hold me anymore, so I did it anyway.

I told myself I wasn't really *scared* of Anderson. I told myself that I was having a hard time finding my voice because I didn't want to cause him pain, and because I was enough of an emotional coward that I didn't want to be there to *see* his pain. That part was true, at least as far as it went. But the truth was, I *was* scared. He was a freaking *god*! And anyone who has even a smidgen of familiarity with mythology knows that gods don't act like human beings. They routinely kill the people closest to them, and they only sometimes show any remorse for having done it.

Despite my pathetic attempts to put on a brave face, Anderson couldn't help but see my fear. I thought even that might make him angry, but when I sneaked a glance at his face, I saw only gentle compassion. I just didn't know whether to trust it or not.

"You don't have to be afraid of me, Nikki," he said in a tone he might use with a frightened animal. "I can tell you have bad news to impart, and I promise I won't kill the messenger."

They were the right words, delivered in the right tone, and yet I still didn't trust him. "I've seen your temper before," I said, looking at the floor because I couldn't bear to face him. "I saw you torture a couple of people to death. I saw you stand by and watch your wife being killed before your eyes because you were angry at her for betraying you. I saw what you did to all the trees in the clearing." I didn't even mention the times he had threatened to kill me.

He stood up and came toward me, and I had to fight an urge to jump to my feet and run. I was rather proud of myself for staying right there on the edge of the bed until Anderson was an arm's length away. I would have had to look up to meet his eyes, but I felt no temptation to do so.

I practically jumped out of my skin when Anderson reached out and brushed his fingers over my cheek, tucking a stray lock of hair that had escaped my messy braid back behind my ear. The touch startled me enough to make me look up at his face.

"You have seen me get angry," he said, and there was still that look of compassion in his eyes. "You have seen me be ruthless. You *haven't* seen me truly lose my temper. I learned long ago how dangerous my temper can be. I did . . . terrible things in the old days, before I started consorting with humans. I will never let that happen again. That's why I shut down like I did the other night. It's what I had to do to contain myself." He touched me again, a brief caress of my cheek.

"I would never hurt you, or your loved ones, or any of my people, in a fit of anger."

I looked down, unable to think straight when he was looking at me like that. Maybe I was imagining things, but I thought I'd seen a kind of warmth in his gaze that was almost . . . intimate. Was I really seeing something telling in his eyes? Or was I doing exactly what I'd feared I would ever since my conversation with Maggie and letting the power of suggestion make me see something that wasn't there? I didn't know, and I couldn't afford to think about it.

"Tell me whatever it is you have to tell me," Anderson prompted. "I can sense your urgency."

I can't say I was completely convinced. But he

wasn't wrong about the urgency, and it was time for me to stop stalling.

"Cyrus killed the Descendant who attacked him, but he didn't do it quickly." My gorge rose as I remembered Cyrus's dispassionate account of using his power as a descendant of a sun god to slowly roast his attacker to death. "While he was suffering and dying, the Descendant raved about how Konstantin would win in the end. And he said Konstantin had used Cyrus to—" My voice choked off for a moment, and I forced myself to look up at Anderson once more. He'd put on his unreadable mask, and I had no idea what he was thinking or feeling.

"You might want to sit down," I said, and despite my lingering fear, I felt an urge to reach out and take his hand to comfort him as I delivered the blow. It said something about what he was feeling behind the mask that Anderson actually took my advice and sat down on the bed beside me.

"What did Konstantin use Cyrus to do?"

I took a deep breath in a futile attempt to steady myself. No amount of willpower could force me to look Anderson in the face. "He used *all* of us," I said. "To frame Emma. He was behind the fires, and behind my abduction. He planted the fake letters on Emma's computer. I thought I'd had a lucky escape thanks to the car accident, but that was all part of the plan, too. He wanted the kidnapper to be caught so he would admit what he was hired to do and say he was hired by a woman. It was all a big setup so that you would kill Emma." Never mind that Anderson hadn't killed her with his own hands. We all knew the decision to let her die had been his in the end. And now, he would have to live with having condemned the woman he'd loved so desperately to die over a betrayal she wasn't even guilty of.

My hand was squeezing the bedpost so hard my knuckles were turning white and my fingers were going numb. My pulse was drumming erratically in my throat, and I had to remind myself to draw the occasional breath as I waited for Anderson's reaction. No matter what he'd promised, I feared an explosion of some kind.

The silence stretched, my heartbeat loud in my ears as I held myself tense and ready—for what, I don't know. I finally couldn't stand it anymore and risked a look in Anderson's direction.

His face had a slightly gray cast to it, and his bloodshot eyes were rimmed with red. His lips were pressed together in a tight line, and I saw no evidence that he was even breathing. But when he met my eyes, there was no sign that he had turned into the automaton of the other night, nor that he was about to explode with temper. There was just pain, and a soul-deep sadness that brought tears to my eyes.

I wanted to say something to break the silence, find some words of sympathy, or comfort. Anything to break the tension, if only for a second. But there were no words.

Anderson blinked rapidly a few times, then let out a slow, hissing breath. "Do you know what the worst thing about this is?" he asked in a hoarse whisper.

I shook my head mutely. Everything about it seemed equally awful to me.

He reached up to rub his eyes, as if he could make the haunted expression in them go away. "The worst part is that this doesn't hurt as much as Konstantin hoped it would. Because you see, Nikki, I've done worse."

TWENTY-THREE

I'd been unsure of a lot of things in recent days. However, there was no uncertainty in my mind now. If Anderson had done worse sometime in the course of his long life, I didn't want to know about it. And while he said Konstantin's trick hadn't hurt as much as Konstantin had hoped, it was obvious that it had hurt plenty. Anderson wasn't exploding in rage, but the pain and sadness that wafted from him made my eyes tear up in sympathy yet again.

Not trusting my voice, I cleared my throat before I spoke again.

"Strangely enough, Cyrus doesn't feel the need to protect Konstantin anymore. He suggested you and I might want to hunt Konstantin down and bury him somewhere that no one will ever find him."

Anderson nodded slowly. "He wants us to do the dirty work for him so he can deny having anything to do with his father's disappearance."

"That was my interpretation. So far he and Mark are the only Olympians who know what Konstantin tried to do, and I think Cyrus plans to keep it that way if he can. I don't know if he's trying not to piss off Konstantin's supporters, or if he just doesn't want to give anyone else ideas.

"Anyway, Cyrus told me Konstantin's been moving around constantly, trying to make it hard for me to get a bead on him. But he was apparently staying at Alexis's old place last night. I'm sure he knows by now that his assassination attempt failed, and he's no doubt on the run, but we have a solid starting point, and the moon is still up."

Anderson raised an eyebrow at me. There was still a haunted expression in his eyes, and his face hadn't fully regained its usual color, but he seemed entirely calm and rational. "You mean to tell me you're willing to hunt him now? His revenge has come to its head, and I doubt you and your family are in any danger from him anymore. He was never really after you in the first place."

My shoulders slumped, and I suddenly felt almost unbearably tired. Until that moment, when Anderson challenged me with it, I hadn't even allowed myself to *think* about what I was doing. The pain and anger that swelled in me when I learned what Konstantin had done were so overwhelming that I'd been acting on pure instinct, letting those swirling emotions guide me. I wanted Konstantin dead, and if I could help make him that way, then I was all for it.

But had anything really changed since I'd refused

to hunt Konstantin because my conscience rebelled at the idea of killing for revenge? Sure, Konstantin had hurt more people, but as Anderson had said, his revenge was now complete. At least, it seemed logical to assume it was.

I like to think of myself as a nice person. I've long taken pride in being a bleeding heart, in being a voice of reason when others around me were acting on pure emotion. I'd considered myself above acting out of revenge. And yet even now, when Anderson pointed out the inconsistency of my decision, my conscience couldn't quite rouse itself to try to talk me out of it. Konstantin had hurt too many people, in too many twisted ways. And unlike Emma, or even Justin Kerner, he was not clinically insane. There was no excuse for his actions, not even in my unusually open mind. He was just an evil man, and the world would be a better place without him.

"I still don't believe in revenge killings," I said slowly, thinking over my words carefully. "If there were a way to sentence him to life in prison, I'd be all for it." Even as I said those words, I wasn't sure they were true. Not anymore. In my arrogance, I'd thought there was no situation that could persuade me to believe in the death penalty, ever. Maybe I still didn't. I'd have to wait until my emotions settled down before I would know for sure. But there were exceptions to every rule, and I couldn't deny that in my mind, Konstantin was one of them. "But since we can't imprison him except by burial, which I wouldn't wish even on him, then I guess he has to die. If that makes me a hypocrite, then I guess I'm just going to have to live with it."

Anderson gave me a gentle smile. "I don't think you're being a hypocrite, Nikki. We're being spurred into action by revenge, but that's not all there is to it. Even if he doesn't personally come after us anymore, he will still be an evil person, and countless others will suffer and die at his hands if we don't take him out. There are good, logical reasons to kill him above and beyond our desire to punish him for what he's done."

Everything Anderson said was true. By killing Konstantin, we'd be saving innocent lives, there was no question about it. But I had the sense that I was taking my first step onto a slippery slope, and that there was a long, long fall ahead of me if I wasn't very careful.

"I can wrestle with my conscience later," I said. I glanced at my watch. "We have about an hour and twenty minutes before the moon sets. It'll take us thirty to get to Alexis's place, and that won't leave us a whole lot of time to pick up the trail and figure out where Konstantin has gone." Assuming I could get my power to work on command, which was far from a sure thing.

"Then there's not a moment to waste," Anderson said.

Together, we hurried out into the predawn darkness to hunt the deposed "king" of the Olympians.

I let Anderson drive, on the assumption that once we got close enough to Alexis's mansion for me to start sensing Konstantin, I'd have to do my semiconscious tour-guide impersonation as I'd done with Steph on the night we'd gone hunting together. As soon as we were through the gates, I leaned back in my seat and closed my eyes, trying to let my mind drift in just the right way. The darkness, the early hour, and my exhaustion from a mostly sleepless night threatened to drag me down into sleep. The pressure of the ticking clock, along with the burning need to ensure that Konstantin could never hurt anyone again, kept sleep from winning, but it didn't exactly help me zone out.

The roads were an icy mess, making the drive painfully slow. A couple of times, I felt the car skid, and my eyes opened in alarm. Anderson knew how to drive in the snow and ice, however, and he quickly righted the car.

"Relax, Nikki," he said, reaching over to pat my knee briefly. "I'm not going to crash the car. Trust me."

I gave him a sidelong glance and frowned. The knee-pat had been an almost instinctual, absent gesture, and if he'd realized it was uncommonly familiar, he showed no sign of it. I bit my lip and sank a little lower in my seat. The last thing I needed right now was to distract myself analyzing every nuance of Anderson's behavior when I should be tracking a killer.

"It would be nice if just once I was trying to find someone without being under time pressure," I grumbled. It would be so much easier to relax if it didn't *matter* so goddamn much.

Of course, if it didn't matter so much, then I wouldn't be doing it.

Anderson didn't reply. I let out a long, slow breath and let my eyes slide closed again. I hoped Konstantin hadn't gotten very far away from Alexis's house by the time we got there. We were going to have precious little moonlight left, and if I lost the "signal," we'd be back to square one again by the time the moon next rose. Konstantin was no dummy, and after poking the bear, he was going to be running as fast as he could. With Cyrus mad at him, without the full support of the Olympians, he would have to get out of the D.C. area, and who knew where he would end up? If it were me, I'd get out of the country. And if he left the country, I suspected even *my* hunting skills might not be up to the challenge of finding him.

The urgency made my nerves buzz as if I'd drunk a gallon of coffee. I was tapping the fingers of one hand restlessly against my thigh. I stopped as soon as I noticed the movement, taking another deep breath and urging myself to calm. I searched for that floaty, abstracted feeling I got when I was a passenger on a boring drive.

The car hit a bump, and my eyes popped open again, searching out the dashboard clock before I could stop myself. It was 5:29, and we had less than thirty minutes left before the moon set. My heart sank. Even if Konstantin hadn't found out his assassination attempt failed until Anderson and I had left the mansion—and I was pretty sure he would have known before then—he had a good forty-minute head start. There was no way we were going to catch up with him before the moon set. My powers aren't nonexistent without the moon, but they're spotty at the best of times. I didn't for a moment believe I could find Konstantin during the day. And by nightfall, he'd be long gone, perhaps out of my reach.

The grimness on Anderson's face told me he'd reached the same conclusion, but he wasn't ready to admit it yet.

"Keep trying," he urged me as he turned onto the street that would take us by the front gates of Alexis's home. I would have thought one of the other Olympians would have appropriated it after Alexis's "disappearance," but perhaps Konstantin had wanted to keep it for himself.

I shook my head. "It's too late." I rubbed at my tired eyes, wishing there were some better way for me to control my power. Maybe it would help if I took up meditation. Maybe that would make it easier to relax in tense situations like this one.

"Don't you dare give up on me now, Nikki," Anderson warned in a low growl.

If he thought that was going to make it easier for me to relax into my powers, he was sorely mistaken. But I wasn't in the mood to argue with him, so I closed my eyes. My fingers were tapping away again, trying to vent the nervous energy that still pulsed through my veins. My mind might have decided the search was fruitless, but my body hadn't caught up, still buzzing on the adrenaline of the hunt.

I made only a halfhearted effort to relax myself, knowing there was no way we were going to have time to catch up to Konstantin. Mostly, I was just pretending to try so Anderson wouldn't nag me. My mind was still going a thousand miles an hour, and my token effort to relax hadn't had the slightest effect, when my eyes popped open for a third time, this time with no external prompting whatsoever.

A shiver of dread trailed down my spine as I looked out my window and saw we were passing directly in front of the gates to Alexis's mansion. Once upon a time, I would have considered the fact that my eyes had opened at that very moment to be nothing more than a coincidence. Now, however, I felt sure it meant only one thing.

"Konstantin is still in the house."

Anderson's hands jerked on the steering wheel, and for a moment I feared he was going to take us right into a ditch. He handled the car expertly, smoothly turning into the skid until he regained control and came to an idling stop in the middle of the road.

"He can't be," he protested. "He's arrogant, but not stupid. He had to have arranged for his pet Descendant to contact him when Cyrus was dead, and he *had* to know what it meant when the Descendant didn't do it."

"Maybe he didn't expect Cyrus to sic us on him so quickly," I said doubtfully. Of course, it didn't matter exactly what Konstantin had been expecting. Whether he thought we'd be after him in an hour or a day, he wouldn't be hanging out at his last known location to make it easy for us. "Or maybe Cyrus forced the Descendant to call Konstantin and tell him he succeeded."

"Yes, and he failed to mention that to you when you talked to him. And Konstantin has nothing better to do after assassinating his son than to lounge around in Alexis's house."

Okay, that theory didn't make a whole lot of sense, either. But I really hated the third theory that came into my mind.

There was no parking on the street in this neighborhood, and a snowplow had piled dirty brown snow and ice along the curbs, but that didn't stop Anderson from pulling off the road. The car shimmied and groaned a protest as he forced it over the mounded, icy snow. I clutched the grab bar with one hand and braced against the center console with the other. There was an ominous bang from the undercarriage, and Anderson's side of the car lurched upward while mine lurched downward. I barely kept my head from smacking against the window.

Anderson brought the car to a stop—or maybe the car took the decision out of his hands—and put it in park. We were still at a precarious angle, and I wondered if the tires on his side were even touching anything. Of course, if being hung up on the side of the road was the worst thing that was going to happen, I'd be ecstatic.

"The only reason I can think of for Konstantin to still be here is if this is a trap," I said, giving Anderson a meaningful look. Which would have been more effective—maybe—if he'd bothered to look at me. Instead, he was unbuckling his seat belt with one hand while opening the door with the other.

I grabbed his arm to get his attention. "Let's think about this for a minute before we do something stupid!"

I had no idea what Konstantin was planning. He *knew* Anderson couldn't be killed, not by him, and not by a Descendant. But he must think he had some way to hurt him, some way to prevent Anderson from killing him. There was no other reason I could imagine for him to still be in the house when he had to know we'd be coming after him.

Anderson gave me a steely glare. "Konstantin is here. That's all I need to know."

He turned toward the door again, and again I grabbed his arm. "We also know this has to be a trap. He could have thirty of his closest friends in there with him, just waiting for you to stroll in like a macho idiot."

Anderson snorted. "He'd have to risk letting them find out what I am, and that's something he would never do. He's alone in there. And I suggest you let go of me. I'm in no mood for your interference."

"Well, *I'm* in no mood to get killed because you won't listen to reason."

"Fine. Then stay here." He easily jerked his arm out of my grip and leapt out of the car.

"Dammit!" I fumbled with my own seat belt,

uttering a few choice cuss words under my breath. I couldn't just let Anderson walk in there alone. Sure, I was more vulnerable than he was, but I was also a hell of a lot more *rational,* and right now, that seemed like an important factor. "Wait up!" I yelled, pushing my door open and jumping out. Which turned out not to be my brightest move ever. We had come to a stop at the edge of the ditch, the car's undercarriage hung up on a big chunk of ice. The side of the ditch was covered with ice as well, and given my momentum and the severe angle, I ended up doing an inglorious nosedive into the ditch.

I twisted my ankle during the fall, as well as knocking the wind out of myself. Anderson, radiating impatience, reached down and hauled me to my feet before I was ready. I almost went down again.

"Your delay tactics are getting on my nerves," he said, and if he wanted to think my pratfall was a deliberate attempt to slow him down, then I was happy to let him go right ahead thinking it.

"Just give me half a second to catch my breath. That hurt!"

From the looks of him, half a second was all I was going to get, and grudgingly at that.

"So what's your plan, Rambo?" I asked as I gingerly put my weight on my injured ankle. "Go in the front door and hope he's not expecting you?"

He shot me a glare that would have had me taking a hasty step away if my ankle weren't complaining so loudly. Clearly, he wasn't open to suggestion, nor was he prepared to address my objections. I'd never seen him quite like this before, and frankly, it scared me. I didn't want to let him go in there alone, but I didn't want to get killed—or worse, considering this was Konstantin we were going after—charging in like a stampeding bull.

"I don't care if he's expecting me," Anderson said through gritted teeth. "There's nothing he can do to me."

Apparently that was as much discussion as he was willing to entertain. He turned away from me and started marching through the snow toward the house, leaving me to follow or not as I chose.

Wincing in pain at every step, I took off after him.

Our car had come to a stop well past the driveway, and Anderson and I were approaching the house through the woods. I could have reminded him that there were surveillance cameras in these woods and that it might be best to disable one before plowing heedlessly onward, but I didn't think he would listen to me. I just hoped Konstantin hadn't kept up the security detail that was monitoring the cameras the last time I'd trespassed here.

I had already determined beyond reasonable doubt that Anderson wasn't going to listen to me, but I didn't have it in me to just keep quiet as we knowingly walked into a trap without a plan.

"Konstantin obviously thinks there's *something* he can do to you," I said, panting a bit from the effort of walking through the snow, especially at the brisk pace Anderson had set. "Are you 100 percent sure he's wrong?"

"Yes," Anderson snapped.

"What if he's planning to bury you? Or drown you, like he did Emma?"

"He might find me reluctant to hold still for it. Besides, I'm rather hard to restrain." To punctuate his point, Anderson walked straight through the trunk of a tree.

I wished his reminder and demonstration made me feel better. The walking-through-walls thing was a common ability for death-god descendants. Konstantin had to know Anderson, as a death *god*, could do it, and he was waiting in that house for us anyway. To say I had a bad feeling about this was an understatement.

"But you *can* die, at least temporarily," I said. "I've seen it happen." He hadn't stayed dead anywhere near as long as a *Liberi* with similar injuries would have, but still . . .

"Unless his plan is to stand by my side and kill me every ninety seconds or so, it doesn't matter." He came to an abrupt stop and whirled on me. A hint of white glow was leaking out of his eyes, giving me a glimpse of the terrifying, nonhuman creature that lay behind his facade. "Go back to the car. This is my battle, not yours."

Oh, we were back to that again, were we?

"You're being a pigheaded, mindless jackass," I retorted. "Don't you see that Konstantin has been pulling our strings from the very beginning?" I myself was only now beginning to see how thoroughly Konstantin had manipulated us all. "He didn't trick you into killing Emma just to hurt you. He did it because he knew it would make you act exactly like you're acting now." And his attack on Cyrus was never supposed to succeed, was only meant to prompt Cyrus into giving up his location. "This is exactly the endgame he planned. We're here because he wants us to be, and we'd be idiots to fall for it."

Anderson moved so fast that all I saw was a blur. Then there was a hand at my throat and I was being propelled backward until I crashed into a tree trunk. I probably would have lost my footing in the snow and ice, but Anderson kindly held me up. Unfortunately, he was holding me up by the throat, but what's a little choking between friends?

"I told you I would never hurt you in a fit of temper," Anderson growled, the white light in his eyes now bright enough to make me squint. "Don't make a liar out of me."

I swallowed hard. Anderson can be one hell of a scary guy when he wants to be. But I also noticed that the hand around my throat wasn't really digging in, and that my impact with the tree had been much more surprising than painful. He was in better control of himself than he wanted me to think, which was sort of scary in itself. If he was in control of himself and *still* wanted to storm the house, if it wasn't just some hotheaded momentary madness, then there was no chance in hell I was talking him out of it, no matter how sound my reasoning.

Anderson took my silence for capitulation, and he let go of me. When I started following after him yet again, he gave me an exasperated look over his shoulder.

"I'll shut up," I promised him, holding my hands up in surrender. "But I'm coming with you."

I didn't know if I could possibly be any help. Konstantin had to be expecting both of us, after all, and that meant he had a plan to deal with both of us. But I wasn't letting Anderson walk in there alone. I fished my gun out of my coat pocket, rechecking the cylinder to make sure it was loaded and ready to go. Not because I had any doubts, but because I wanted to look tough and ready for action, instead of scared out of my wits.

The show must have been at least marginally convincing. Anderson turned from me once again and started heading toward the house. I followed.

TWENTY-FOUR

We approached the house from the back, staying under the cover of the woods for as long as we could. I tensed as we broke through the trees and onto the back lawn, but no gunshots shattered the darkness, and there was no one lurking nearby to jump us.

My twisted ankle had healed already, but Anderson was still walking fast enough that it was hard to keep up. I wished I had longer legs, and bit my tongue on a request that he slow down. He'd made it clear he was through waiting for me.

To get to the back door of the house, we had to walk by the pond that had been Emma's personal torture chamber for the better part of a decade. It was completely frozen over, its surface hidden under a layer of snow. Someone not familiar with the house might not even have realized it was there, though if you looked carefully you could see the outline of its banks under the snow.

I'm sure it cost him something, but Anderson resisted looking at the pond as we made our way past it. There was no way he wasn't aware of its presence, wasn't thinking about what Emma had gone through, wasn't thinking about what Konstantin had manipulated him into doing, but he was in a painfully single-minded state, so focused on his revenge his footsteps didn't falter.

There were no lights on in any of the windows that looked out over the back of the house, but that didn't mean there wasn't anyone on the lookout for intruders. I wanted to maybe do the kind of crouching run you often see people doing in action movies, but that only worked if there was cover to hide behind. Anderson and I were two moving dark blotches in a sea of pristine white snow, and if anyone was watching for us, there was no way in hell they could miss us.

The thought made me utter a few more curses under my breath. Anderson could make himself invisible. If he'd been willing to take the time to formulate a plan, perhaps we'd have been able to figure out a way to take advantage of his ability. But no, he'd rather charge in immediately, too impatient for his revenge to waste time on such trivialities as trying to figure out how to get at Konstantin as safely and easily as possible.

We reached the back door without any alarms sounding or traps springing, but that didn't make me feel any better. If Konstantin had set a trap of some sort, it made sense that it would be inside the house.

Anderson tried the door. Surprise, surprise, it was locked, but there was no way that was going to slow down a death god, much less actually stop him.

Anderson walked right through the door, and I had a momentary fear that he was going to leave me outside to find my own way in while he continued on without me. Before the worry took on a life of its own, I heard the locks turning, and Anderson considerately opened the door for me. I had the guilty thought that I'd probably have been better off if he'd stranded me outside, but that didn't stop me from stepping through the doorway.

"What now?" I asked in a bare whisper.

"Take me to him," Anderson responded. The edge of impatience in his voice made me bristle.

"I'm not a bloodhound!" I held up my wrist and pointed to my watch. "The moon set three minutes ago. I have no idea where he is." There was a flash of white light in Anderson's eyes again. "And getting angry at me isn't going to make my powers suddenly come back."

He blinked a couple of times, and the light went away. "The moon may help you, but you aren't powerless without it. You should be able to track Konstantin when he's so close."

He was right, and I knew it. But my pulse was tripping, and my chest was tight with anxiety, and I wasn't in any state to pick up the subtle nuances of my subconscious. My conscious mind was fully in control—telling me I should get the hell out of the house while there was still time—and any subconscious cues I might be getting were drowned out by the yammering.

I made a helpless gesture and shook my head. At this point, I almost hoped Konstantin changed his mind about whatever he was planning and decided to run instead. I was too frazzled to follow him, and it meant I would probably never be able to find him again, but I suspected that might be the lesser of two evils.

Anderson grunted. "Guess we'll just have to search the whole house then."

And what a joy *that* was going to be. The damned house must have been fifteen thousand square feet at a minimum. Searching it was going to take forever. Maybe it would be boring enough that I'd be able to hear my subconscious eventually. Or maybe Konstantin's trap would be in the first room we checked.

Anderson reached out and took my left hand. I wasn't expecting it, and I was jumpy enough that I tried to snatch my hand away. Anderson kept a firm hold, but disappeared from my view. I could still feel him there, still feel the pressure of his fingers against mine, but though I was looking straight at him, all I saw was the wall behind him.

"Be ready to shoot at a moment's notice," his disembodied voice said. "And try not to shoot *me,* even though you can't see me."

"I'll do my best."

There was a noise behind me. I jumped and gasped, whirling in that direction before logic caught up with me and informed me it was just the heater switching on. Luckily, I resisted the urge to pull the trigger.

Anderson made a sound that could have been a snort of disdain or a muffled laugh. Without being able to see his face, I couldn't tell. My hand was sweating in his. I did one more quick scan of the entryway, and that was when I noticed Anderson wasn't completely invisible, as I'd thought. I could sort of see him as a vague shadow, a deep black against the predawn darkness, but only out of my peripheral vision. If I looked straight at him, it was as if he wasn't there.

"I'll go first around every corner," Anderson told me, giving my hand a little tug and leading me through a laundry room that was to the right of the entry.

That sounded almost like the beginnings of a plan. Emphasis on *almost*. Being mostly invisible, Anderson wasn't likely to get shot or otherwise attacked when he walked into a room, so it made sense for him to go first. It would have made *more* sense if we'd had some idea of what we'd do if he rounded a corner and found Konstantin waiting. The way Anderson was acting, I thought it more than likely he'd dispense with any hint of caution and rush into mortal combat. The best I could do in that case was zip in after him and hope I could get a shot at Konstantin before he sprang whatever surprise he had waiting for us.

To say I wasn't happy with our "plan" was an understatement, but I followed Anderson into the belly of the beast anyway.

The house was as huge as I'd expected, and I couldn't help wondering what a single guy needed with all that. My dearly departed condo had been a little over two thousand square feet, and I'd thought *that* was more than enough. The floors, when they weren't covered with Persian rugs, were all marble or hardwood, and my rubber-soled boots made squeaking noises when I walked no matter how carefully I stepped. Anderson and I both ended up taking off our shoes and leaving them in the hallway for the sake of stealth. I left my parka as well.

There was a faint musty smell in the air, and even in the darkness, I could see that some of the furniture was collecting dust. The aura of genteel neglect made me feel like I was picking my way through a haunted house. The unsettling half glimpses I kept getting of Anderson out of the corner of my eye weren't helping any, nor was the feeling of his invisible hand on me. It wasn't just my hand that was sweaty anymore. The heat was turned on too high for my tastes, but it was the nerves that were making me perspire. Whatever was about to happen, I wished it would just happen already.

A thorough search of the first floor failed to reveal Konstantin. I couldn't decide if I was relieved or disappointed. Anderson tugged me toward the staircase leading up to the second floor. I was still taut as a guitar string about to break, but as soon as I'd walked up those first few steps, I felt a strange reluctance to go any farther. Maybe it was just because it was so dark at the head of the stairs that I couldn't see where we were going.

No . . .

"Wait," I whispered, giving Anderson's hand a little tug for emphasis. I tried to sort through what I was feeling, tried to isolate whatever sense made me reluctant to go up the stairs, but the more I tried to focus on it, the vaguer it became, until I wasn't sure it wasn't all my imagination.

"What is it?" Anderson asked when I just stood there.

"It might not mean anything," I hedged. "But for some reason I didn't want to go up the stairs. The feeling is gone now."

I heard a sigh that echoed how I felt. I wished my damn powers would provide blinking neon signs instead of subtle, ephemeral hunches.

"It means something," Anderson said, and I felt him changing direction and starting down the stairs.

When hunting monsters, even those in human form, the last thing I want to do is go exploring dark basements, but it looked like that was what I was going to have to do.

"I don't like this," I muttered.

"Just stay behind me," was Anderson's only reply.

During our search, we'd found two doors that opened on stairs leading down. Whether they led to two separate basements, or were two ways to the same basement, was yet to be determined. I didn't feel any strong preference for one stairway or another, so Anderson and I chose the one closest to us.

There's nothing quite like looking down pitch-black stairs to raise the hairs on the back of your neck, especially when you're stupid enough to be descending them into the darkness. We'd been making our way through the rest of the house with the aid of the predawn light that filtered through the various windows, but we would have no such help in the basement. I hated the idea of lighting a beacon to let anyone in visual range know we were coming, but we wouldn't have much luck finding Konstantin if we couldn't see our hands in front of our faces.

The constant pinging of my nerves was making me punchy, and I almost laughed as I thought that Anderson couldn't see his hand in front of his face regardless. I swallowed the laugh and tugged my hand out of Anderson's grip. I was holding the gun in my right hand, and there was no way I was putting it away to get my cell phone out of my pocket. Anderson made a small sound of protest.

"Flashlight app," I hissed in explanation. I had my phone set to airplane mode so it wouldn't make any inconvenient sounds that might give us away, but I supposed if I was going to use it as a flashlight, that was a wasted effort.

I worried for a moment that Anderson would try to veto the flashlight, but he had to know fumbling around in the dark wasn't going to do us any good. With another sigh, he became fully visible again.

"Don't suppose there's any point in hiding anymore," he mumbled under his breath. "Stay behind me anyway."

It seemed to me like the person with the flashlight should lead the way, but I didn't think Anderson was going to let me take point. Mutely, I handed him my phone, and he took it without comment. We continued down the stairs.

The light from the phone wasn't exactly powerful, and the darkness of the basement was oppressive as all hell, even once we made it safely out of the stairwell. The stairs opened onto a somewhat puny gym, with a small collection of free weights and an ancient-looking treadmill. However, I smelled chlorine in the air, and sure enough, when we made it through the gym, the next door opened onto an impressive lap pool. The pool was big enough that my light couldn't illuminate the far end of it, but when Anderson and I made a circuit of the deck, we still saw no sign of Konstantin. We peeked behind a couple of closed doors that turned out to be changing rooms, and then we found yet another stairway, this one leading even farther down.

How many freaking floors did this mansion have?

The hairs on the back of my neck prickled yet again. This stairway was far narrower than the previous one, the steps nothing more than bare planks. We weren't going to be finding any fancy exercise equipment down there.

Anderson looked at me, and I shrugged. My instincts weren't talking to me, and I had no idea whether we should continue down these stairs or go back up to the ground floor and try the other stairway we'd seen up there. We hadn't found any evidence of it opening onto this first basement anywhere.

"We might as well check it out while we're here," Anderson whispered, though why he was bothering to whisper when the flashlight was giving us away, I don't know.

He went first down the stairs, and I followed reluctantly. It was so tight and claustrophobic, even with the flashlight, that I had a hard time forcing myself to take each step. The wooden steps seemed rickety, and they creaked, further removing any hope we might have of keeping the element of surprise. Not that I thought we had it in the first place.

I was about halfway down the stairs, and Anderson was about two thirds of the way down, when suddenly, the pitch-black staircase was flooded with blinding white light, so bright I couldn't possibly keep my eyes open. I heard Anderson's cry of dismay, and heard what I presumed was my cell phone thunking to the floor. I tried to force my eyes open in search of something to shoot, but the light was overpowering after the heavy darkness.

A step creaked behind me, and a gunshot nearly shattered my eardrums. Anderson made a strangled sound, which I could barely hear through the sudden ringing in my ears. I felt the vibration under my feet as he fell. The light hurt, stabbing through my head like ice picks, and there was no way I could open my eyes. I turned, meaning to shoot blindly up the staircase behind me. I didn't know if my supernatural aim could work if I had no idea what my target was, but it was worth a try.

Whoever was behind me moved faster than I did,

and something hard and heavy smashed into the side of my face. Pain short-circuited my brain, and I tried to take a step backward to steady myself. Not such a great idea on a staircase. My foot came down on empty air, and I plummeted downward. My reflexes tried to save me, but there was nothing to grab on to, and all I could do was drop the gun. The light dimmed, and I managed to squint my eyes open just a tiny bit.

Enough to see Cyrus, wearing wraparound sunglasses and holding a gun, standing on the stairs and watching me fall.

TWENTY-FIVE

I went down the last of the stairs in a painful and undignified tumble. My ears were still ringing from the gunshot in the enclosed space, and I felt more than I heard the ominous crack a fraction of a second before white-hot pain stabbed through my chest.

There's nothing that hurts quite so much as a broken rib, and if I'd had any air in my lungs I'd have screamed at the pain. The rib jolted again when I landed in a heap at the base of the stairs, my body piled atop Anderson's. The light was no longer blindingly bright, but it was as if I'd stared directly at the sun, the afterimage burned into my retinas. Cyrus was nothing more than a shadowy form descending the stairs toward me.

The pain got the better of me and I blacked out.

I don't think it was for very long. Only enough for Cyrus to reach the bottom of the stairs and crouch over me. He tucked his gun into a holster on his belt, then grabbed mine from where it had landed on the basement floor. He was smart enough to unload it before sticking it in his pocket, though in the state I was in, I wasn't wrestling it away from him anytime soon. My rib screamed with every breath I took, my exposed skin seemed to have gotten a serious sunburn from the bright light, and my face throbbed where Cyrus had hit me. I probably had a bunch of other injuries, too, but my rib and face hurt the worst. My head was a little woozy, and it took me a heartbeat or two to realize I was no longer lying atop Anderson's body.

"I'm sorry about this, Nikki," Cyrus said, flashing me a sad and sympathetic smile. He took off the wraparound glasses and stuck them into his shirt pocket. I guess the light had been so bright that even the descendant of a sun god needed protection from it.

Before I could tell him what to do with his apology—before, in fact, I was conscious and coherent enough to do or say much of anything—he had turned me over onto my stomach. My rib didn't appreciate the movement, and I couldn't suppress a scream of pain, even though the scream itself hurt just as much.

"Sorry," Cyrus said again as he hauled my arms around behind my back and fastened what felt suspiciously like handcuffs around my wrists.

I was in no position to object to his rough treatment, and the breath-stealing pain kept me from retorting. Once my hands were bound, Cyrus sat on my legs, and I felt him pulling up the cuffs of my pants. The clinking sound of metal warned me what he was about to do, but with my hands behind my back and his weight holding me down, there was nothing I could do to stop him from shackling my ankles together.

I blinked away tears of pain and tried to breathe. When Cyrus had turned me over, I'd come to rest with my head facing the base of the stairs, giving me a disturbing view of a large pool of blood. I presumed it was Anderson's, since as far as I knew, I wasn't injured enough to leak that much. It was enough blood that I knew Anderson hadn't moved himself out from under me, and that meant Cyrus wasn't alone.

Steeling myself against yet another blast of pain, I turned my head so that I was facing the main part of the room.

Actually, calling it a "room" was a bit of an exaggeration. It was really just an unfinished, unadorned basement. The floor was ugly gray concrete, and the walls were cheap Peg-Board, like you might see in some handyman's garage, only there were no tools on any of the pegs.

In the center of the floor was an ominous black hole, about the size of a manhole, though I didn't think there were too many people who had manholes in their basements, and I saw no sign of a cover anywhere. Beside the hole, there was a large collection of what looked like steel girders, only they'd been cut up into little sections, maybe six or eight inches long and piled about three feet high. And beside those girders, looming over Anderson's limp body, was Konstantin.

Having finished securing my legs, Cyrus grabbed me under my arms and pulled me into a seated position, dragging me a couple feet so my back could rest against the wall. I could tell he wasn't actively trying to hurt me, but when you've got a broken rib, *everything* hurts. He winced in what looked like sympathy. Some of my hair was sticking to the tears on my cheeks, and Cyrus reached out to brush it away and tuck it behind my ear. I jerked away from his touch, practically knocking myself out as my head reminded me I'd been pistol-whipped about two minutes ago.

Cyrus pulled his hand away, and I saw that his fingers were wet with blood, rather than tears. "I didn't want the wound to heal around your hair," he said.

How considerate of him.

"Guess everything you told me on the phone this morning was a lie, huh?" I asked. I'd thought after seeing him kill Emma with such cool dispassion that I'd allowed myself to see Cyrus as he truly was, that I'd gotten over thinking he wasn't really such a bad guy. But the stab of betrayal as my head cleared enough for me to figure out what was happening said I hadn't quite gotten there yet.

" 'Fraid so," he said, sitting back on his haunches.

"Why?" I shook my head, hardly able to believe how wrong we'd all been about him, thinking him a lesser evil than Konstantin.

Cyrus glanced over his shoulder briefly, taking in the sight of his father looming over Anderson. When he turned back to me, there was an expression of grim determination in his eyes.

"Because when Anderson's gone, Blake will have no choice but to rejoin the Olympians."

My jaw dropped open. I hadn't even come close to seeing that one coming.

"How I managed to raise a son with a sentimental streak, I'll never know," Konstantin said, and there was no missing the disdain in his voice.

"You don't have to understand," Cyrus said tightly without looking at his father. "You just have to stick to the deal."

My stomach felt like it was doing the cancan, and I wasn't sure whether it was because I was sickened by what Cyrus was doing, or if he'd actually given me a concussion when he'd hit me. Maybe both.

My head wasn't as clear as I would have liked, and my sense of time was definitely out of whack, but I was pretty sure it had been at least a couple of minutes since Anderson had been shot. If I could keep father and son talking long enough for him to come back to life . . .

"I thought you were enjoying your Blake substitute," I said, trying to sneer. I think it came out more like a grimace of pain, but Cyrus was appropriately needled anyway.

"Why settle for a substitute when I can have the real thing? Blake never belonged with you people anyway. He really wants to be one of the good guys, but it just doesn't suit him."

"And you think taking out Anderson and letting your daddy kill the rest of us is going to send Blake running into your arms?" It was a little easier to muster a real sneer this time. I hadn't thought much of Blake when I'd first met him, and I still didn't think a whole lot of him dating my sister. But I *did* think he was basically a good guy, with a good heart. It was hard to imagine what he'd ever seen in Cyrus—at least, it was hard for me to imagine it now, when Cyrus was flaunting his true nature—but I didn't for a moment believe Blake would forgive and forget.

Cyrus shrugged. "If his choices are run into my arms or die, he'll run into my arms." One corner of his mouth tipped up in a fond smile. "He's a survivor." The smile faded quickly, and Cyrus's voice dropped to a whisper. "I'll save as many of your people as I can, Nikki. I'm not doing this because I want anyone to get hurt."

Words couldn't describe how much he disgusted me in that moment. I felt a chill of fear as I thought about what would happen to the rest of Anderson's *Liberi* if Anderson were no longer around to protect them. Leo, Maggie, and Blake might be able to become Olympians, if they could stomach it. They were all descended from Greek gods, which was the primary membership requirement for the Olympians. But Jack, and Logan, and Jamaal . . .

And let's not even talk about what would happen to *me*. I might not be Olympian material despite my ancestry, but I was a rare and useful tool, and I held no illusions that there would be a quick and easy death in my future.

But of course, nothing was going to happen to

Anderson. He was a freaking god, and he was going to come back to life any second now. Once he did—

Another gunshot rang out. Cyrus flinched and ducked, his hands going up to his ears. He quickly lowered them again and glared over his shoulder at Konstantin.

"Some warning would be nice next time," he shouted. At least, I was pretty sure he was shouting, because otherwise I wouldn't have been able to hear him over the renewed ringing in my ears. If I were an ordinary mortal, I'd be seriously worried about permanent hearing damage.

Of course, the ringing ears weren't the worst of my problems. Konstantin had just shot Anderson a second time, which meant any healing progress was back to square one. Killing Anderson every few minutes was a surefire way to keep him out of the picture, though obviously Konstantin had something else in mind. The yawning hole in the floor suggested that some kind of burial was forthcoming. Anderson had dismissed potential burial as a threat—maybe he could move through the earth as easily as he could move through walls—but I wasn't exactly eager to put it to the test.

"If you don't like it, hurry up and finish your touching good-bye before I have to do it again," Konstantin replied.

"It's not really a good-bye," Cyrus hastened to reassure me. "You don't have to take my word for it, even. You know you're too valuable to kill."

"Actually, that doesn't make me feel any better," I said between clenched teeth.

"If you can find it in yourself to cooperate, things will go much easier for you."

My rib was still hurting like hell, but I managed to suck in a deep breath of indignation anyway. "You advising me to lie back and think of England?" I growled at him.

He wouldn't meet my eyes. "It's the best advice I can give under the circumstances."

"As if I would ever take advice from *you*," I replied in disgust, hating myself for letting his charming smile lull me for even a moment. "You're nothing but a liar and a fraud. I should never have believed a single word that came out of your mouth."

"I can't argue that I'm not a liar," Cyrus admitted. "But for what it's worth, I was telling you the truth most of the time. I didn't know my father was behind any of this until last night."

Konstantin interrupted with an exaggerated snort. "Now tell her if it would have made a difference if you had."

"It might!" Cyrus snapped over his shoulder, and his father laughed at him.

"As long as I promised to give you Blake, you'd have done whatever I told you to do."

Cyrus's face flushed with anger. I didn't know why he was getting so pissed off. Did he really think it made a difference whether he'd been lying from the beginning or just since his phone call this morning? "Then why *didn't* you tell me?" Cyrus countered.

"Because I would have had to watch you wring

your hands and listen to you whine about it." Konstantin gave Anderson a nudge with his foot, as if to reassure himself that he was still dead. Then he turned to me. "My dear son has pretensions of moral superiority. He doesn't mind making an omelet, as long as he doesn't have to break the eggs himself."

The anger that flared in Cyrus's eyes made me hope he and Konstantin were going to get into a fight. I didn't know exactly how I was going to take advantage of that fight, but I was sure I would find a way to do *something* useful while they weren't looking.

Unfortunately, they weren't stupid enough to give me the opportunity.

Cyrus stood up straight, wiping the remainder of my blood off his hand and onto his pants. "I don't think it's a character flaw that I don't enjoy hurting people."

Cyrus had his back to Konstantin and couldn't see his father rolling his eyes. For once, Konstantin and I were in agreement about something. It might make Cyrus more comfortable if someone else did the dirty work for him, but the fact that he didn't enjoy it and would rather not see it didn't make him a better person. Nor did the fact that he seemed to feel at least a little bad about it.

"You're worse than *he* is," I said to Cyrus. "At least he's not a hypocrite!"

Cyrus hung his head in what looked suspiciously like shame. The look on his face said he actually did feel more than a little bad about what he was doing, and I suspected he was fully aware of the hypocrisy of his own position. The question was, was there some way I could take advantage of his vulnerabilities and turn him against his father? Because I didn't care *what* Anderson had told me about how Konstantin couldn't do anything to him. Konstantin had a plan, and a reason to believe it would work. Anderson might be a god, but that didn't mean he was never wrong, and this would be the world's worst time to prove it.

"Don't do this," I begged. "Blake still cares about you. I can hear it in his voice when he talks about you. You can work things out with him if you want to. But not if you kill all the other people he cares about. You do that, and he'll hate you, and you'll never have what you really want."

My impassioned plea missed its mark.

"He'll hate me at first," Cyrus conceded. "But you know what they say about time healing all wounds. I'm willing to wait." A tiny smile played along his lips. "And I think I'll enjoy the challenge of trying to seduce him and win him back."

Cyrus stepped over my outstretched legs, carefully avoiding the pool of Anderson's blood as he put his foot on the first step. I realized that meant he wasn't going to stick around and watch whatever Konstantin was planning to do to Anderson and me. I also realized that meant whatever unpleasantness was in store for us would likely start as soon as he left the basement.

I did *not* want him to leave the basement.

"Cyrus! Wait!"

I had no arguments left to make, no hope that Cyrus was going to change his mind. In fact, I had only two hopes left: that I could keep delaying things until Konstantin got careless and didn't shoot fast enough to keep Anderson dead; or that Anderson was right and there truly was nothing Konstantin could do to him in the long run. Neither one felt like a spectacularly strong possibility to pin my hopes on, but Cyrus shattered hope number one when he ignored me and started up the stairs.

"I'm sorry, Nikki," he said again, shaking his head.

I let out an incoherent cry of rage and frustration—and not a little fear—as the stairwell swallowed Cyrus. Moments later, I heard the door at the head of the stairs open and close.

And it was time to find out exactly what Konstantin had planned.

TWENTY-SIX

Konstantin stared at the ceiling. Possibly, he was listening to Cyrus's retreating footsteps, but all I could hear was the rushing of my blood in my ears. My rib still sent daggers of pain through my body with every breath, but I no longer felt blood trickling down the side of my face. All in all, I was in a lot better shape than Anderson was.

To make sure that remained the case, Konstantin shot Anderson yet again.

Anderson's head was a bloody mess. He was never going to recover unless I could find a way to stop Konstantin from shooting him every couple of minutes. My stomach lurched unhappily. I told myself I had a concussion, because a tough chick like me had no business vomiting at the sight of blood. Never mind that I'd once tossed my cookies looking at crime-scene photos.

"Did you tell Cyrus Anderson's big secret?" I

asked. Not that I actually cared. I was just looking for an opening, some way to distract Konstantin long enough to let Anderson heal.

For one unguarded moment, I saw shock on Konstantin's face. He hadn't realized I knew that Anderson was a god. He hid his emotions quickly, but I cursed myself for opening my big mouth. Konstantin didn't want anyone to know Anderson was a god, because he didn't want anyone getting the idea that he himself wasn't the most powerful being in the universe. And I might have just signed my own death warrant by admitting what I knew.

The scary thing was, I would probably be way, way better off if Konstantin killed me than if he kept me alive.

"I didn't see any reason to burden him with that knowledge," Konstantin said, giving me a once-over that made my skin crawl. I couldn't have looked that appealing with my face all bloody and my hair scraggling out of its braid. My flannel shirt was blandly shapeless and buttoned to the top for warmth. And yet Konstantin's leer told me he liked the way I looked just fine.

Maybe he just liked how a woman looked in chains.

It was hard not to squirm when Konstantin looked at me like that. I knew he was a rapist, and I hoped like hell that Anderson was going to come back to life sooner rather than later, before Konstantin decided he was in the mood to play.

"So what's your big plan, anyway?" I asked as

nonchalantly as I could. "Are you going to stand there and shoot Anderson in the head every couple of minutes for the rest of eternity? Because personally, I think that would get old after a while."

I was trying to get under Konstantin's skin, but his smile said he was finding me more entertaining than annoying. On another man, the smile would have looked genuine and disarming. Konstantin wasn't traditionally handsome, but he knew how to make the most of what he had. His neat black beard disguised what I suspected was a weak chin, and I'd never seen him wearing anything other than designer suits. Today was no exception, though the suit was well on its way toward being ruined. Anderson's blood spotted his pants legs and the bottom of his jacket.

"Actually, I've quite enjoyed it," Konstantin said, his smile morphing into a phony frown. "Though I'd enjoy it more if he were alive to feel it."

I shuddered. Cyrus might not enjoy hurting people, but Konstantin sure did. I wished Anderson had listened to me, though truthfully, I'm not sure what kind of plan we could have made to avoid this. We couldn't have gotten to Konstantin without descending the stairs into the basement, and once we were in the stairway, we were sitting ducks.

Konstantin's smile returned, and there was now an unpleasant gleam in his eyes to go with it. "But no matter. I'm sure I can find other ways to entertain myself once I've removed this thorn from my side."

He tucked the gun into the waist of his pants. I hoped it would go off and blow his balls to smithereens. The damage would heal, but I suspected the pain would distract him for a good long while.

Unfortunately, my hopes were in vain. Konstantin bent down and grabbed Anderson's arm, dragging him closer to the hole in the floor. The man might have looked like a fop in a fancy suit, but he was clearly carrying some muscle underneath, because dragging Anderson's lifeless body didn't even make him break a sweat.

My mouth went dry, and my heart rate jumped to red alert. I was aware of Konstantin watching me, savoring my reaction. I tried my best to keep my face neutral, but I don't think I succeeded. I bit my lip when Anderson's head slid over the edge of the hole, flopping limply into the darkness.

Konstantin kept dragging on Anderson's arm, until Anderson's shoulders crossed the edge and his upper body tilted precariously.

One more tug, and Konstantin let go of Anderson's arm, tossing it into the mouth of the hole. The weight of his arm was enough to tip the scales, and Anderson started slipping into the hole, headfirst. I wanted to howl in rage, but I somehow managed to stifle the sound. Still, a little whimper worked its way out of my mouth as Anderson fell. When he hit the bottom of the hole, there was a metallic clang. I didn't know what it meant.

"Anderson can walk through walls," I said, my voice shaking. "He can get out of there."

If nothing else, he'd be able to brace himself against the sides of the hole and inch his way up. But

I knew there was more to Konstantin's plan than just dumping Anderson in a hole.

Konstantin leaned over the hole and fired three quick shots. It would be nice if that were the last of his bullets, but I didn't think he was careless enough to let that happen.

"It's very hard to keep death-god descendants contained," Konstantin agreed. "I found that out the hard way, as you know. I imagine it's even harder with an actual god." He grabbed one of the sections of girder stacked beside the hole, dropping it down. "I don't know if he has some kind of animal he can conjure to dig him out if I bury him." This time, he used both hands and threw two sections down at once. "But I'm not about to take chances."

"What are you going to do?" I didn't know how tossing pieces of steel down into the hole was going to help keep Anderson trapped, but I had a sick feeling I would soon find out.

"After my mistake with Justin, I've decided a little overkill is in order." He got impatient with throwing the steel down one piece at a time, positioning himself behind a stack of pieces and giving them a mighty shove.

I winced, even knowing that Anderson was currently dead down there and couldn't feel all those heavy pieces of metal raining down upon his vulnerable flesh.

Konstantin looked over the edge of the hole and nodded in satisfaction. "That ought to be enough," he said, more to himself than to me.

He held out both his hands toward the hole. "I reinforced the hole with steel pipe, and put a good size layer of girders on the bottom."

A blast of heat sucked all the moisture from my eyes and mouth. I couldn't see very well from where I was sitting, but my skin felt seared and raw from the heat, and the edges of the hole began to glow, first red, then white.

The steel was melting.

I screamed out a protest as the sides of the hole began to melt and run, flowing downward into the hole. I thought of all those pieces of metal Konstantin had tossed down there, melting around Anderson's body, burning the flesh from his bones.

Konstantin smiled and made a big show of dusting off his hands. "Even a god will take some time to recover from the damage all that molten metal will do. And when he does, the steel will have cooled around him. He'll be trapped like a bug in amber."

I was crying again, dammit. I tried to hold on to the hope that Anderson was as indestructible as he'd thought he was. "B-but, he can walk through walls. He can get out of the metal."

Konstantin took one last, satisfied glance at the hole, then sauntered toward me. I wanted to scoot away from him, but there was nowhere I could go. The best I could do was draw my bound legs up toward my chest as he squatted beside me with that smug, sadistic smile.

"Let me explain some basic rules of physics to you," he said. "A human body cannot pass through a solid object. Death-god descendants pass through walls by making themselves incorporeal, but they can't actually move themselves when they're incorporeal. Imagine them like astronauts, floating through the vacuum of space. If you give them a push, then the momentum will keep them going indefinitely. But if you could drop them into the vacuum in complete stillness, then they'd have no momentum to move them, and nothing to push against to give them momentum. A death-god descendant takes a step toward whatever barrier is in his way, giving himself momentum. Only then can he go incorporeal and keep moving.

"Anderson will awaken completely immobilized by his metal casing. He can go incorporeal all he wants, but with no momentum, all he can do is flail around." Konstantin frowned dramatically. "It might have been enough just to immobilize him by burial. After all, Kerner could go incorporeal, but he couldn't get out of his grave until his jackals dug him out. But, as I said, overkill seems like a good idea."

Konstantin sat back on his heels with a happy sigh as I tried to absorb the horror of what he'd just told me. I really wanted to find a flaw in his theory, or at least to believe he was lying. But no, he was way too happy and self-satisfied. He was sure Anderson wasn't getting out of that hole. Ever. And I was beginning to fear he might be right.

TWENTY-SEVEN

I was deathly afraid of whatever Konstantin was going to do next. Even if there was some miraculous way Anderson could escape when encased in solid metal, I was sure it would take a while. Hell, it would probably take a while before he could possibly come back to life. I had no idea how long it would take that molten metal to cool, but I was sure its temperature would be lethal for quite some time.

Meanwhile, I was chained hand and foot and trapped with a man who thought rape and torture were fun. The only other living person who knew where I was was Cyrus, and he'd made it abundantly clear that he had no intention of saving me.

In short, it was looking spectacularly bad for the home team, and I was fighting the very reasonable urge to panic. I tried to wriggle my hands out of the cuffs, willing to take off as many layers of skin as necessary to escape them, but I didn't think I was getting out of them without removing a few pesky bones from my hand.

Konstantin licked his lips, and I couldn't tell if it was an unconscious gesture, or if he was trying to feed my panic. He smiled over his shoulder at the hole in the floor, the contents of which were still emitting a faint red glow.

"I'm sure that will hold him," he said, turning back to me, "but a little more overkill can't hurt."

I tried to flinch away as he reached for me. All I managed to do was tip myself over. Konstantin grabbed me by the waist, then flung me over his shoulder in a fireman's carry. I wished I could struggle more effectively, but it's hard to do much of anything when your hands are cuffed behind your back and your ankles are shackled.

"Patience, Nikki dear," Konstantin said as he started up the narrow stairs. "I'll give you plenty of things to get excited about later, but being carried up the stairs isn't one of them. You might want to save your energy."

Raw terror coursed through my veins with every beat of my heart. There was nothing I could do to get his hands off me. The sense of helplessness and dread was crushing, but I was never, ever going to give up fighting. I struggled and squirmed, not caring that getting free of Konstantin at this moment meant another painful tumble down the stairs, but I'm a small woman, and Konstantin was way too strong for me.

Konstantin paused when we reached the pool deck.

"I wonder how long it would take you to bend to my will if I dropped you in the pool for a while. It certainly helped put our dear, departed Emma in a more accommodating state of mind."

I struggled even harder as Konstantin walked to the edge of the pool. I didn't want to die ever again, and from everything I'd heard, drowning is a very unpleasant way to go. A life that alternated between drowning and being suspended in the airless dark of death wasn't worth living. Maybe I should have been hoping he followed through with the threat, because at least while he was drowning me, he wouldn't be raping me, but I wanted to live. Where there's life, there's hope, right?

Konstantin sighed in mock regret. "Such a shame the pool is too shallow. Of course, there is that lovely pond out back. As you might have noticed, I wouldn't have any trouble melting all that inconvenient ice."

Oh good, I wasn't going to be drowning in the next five seconds. One could argue that things were looking up.

Konstantin continued on past the pool, carrying me up to the ground floor and then wending his way through the house to the back door. I remembered his previous comments about overkill and wondered what the hell he was up to. If he was planning some additional safeguard to reassure himself that Anderson was trapped, then why was he leaving the house?

I hadn't realized my clothes were damp with sweat until we made it outside and a blast of wind plastered them tightly against my skin. I started shivering almost immediately. Konstantin wasn't wearing a coat, but the cold didn't seem to bother him. Maybe he could generate his own heat using his powers. Or maybe his excitement over whatever torture he had in mind was enough to keep him warm.

I had mostly stopped struggling. I was just too exhausted to keep it up, and while I was determined to fight to the bitter end, I had decided to conserve my energy for that mythical moment where fighting might actually do some good.

Slung over Konstantin's shoulder as I was, I couldn't see where we were going, but then I didn't *need* to see. We were going to the pond, of course. Whether he truly meant to toss me in there or was just trying to push my fear to the max, I didn't know.

I didn't have a properly scaled map of the property in my head, but when Konstantin came to a stop, I knew we weren't anywhere near far enough away from the house to have reached the pond yet. Konstantin let go of me and ducked his shoulder so I would roll helplessly off. I hit the snow with a cry of pain as my broken rib reminded me it hadn't finished healing yet.

"You might want to watch this," Konstantin said, reaching down and dragging me into a sitting position by the collar of my shirt.

I sat panting and shivering in the snow, my eyes squeezed half shut as I waited out the pain. Konstantin stood slightly in front of me and held out his hands like he had in the basement. Ignoring the biting cold, I let my fingers sift through whatever snow they could reach, hoping to find something I could use as a weapon. There was no way I could throw anything with my hands bound behind me, but I might be able to use my feet.

It was a long shot, no doubt about it. But a long shot was better than no shot, so I kept searching.

Once again, I felt a blast of heat, and something like an invisible fireball shot from Konstantin's hands toward the house. I could track its progress as it evaporated the snow in its path. It expanded as it traveled, growing wider until when it hit the house it was almost wide enough to engulf it.

The moment Konstantin's fireball hit the house, it went up in flames, the walls practically melting away. The fire spread instantly, racing around the walls and over the roof. Windows shattered, and the flames crawled in like living things, all blue and white with heat. I'd been shivering and cold a moment ago, but now I felt like I was sitting in an oven.

In a matter of seconds, the entire house was ablaze, the flames roaring with the fury of a forest fire. Konstantin basked in the glow of the fire for a moment, then frowned.

"Hmm," he said. "Perhaps we're still standing a little too close."

It was almost unbearably hot, and I was more than happy to put some more distance between myself and the fire. I'd have liked it a lot better if Konstantin hadn't moved me by grabbing hold of my braid and dragging me through the melting snow. Despite the pain, I kept trying to sift through the snow with my fingers in search of a weapon. Unfortunately, the snow was covering a lawn, and there aren't a whole lot of useful throwing weapons lying about on your average lawn.

Konstantin had dragged me all of about five feet when there was a deafening, earthshaking *boom*. He let go of my hair and dropped to the ground as the flaming house collapsed, the walls falling in upon themselves. Out of the corner of my eye, I saw Konstantin covering his head, and I wished I could do the same. There was another blast, even louder than the first, and a huge cloud of smoke and dirt and debris fountained into the air.

I had no way to protect myself as the debris came raining down. The best I could do was curl into the smallest ball possible and hope nothing too big and lethal landed on me. Flaming pieces of house dropped to the ground all around me. A couple of the missiles hit me, including one that nearly lit my pants leg on fire, but I rolled enough for the wet snow to snuff it out.

When the debris rain had lessened enough for me to risk it, I sat up and looked all around me.

The house was completely gone, nothing but a burned-out, debris-filled, smoldering crater where it had once sat. Konstantin had seemed to know the explosion was coming, and I figured that meant he had set up explosives so that the house would fall down directly over the basement where he'd stashed Anderson. Now I saw what he meant by overkill, though to tell you the truth, if being encased in metal didn't keep Anderson contained, I doubted the weight of an entire mansion crumbling on top of him would, either. Still, it made for quite the spectacular show.

I hoped that a stray piece of debris had crushed Konstantin like the bug he was, but he'd actually gotten us pretty close to the edge of the debris field before the charges went off. There were bits and pieces lying on the still-melting snow around us, but most of the heavy stuff had come down closer to the house, and except for his seriously destroyed designer suit, Konstantin was unharmed. His eyes were practically glowing with pleasure as he eyed the destruction.

For the moment, his attention was not focused on me, and I knew I had to take advantage of his distraction in any way I could. The nice, grassy back lawn had been a poor candidate for providing a projectile weapon, but thanks to Konstantin's overkill, there was now a lot of potentially handy debris lying about.

I searched the ground around me. I needed something heavy enough to do some damage, yet small and light enough that I could either lift it with my bound feet, or at least slip my feet under it so I could give it a kick. And it also needed to be close enough that I could get to it before Konstantin noticed I was getting ready to try something.

Moments ago, I'd been glad we were out of the worst of the debris field, but now I wished I had more larger chunks around me. Most of it was too small to do any significant damage. However, I did spot a broken piece of brick not too far away. A normal person wouldn't have been able to do any damage with that piece of brick unless they could really wind up and throw it like a baseball, but I thought it possible that with my aim, I might be able to do it.

Keeping an eye on Konstantin, I wriggled and squirmed my way toward the brick, angling my body so my feet would get there first. Despite the fact that my socks were soaking wet from melted snow and my feet beneath them felt frostbitten in places and burned in others, I was glad I'd taken off my boots while in the house, because I was definitely more agile without them.

I managed to wriggle my toes under the piece of brick, then positioned myself so I could get the best momentum behind my kick/throw. Konstantin was still looking at the crater. The brick felt alarmingly light under my feet, and I knew it was all going to come down to perfect placement. I had to hit Konstantin in just the right spot to disable him, and in my experience, the eye is just about anyone's most vulnerable spot. Lots of soft tissue to damage, some delicate bones that can shatter, and let's face it, there's a certain terror factor to feeling your eye squish.

I needed him facing me, and closer.

"Are you posing for a picture or something?" I jeered, and he finally managed to drag his attention away from the ex-house.

"I was observing a moment of silence for Anderson," he replied with heavy sarcasm, and though he was looking at me, I could tell his attention was still divided. Which was good, because if he realized I had a weapon within my reach (sort of), he might decide to shoot me before coming any closer.

"But if you're impatient to find out what I have planned for you, I'll be happy to hurry things along."

He was smiling his smug smile, jovial, arrogant, secure in his victory. Just the way I wanted him. He took a whopping two steps in my direction before he noticed the positioning of my feet. His eyes widened, and as he stepped backward, he reached for the gun still sticking out of his pants.

I wanted him closer, but it was now or never.

Putting every bit of strength I could muster into it, I scooped up the piece of brick, using the backs of my feet rather like a lacrosse stick, and kicked my bound legs as hard as I could toward Konstantin's face.

I had taken Jamaal's eye out once with a well-aimed toss of a stiletto-heeled shoe, but I wasn't quite as lucky this time. The brick hit Konstantin's eye, and he fell to the ground with a gratifying scream of pain, but though he clutched the socket, there was no sign of blood leaking through his fingers.

I hadn't taken out his eye, but for a few precious moments, he was going to be in too much pain to retaliate. I couldn't let him have time to recover.

I spotted another piece of brick, even smaller than the first, positioned between me and Konstantin. I wriggled toward it and kicked it at Konstantin's head. He was protecting his wounded eye with his hand, but his other eye made a good target.

The second piece of brick didn't hurt him as much. The hand that wasn't clutching his wounded eye pulled his gun from his belt, and I had to duck as he fired a couple of blind shots in my direction. I suspected he'd get me with a lucky shot before I was able to pitch enough debris at him to incapacitate him, so I needed another plan.

I hunched in on myself, making myself as small a target as possible, then tried to contort myself enough to get my cuffed hands down below my butt. I'd tried this maneuver when I'd been duct taped in the trunk of the car and hadn't been able to manage it, but I had a lot more freedom of movement out here in the open. I practically tore both arms out of their sockets to do it, but I managed to get first my butt, then my legs, through the circle of my arms so my hands were in front of me. Still cuffed together, but it was an improvement.

Konstantin fired off another shot, and it splashed up muddy snow way too close to my head for comfort. He tried to fire again, but he was out of ammo.

"Probably shouldn't have wasted so many bullets on Anderson," I taunted, because I couldn't resist.

Konstantin dropped his hand from his eye, and though it was closed and swollen and obviously painful, he was going to be back to full capacity way sooner than I would like.

"I have more," he growled at me, reaching into his pants pocket.

Of course he did.

Bracing myself with my hands, I pushed to my

feet. I could move a little by shuffling, but by the time I got anywhere, Konstantin would be reloaded. He might not be able to aim as well as he'd like with one eye swollen shut, but I doubted he'd have any trouble hitting me with a full clip at his disposal. So instead of taking little shuffle-steps, I bunny-hopped.

I probably looked pretty ridiculous, but aesthetics were the last thing on my mind. I hopped toward another piece of debris, then bent to retrieve it and hurl it at Konstantin's hands. I didn't even know what I had thrown. It wasn't big or heavy enough to do damage, but it did cause him to drop his clip in the snow. I thought that was an improvement, until he abandoned the gun and clip and surged to his feet.

Even if I hadn't been bound hand and foot, Konstantin didn't need a gun to hurt me. He was a big, strong guy, and I bet he had plenty of experience wrestling women into submission.

I hopped away from him as fast as I could, my eyes frantically scanning the grass and snow for the perfect weapon.

I saw it about six feet away, a big chunk of concrete that might have come from the foundation. I wasn't going to be able to hop that distance before Konstantin tackled me, so I threw myself forward in a headfirst slide, my hands outstretched.

I might have put a little more oomph into that slide than was strictly necessary. I jammed my fingers against the concrete, breaking a few nails and possibly dislocating my middle finger. I swallowed the pain and wrapped my hands around the concrete, rolling into a sitting position so I could get some momentum on the throw.

At the last moment, Konstantin, who was almost on top of me, seemed to realize he had made a mistake. He tried to skid to a stop, holding his hands out in front of him. I think he was trying to summon another blast of heat, but it was too late.

I put my whole body into the awkward, two-handed, side-arm throw, and the chunk of concrete hit Konstantin right between the eyes.

He staggered and went down to his knees, blood streaming from his nose and from a large cut on his forehead. My throw had been too awkward, and he'd been too close for me to get enough momentum to knock him out. However, it had obviously made him woozy.

He flailed at me as I hopped over toward the chunk of concrete, but I think he was seeing double or triple, because he didn't come close to hitting me. I raised the concrete over my head, and this time I had a nice downward angle for my throw.

The concrete caved in the back of Konstantin's head, and he went down for the count.

TWENTY-EIGHT

I gave myself all of about three minutes to bask in my victory and enjoy the relief that flooded my system. Konstantin wasn't going to get his chance to rape and torture me, and though I was hurting in any number of places, the damage I'd sustained was all superficial enough that it would heal completely within an hour or two. Considering how grim my situation had been when Konstantin had carried me out here, it was quite a gratifying turnaround.

It didn't take long, however, for the logistics of my current situation to sink in.

Konstantin was dead, sure. But I was neither a mortal Descendant nor a death god, so he wasn't going to stay that way. I was still bound hand and foot. My phone was somewhere in the rubble beneath the house. We'd driven here in Anderson's car, and the keys were probably somewhere down there with my phone. Not that I liked my chances of making it to the car before Konstantin came back to life and tracked me down. Hopping wasn't the most efficient means of travel, and my legs were already feeling the burn. It didn't help that my supernatural healing ability sapped so much of my energy. It would probably take me hours, and plenty of rest stops, to get to the damn car, even if I had the keys. And let's not even talk about how I would be able to drive!

I was squeamish enough that I'd have preferred not to look at Konstantin's body. There was a lot of blood, and an obvious concave spot on his skull. However, unless I planned to stand here indefinitely in the freezing cold and conk him on the head every time he started to come back to life, I was going to have to get out of the handcuffs and shackles.

Praying under my breath that he would have the keys on him, I dropped to my knees beside him and started gingerly exploring his pockets. I kept my eyes narrowly focused on his body, not letting them stray to his ruined head, but my stomach was queasy anyway.

The good news was I didn't hurl. The bad news was, there were no handcuff keys on him. In another case of good news/bad news, he had a cell phone, but either he'd broken it during our struggle or its charge was dead. I had no way to get out of the handcuffs and shackles, and no way to call for help. It was possible one of the neighbors had heard the blast and called the cops, but I didn't think that would be a good thing. I did *not* want to try to explain the current situation to cops, and if Konstantin came back to life while there were witnesses . . .

I scanned the sky, trying to judge how likely it was that I had to start figuring out a cover story. The blast had been incredibly loud from close range, but in this neighborhood, there were acres of land between houses. I could imagine someone nearby being roused from their bed by the blast. They might even go look out their window in case they could see what had caused it. However, you couldn't see Alexis's ex-house without actually trespassing on the grounds. The fire had burned so fast and fierce that it had burned itself out already, but there was still plenty of smoke rising from the smoldering wreckage. The darkness wouldn't hide the smoke for long, which meant I had until dawn to get myself and Konstantin's body out of here.

I was frankly at a loss for what to do. With a lot of work, I *might* be able to drag Konstantin's body past the tree line, where he was less likely to be found right away. What I really needed was a *Liberi* extraction team to come get me. We would then have to find someplace secure where we could bury Konstantin's body. I still didn't like the idea, no matter how evil Konstantin was, but until we could get Anderson out from under all the rubble and saw through his metal casing, we didn't have anyone who was capable of making Konstantin's death permanent.

I now had something new to add to my list of things I didn't want to think about: how to get Anderson out. We would need a freaking excavation to get down to where he was, and somehow I didn't think it would be so easy to arrange an excavation on land that didn't belong to us.

I'd spent about fifteen minutes dithering, trying to come up with a plan that didn't suck, to no avail. Maybe it was my imagination, but when I forced myself to look, I thought the depression in Konstantin's skull was shallower than it had been.

Hitting a dead man in the head with a hunk of concrete shouldn't bother me so much. It wasn't like he could *feel* it. But it was still remarkably hard to get myself to do it. I'm just not the violent type. However, I couldn't risk him coming back to life.

Closing my eyes and turning my face away, I brought the concrete down on Konstantin's head. The nasty crunching sound it made when it hit his skull made my stomach turn over, and it took everything I had not to throw up. I was just not cut out for this sort of thing.

I put down the hunk of concrete, then lowered my face into my hands, momentarily overwhelmed. It didn't help that the heat from the fire had dissipated. I was shivering, and I couldn't feel my feet. It was bitterly cold out, and ice was forming on the surface of the puddles the melting snow had formed. Frostbite couldn't kill me, but it could make getting myself out of this mess even harder.

I was still hanging my head, my mind cycling through each of the possible things I could do next and hitting the same brick walls, when the sound of a throat clearing behind me made me scream and jump to my feet. The screaming part of that equation worked just fine. Jumping to my feet, not so much. It's amazingly hard to stand up when you can't feel your feet, especially when your ankles are shackled together.

I landed in a heap in the snow.

"I'm sorry," Anderson said. "I didn't think there was any way I could make my presence known without scaring you."

My jaw gaped open, and I turned to look at the smoldering ruins of the house. Then I turned to look at Anderson. My gaze dropped to his feet when I realized he was stark naked. He was standing in a pristine patch of snow about ten feet away from me, past the debris field and past where the heat from the fire had melted the snow. Which made the lack of footprints anywhere around him noticeable even while my mind was trying to encompass the idea that he was alive and free.

"H-how . . ." I gestured at the ruins and shook my head, unable to form a coherent question.

"I'm not sure exactly what happened," he said. He had to be freezing standing there in the snow in the nude, but there was no hint of shivering in his voice. "I take it I was inside when the house came down?"

Of course he wouldn't know what had happened. He'd been dead for most of it. I could have given him a blow-by-blow recap of what he'd missed. But only if my brain had actually been working.

"M-molten metal," I stammered incoherently.

"You were encased in molten metal and h-he brought the house down on t-top of you." The fact that I was well on my way to turning into a human Popsicle wasn't making my dialog any wittier or easier to understand.

I saw him nod out of the corner of my eye. He was completely unself-conscious about his nudity, but I couldn't say the same of myself.

"I can see why he'd have thought that might work."

I sucked in a deep breath, hoping it would help steady me. Instead, I merely froze my lungs a little more. "H-he said you wouldn't be able to move."

"He was right about that, at least." There was a hint of smugness in his voice, and I couldn't resist looking at him despite his nudity.

"Then how—?"

"I'm the son of Death, Nikki. There is one way to kill me, and it was not in Konstantin's power to do. But there is no power on earth that can contain me." He walked through the snow toward me—leaving footprints this time—and crouched so he was about at eye level. "You remember the Underworld, don't you?"

I shuddered and nodded. When I'd been hunting Justin Kerner, I'd discovered that some death-god descendants are able to use cemeteries as gateways to the Underworld. I couldn't tell you exactly what the Underworld *is*, even though I've been there, but it's not a place we mere humans can get to without aid. I knew that Anderson was able to use cemeteries that way—after all, he'd come into the Underworld to rescue me—but we weren't in a cemetery right now.

"Neither Alexis nor Konstantin was stupid enough to bury bodies on their own land, so unless we're sitting on top of some ancient burial ground, this isn't any form of cemetery," I said.

"Death-god descendants get to the Underworld by *creating* a gateway. I, on the other hand, *am* a gateway. I can create an entrance to the Underworld wherever I am. I told you Konstantin couldn't trap me by burial or drowning."

"You didn't mention being encased in molten metal."

He smiled. "I'm glad you still have your sense of humor."

I didn't actually find it all that funny. If Anderson had just come right out and *told* me this in the first place, instead of being so cryptic in his impatience . . .

I sighed. It wouldn't have made a bit of difference. He hadn't been able to come back from the dead until after I'd already finished off Konstantin. He wouldn't have been able to help me, and no matter what he'd told me, I wouldn't have believed he could really escape until I actually saw it.

"We have to get out of here," I said, glancing up at the sky. It was still dark, but I thought I was beginning to see the first hints of predawn light.

Anderson stared at Konstantin's inert form. I guess I was getting to know him pretty well, because I knew what he was thinking.

"Unless you can get these shackles off of me," I

said, "you're going to have to carry me to the car if we want to get there before next Wednesday. I know you're strong, but can you carry me *and* Konstantin at the same time?"

Anderson was the son of Death, but he was also the son of a Fury. I'd certainly hurt Konstantin when I'd pelted him with bricks and dropped a hunk of concrete on his head, but when Anderson killed someone, they *suffered*. Unless their human shell was already dead, that is.

"A quick death is too good for him," Anderson said through gritted teeth.

"Maybe. But how about you worry about what's good for *us* instead? We really don't want to be here when the police come knocking, and the house is going to be sending up smoke signals like no one's business when the sun rises. We need to go. The sooner the better."

For a moment, I thought Anderson's need for revenge was going to overcome his common sense. He had that angry light in his eyes, and I could feel the malice rolling off of him in waves. Then he shook his head violently and closed his eyes.

When he opened them again, the white light was gone, and he had a look I could only describe as haunted. "I let my need for revenge control me once before. I swore to myself I would never do it again."

He didn't seem to be talking to me so much as to himself. He'd told me before that he'd done "terrible things" in his past, and it seemed like a good guess those "terrible things" had been done in revenge.

I was too nosy not to be curious, but now was not the time for questions. And I didn't think Anderson would answer them anyway.

"If it makes you feel any better," I said, "at the last moment before I hit him with the rock, Konstantin realized he'd made a mistake and he was going to get killed by a five-foot-two woman with chains on her wrists and ankles. I suspect that knowledge counts as suffering in his book."

Anderson flashed me a weak smile. Then, his face saying it was killing him to do it, he reached out with a glowing hand to touch Konstantin.

TWENTY-NINE

Not having keys turned out not to be a problem, as Anderson kept a spare set in the glove compartment; however, we had to get underneath and chisel away at the hunk of ice we were hung up on. It didn't actually take all that long, but if another car had come along while we'd been at it, it would have been ... awkward. It's not every day you see a naked man and a woman chained hand and foot having car trouble by the side of the road. Anderson had helped himself to Konstantin's suit jacket after Konstantin was dead, but it was speckled with blood, which would have been hard to explain if anyone had stopped to try to help us. He'd tried the pants, too, but Konstantin was both taller and broader, and there was no way to keep the pants up.

At least the jacket, bloodstains and all, kept Anderson from looking like he was completely naked when we passed the police cars that blew by us only moments after we'd gotten back onto the road.

As I defrosted in the car on the way back to the mansion, I told Anderson everything he had missed—including that Cyrus had set us up. The fury that darkened his face made me wonder if I should have left that part out. The Olympians had clearly broken the treaty, but even though Konstantin was dead, nothing had really changed from our standpoint. We could *not* afford a war against the Olympians, no matter what Cyrus had done.

Anderson was quiet for a long time, stewing in his rage. I thought about reminding him of all the reasons why we couldn't afford a war, but decided my best course of action was to let him figure that out himself.

Of course, the decision of whether or not we were going to war against the Olympians wasn't entirely up to us. Konstantin had never dared start a war because he knew Anderson could kill him, but Cyrus had no way of knowing our puny little team could actually hurt him and his Olympians, and he was bound to be upset when he found out we'd taken out his dad.

Anderson let out a heavy sigh when we drove through the gates of home sweet home.

"Cyrus is a conniving, selfish, morally bankrupt bastard," he said. "And he's a huge improvement over Konstantin."

"He's going to assume we buried Konstantin somewhere," I replied. "He and his daddy might not have had the most loving relationship, but Cyrus is going to want revenge anyway."

"He might want it, but he won't dare try to get it." Anderson smiled, and there was a touch of cruelty in his expression. "If he kills us—or if he just pisses me off enough—he'll lose all hope that we might some-day tell him where Konstantin is buried."

It was the same tactic Konstantin had used with Emma. Anderson had wanted to kill him for a long time, but he hadn't dared kill the one man who might be able to give Emma back to him. The fact that there was absolutely no reason to believe Kon-stantin would ever do it had never killed the little ray of hope. Maybe Cyrus would fall victim to that same hope. Obviously, I was completely worthless when it came to guessing what Cyrus was going to do.

"What are we going to tell Blake?" I asked as we pulled into the garage. The relief of being home was strong enough to bring tears to my eyes.

Anderson frowned and turned off the car. "The truth, I suppose. I think he's past being disillusioned by Cyrus anymore."

"Yeah, maybe he'll be flattered that Cyrus went through all that trouble just to get him back," I said sarcastically. I didn't think it was possible to find out that your onetime lover had planned to kill or enslave every one of your friends to force you to come back to him, without feeling some serious pain and disil-lusionment. After all, Blake still seemed to like Cyrus in a guarded sort of way.

"Don't worry, you don't have to tell him. I'll do it myself. He deserves to know."

To that, I had no argument.

I was too exhausted to hop, so I made no objection when Anderson offered to carry me into the house.

EPILOGUE

The email hit my in-box at eight in the morning. I knew we were in trouble the moment I saw the subject line: ANDERSON IS A GOD.

To whom it may concern,

If you're reading this, then I am most likely dead. My murderer is Anderson Kane, and he is a god. His father was Thanatos, the Greek god of death. I never did find out the identity of his mother. He pretends to be one of the *Liberi,* but I have seen him in his true form. He can kill *Liberi* with a touch of his hand, and if the screams are any indication, it's a terrible way to go. Long ago, we negotiated an agreement whereby I would keep this information secret, but my death invalidates that agreement. I don't know why it is so important to him that this information not get out. Maybe he doesn't want to alienate his people with the knowledge of who and what he really is, and my revenge will turn out to be nothing but a petty torment. But I suspect there is more to it than that.

I have arranged for this email to be sent to all of Anderson's people, as well as all the Olympians. But just in case that doesn't inconvenience him enough, I've also arranged for it to be propagated via spambot. Soon, millions upon millions of people will see this email. Most will delete or ignore it or just think I'm a crackpot. But Anderson, if there's someone out there you're trying to hide from, if *that* is the reason you don't want anyone to know your true identity . . . Well, I'm afraid that cat is now out of the bag.

Isn't it funny how sometimes even when you win, you lose?

Konstantin Galanos

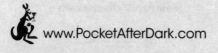

KICK-BUTT URBAN FANTASY
from Pocket Books!

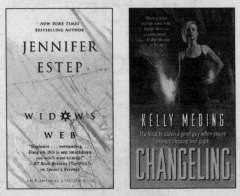

Available wherever books and eBooks are sold.
SimonandSchuster.com

More bestselling
URBAN FANTASY
from Pocket Books!